RANDOM HOUSE

LARGE PRINT

# Property of a Noblewoman

# DANIELLE STEEL

## Property of a Noblewoman

A Novel

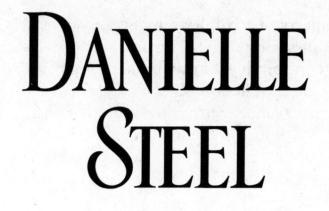

RANDOM HOUSE
LARGE PRINT

Copyright © 2016 by Danielle Steel

All rights reserved.
Published in the United States of America by Random House Large Print in association with Delacorte Press, an imprint of Random House, a division of Penguin Random House LLC, New York.

Cover illustration © Alan Ayers

The Library of Congress has established a cataloging-in-publication record for this title.

ISBN: 978-0-7352-0649-6

www.randomhouse.com/largeprint

FIRST LARGE PRINT EDITION

Printed in the United States of America

10  9  8  7  6  5  4  3  2  1

This Large Print Edition published in accord with the standards of the N.A.V.H.

To my so greatly loved children,
Beatrix, Trevor, Todd, Nick,
Samantha, Victoria, Vanessa,
Maxx, and Zara,

May you be greatly loved at every age,
courageous in your lives,
and honest and forgiving with others
and yourselves.

May your lives be filled with joy and hope,
and may you be blessed in every way.
And may you always know how
much I love you.

                              Mommy/d.s.

"What blesses one, blesses all."
—MARY BAKER EDDY

# Property of a Noblewoman

# Chapter 1

It was one of those January days in New York
that feels like winter will never end. There had
been record-breaking snows since November. And
the morning's snowfall, the second one that week,
had turned to sleet with a bitter wind. People were
slipping and sliding on the ice, and wincing in
the wind as it stung their faces. It was a good day
to stay indoors as Hal Baker sat at his desk at a
branch of the Metropolitan Bank on lower Park
Avenue.

Just over three years before, the bank was on
the dividing line of the part of New York that had
lost power in the epic hurricane that devastated
the city. A few blocks north of the power outages
and floods, the bank had continued to function
and serve its clients, and even offered trays of sand-

wiches and coffee to flood victims in a gesture of civic compassion.

Hal was in charge of the safe deposit boxes, a job others found tedious and that he had always liked. He enjoyed the contact with their older clients, as they came in to riffle through their belongings, check their stock certificates, or deposit new wills in the boxes they rented. He chatted with them if they wanted to, which they often did, or left them alone if they preferred. He knew most of the safe deposit box clients by sight, and many by name. And he was sensitive to their needs. He liked meeting the young clients too, particularly those who had never had a safe deposit box before, and explained to them the value of having one for their documents and valuables, since they lived in apartments that weren't always secure.

He took his job seriously, and at sixty, he was five years away from retirement, and had no burning ambitions. He was married, had two grown children, and running the safe deposit box department suited his personality. He was a "people person," and had been at the branch for twenty-eight years, and at another branch of Metropolitan for ten years before that. He was hoping to complete the final years of his career where he was. The safe deposit boxes had always felt like an important responsibility to him. They were entrusted with their customers' most valuable possessions, and sometimes darkest secrets, where no one else could go or pry, see or touch them, save themselves.

The bank was located in the East Thirties on Park Avenue, a previously elegant, entirely residential neighborhood called Murray Hill, which had long since become interspersed with office buildings. The bank's clients were a mixture of people who worked in the area, and the genteel older customers who lived in the remaining residential buildings. None of their elderly customers were venturing out today. The streets were slick from the sleet, and anyone who had the option would stay home, which made it a good day for Hal to catch up on the paperwork that had been gathering on his desk since the holidays.

Hal had three matters to deal with today. Two of the smaller safe deposit boxes had not been paid for in exactly thirteen months, and the clients who had rented them had not responded to the registered letters he'd sent them a month before, reminding them of that fact. The lapse of payment usually meant that customers had abandoned them, although not always. After waiting a month past the unpaid year, with no response to the registered letter, Hal could now call a locksmith to drill them open, and assumed he would find the boxes in question empty. Some people didn't bother to tell the bank they no longer wanted them, stopped paying the monthly fee, and threw away the keys.

In those two cases, if the boxes were empty, Hal could then turn them over to the waiting list he had of people in need of safe deposit boxes. It was usually a long list for the smaller ones. And it was frustrating waiting thirteen months to reclaim them, but it was the accepted legal procedure at any bank in New York, once clients stopped paying for a box. It would have been easy to notify the bank, relinquish the box, and hand in the keys. But some people just didn't bother. They forgot about it or didn't care.

The third box he was planning to deal with that day was a different situation. He had seen the client a few times over the years, and remembered her distinctly. She was a very distinguished-looking older woman, who was polite but never chatted with him. He hadn't seen her in nearly five years. And payment for the box had stopped three years and one month before. He had sent the standard registered letter one year after the payments stopped and then waited the month as required by law before the box could be drilled open in the presence of a notary public. It was one of the five largest boxes available at the bank. And in front of the notary, he had carefully inventoried the box's contents, as he was supposed to do. There had been several folders with the owner's neat handwriting on them, one with photographs in it, another with documents and papers, including several expired passports, both American and Italian, issued in

Rome. There had been two thick bundles of letters, one in an old-fashioned European handwriting, written in Italian, with a faded blue ribbon holding the letters in a neat stack. And the other letters, tied with a pink ribbon, were in English, in a woman's handwriting. And there were twenty-two leather jewelry boxes, most holding a single piece of jewelry, which he had noted but not examined closely. But even to his untrained eye, the pieces looked valuable. He had listed them simply as diamond ring, bracelet, necklace, pin, without further detail, which would have been beyond his competence on the subject, and was not required of him. He had also looked for a last will and testament, should the box holder prove to be deceased, and he had found none among her documents. The client had rented the box for twenty-two years, and he had no idea what had happened to her. And also as required by law, he had waited exactly two years after the box had been drilled open, and there had been no response from the client. His job now was to notify the surrogate's court of New York of the existence of the abandoned box, the lack of a will, and turn the contents over to them.

They would be obligated to try and determine if the renter of the box was deceased, and in the absence of a will, or noted next of kin, they would place an ad in newspapers, inviting relatives or heirs of that person to come forward to claim her belongings. If no one turned up within a month, the surrogate's court would move forward to sell her possessions as abandoned goods, and the proceeds of a sale would go to the State of New York. And any papers or documents would have to be held for another seven years in case a relative showed up. There were very strict laws that governed intestate estates, where there was no will. And Hal always followed what was required of him scrupulously.

He would be moving into the second phase of action today, notifying the surrogate's court of the abandoned box. And since the woman who had rented the box would be almost ninety-two years old, there was a strong possibility that she was no longer alive, and the court would have to determine that, before taking action to dispose of her possessions. Her name was Marguerite Wallace Pearson di San Pignelli. And Hal had had a gnawing suspicion for two years that the jewelry he had inventoried might be of considerable value. It would be the surrogate's court's job now to find someone to appraise it, if its owner was in fact deceased and had left no will, and no heirs came forward. The court would have to determine its value before it went to auction to benefit the state.

As part of the routine, Hal called the locksmith first for the two smaller boxes, and then called the surrogate's court to ask them to send someone to examine the contents of the larger box with him. He figured they would take their time before they came. They were understaffed and always busy and backlogged, handling the property and affairs of people who had died leaving no will.

It was eleven o'clock by the time Hal called the surrogate's court and Jane Willoughby answered the phone. She was a law student interning for the surrogate's court for a trimester for credit, before she graduated from Columbia Law School in June, and took the bar exam that summer. Clerking at the surrogate's court wasn't the assignment she had wanted, but it had been the only one open to her. Her first choice had been the family court, which was the specialty she hoped to go into, focusing on advocacy for children. And her second choice had been the criminal court, which seemed interesting, but nothing had been available in either court. She had only been offered clerking positions in probate court and the surrogate's court. She thought both courts were so depressing, dealing only with the affairs of dead people and endless paperwork, with little human contact. She took the surrogate's court, felt stuck there, and disliked the woman she worked for. Jane's boss, Harriet Fine, was a tired, faded-looking woman, who clearly didn't enjoy her job but needed the money and had never had the guts to quit. Her constantly negative comments and sour attitude made Jane's job harder, and she couldn't wait for her assignment to end. She was almost finished with her law studies, except for two final months of classes, and a term paper she still had to turn in. The clerkship was a final step toward graduation, and she needed a good report from Harriet to add to her résumé. She had been applying to New York law firms for the past two months.

Jane answered the phone on her desk on the second ring, and Hal explained the situation to her in a pleasant businesslike voice. She wrote down the information he gave her about Mrs. di San Pignelli's safe deposit box, and knew that the first thing she had to do was determine if the box holder was deceased. After that, they could proceed from there, and someone from the court would meet Hal at the bank, to go over the inventoried items with him, and claim them for the state, pending an answer to the ad they would place to locate heirs. It was always interesting to see who would respond to the ad, if anyone did. The surrogate's court had recently handled a case with no heirs, which had resulted in a sale at Christie's, and a nice tidy sum for the state, although Jane hadn't worked on the case. Harriet, her boss, acted as though it was a personal victory when no heirs appeared, and she could turn the proceeds of a sale over to the state. Jane preferred the more human aspect of people coming to claim items they didn't expect to inherit from relatives they barely knew, scarcely remembered, or in some cases had never met. It was found money for them, and always an agreeable surprise.

"How soon do you think you can be here?" Hal

asked her politely, as Jane glanced at her calendar, knowing full well she couldn't make the decision on her own. She'd have to be assigned, and Harriet would probably give it to someone else, since she was only a temporary clerk. Hal mentioned to her discreetly that he thought some of the items in the box might be of considerable value, and would have to be appraised accordingly, possibly by jewelry experts.

"I don't know when someone can be there," Jane said honestly. "I'll do the research on Mrs. Pignelli, to find out if she's deceased, and I'll have to turn the information over to my boss. It's up to her who to send, and when." Hal stared out the window as she said it. It was snowing harder, laying a thin white carpet over the icy sleet. The streets were getting more treacherous by the minute, which was often the case at that time of year.

"I understand," Hal said, sounding matter-of-fact. He knew the court had an overload of cases. But he had done what he was supposed to do, and followed procedure to the letter, as he always did. Now it was up to them.

"We'll notify you of when we're coming," Jane assured him, thinking of what he had told her about the possible value of the contents, and a moment later they hung up, as she sat watching the icy rain from her office. She hated days like this, and couldn't wait to go back to school and finish. And the holidays had been depressing too.

She hadn't been able to get home to her family in Michigan for Christmas, and she and John, the man she lived with, had been trapped in the apartment, studying for months. He was getting his MBA at Columbia Business School, and was due to graduate in June too, and with the pressure of papers and exams, things had been stressful between them. They had lived together for three years, and had gotten along well until the past six months, in the mounting tension before graduation. And both of them were starting to look for jobs, which was causing them anxiety too.

He was from L.A., and they had met in school. They shared a small, unattractive, furnished apartment near Columbia, in a rent-stabilized building on the Upper West Side, and their battle against the cockroaches that infested it made it a less than charming place to live. They were hoping to rent a nicer place when they both found jobs after graduation and could afford it, although her parents still wanted her to come back to Grosse Pointe to live, which wasn't in her plans. She was going to stay in New York and wanted to practice law there. Her father was the CEO of an insurance company, and her mother was a psychologist, although she hadn't practiced since Jane was born. And they were unhappy that she didn't want to return home, since she was their only child. She hated to disappoint them, but she was excited about pursuing a career in New York, and had warned them of it all along.

Jane knew that no matter who got assigned the Pignelli case, Harriet would expect her to check the death records first, to determine if Mrs. di San Pignelli was still alive, and she rapidly typed her name and date of birth into the computer. The response she got was quick. Marguerite Wallace Pearson di San Pignelli had died six months before. Her last known address was in Queens, and she had died there. It was not the same address that Hal Baker at the bank had in his records, which was an address in Manhattan near the bank. And given Mrs. di San Pignelli's age, Jane wondered if perhaps she had no longer remembered she had the safe deposit box, or had been too ill to remove her belongings from it before she died, and dispose of them herself. In any case, she was no longer alive, and someone from the surrogate's court would have to go through the contents of the box more thoroughly to see if they could find a will among her papers.

Jane filled out a form with the details, and walked it to Harriet's office, just as she was leaving for lunch, bundled up in a down coat with a knit cap and scarf and heavy boots. She often went home to check on her mother during lunch, and looked like she was going to the North Pole as she glanced at Jane when she walked in. Harriet had the reputation of being tough on clerks and law students, and she seemed to be unusually hard on Jane. Jane was a pretty young woman, with long blond hair and blue eyes and a terrific figure, and had the look of someone who had grown up with money, no matter how discreet she was, and had all the advantages Harriet had never had. At twenty-nine, Jane had her whole life ahead of her, and an interesting career.

In contrast, Harriet had lived with and cared for her sick mother, was in her early fifties, hadn't had a relationship in years, and had never married or had children. Her life and job felt like a dead end.

"Just leave it on my desk," Harriet said when she saw the form in Jane's hand.

"Someone will need to go to the bank," Jane said quietly, not wanting to annoy her. "The subject died six months ago. They've been holding the box for three years, according to procedure, and they want us to empty it now."

"I'll assign it after lunch," Harriet promised as she hurried out.

Jane went back to her office and ordered a sandwich from a nearby deli to eat at her desk. It seemed better than going out in the miserable weather. While waiting for her lunch to come, she did some minor paperwork.

She had made good headway with the routine tasks she had at hand by the time Harriet came back from lunch, looking worried, and said her mother wasn't doing well. Jane had left two completed files on her desk. It was tedious work, but Jane was meticulous and had made few mistakes while she was there and never the same one twice. She had been a paralegal before going to law school, and Harriet admired her work ethic and attention to detail. She had even told several people in the office that Jane was the best intern they'd had, but she was sparing with her praise to Jane. She called Jane into her office an hour after she returned from lunch.

"Why don't you go to the bank, and go through the contents and their inventory," she said, referring to the Pignelli case. "I don't have anyone else to assign to it for now." She handed her back the sheet on the Pignelli case, and Jane nodded. She had been to only one other inventory since she'd been there, but it didn't seem complicated to her. All she had to do was confirm the bank's inventory, and bring the contents of the safe deposit box back with her, to be put in the safe at the surrogate's court, until the items of value could be sold, and the papers archived for the next seven years.

Jane called Hal Baker at the bank that afternoon to make the appointment, which was sooner than he had expected, and he explained apologetically that he was going on vacation for the next two weeks, and had a training session the week after that. They made the appointment for four weeks later, on the day after Valentine's Day, which Jane didn't point out to him, but it was fine with her anyway. There was no rush, and it gave them time to place the regulation ad in the newspapers. She jotted down the appointment and they hung up, as she took out the standard form for the notice. The process of trying to locate Marguerite di San Pignelli's heirs had begun. It was just another ordinary day at the surrogate's court, trying to track down heirs, and dispose of estates when there were none.

# Chapter 2

Jane took the subway to the stop nearest the Metropolitan Bank, four weeks to the day after her initial conversation with Hal Baker. It was the day after Valentine's Day, and that morning and the day before had been rocky. She and John had had an argument while she was rushing to make toast, pour cornflakes into a bowl for herself, and make coffee for both of them. She burned the toast she had put in the toaster without bothering to check the setting, and spilled the cornflakes just as John ambled into the kitchen in boxers and T-shirt, looking dazed. He'd been out studying with friends the day before, at someone's apartment. She had heard him come home at three o'clock in the morning, but fell back to sleep before he made it into bed. And he totally forgot it was Valentine's Day, although she had bought him a box of chocolates and some cards, and left them in the kitchen for him that morning. He took the box of chocolates with him to share with his study group, and he had no gift, flowers, or cards for her. As far as John was concerned, Valentine's Day had been canceled this year.

"What are you in such a hurry about?" he asked, helping himself to the coffee she'd made, while she swept up the cornflakes and then buttered the piece of burnt toast for herself. He looked exhausted and was clearly not in a good mood as he sat down at the kitchen table and took a sip of coffee. He still hadn't acknowledged Valentine's Day, neither the day before nor today. He was never great about holidays, or dates, and with two major papers due, Valentine's Day meant nothing to him this year. He was totally focused on his work at school. He had been good company and fun to be with until he got overwhelmed in the final months before they graduated. Normally independent but good-humored before, now all he thought of was himself and what he had to do to graduate and get his MBA degree. Some days she felt like she didn't even exist to him.

"I have to inventory an abandoned safe deposit box today," she said, looking pleased about it. At least it was something more interesting to do than her usual fare, buried in the paperwork on her desk.

"Is that a big deal?" He looked unimpressed. It sounded boring to him.

"Probably not, but it gets me out of the office, and it gives me a chance to do a little detective work. We placed a notice in the newspapers to alert possible heirs, and we've had no response in four weeks."

"What happens if no one turns up?"

"Then we sell anything of value in the box, after it has been abandoned for three years and a month, but we keep the papers for another seven years. The money goes to the state."

"Is there anything important in that box?"

"Supposedly some jewelry that might be valuable, according to the bank. I'll check it out today. It's kind of sad, but interesting too. It's hard to imagine that people would just forget about their stuff, but the woman was pretty old. Maybe she died suddenly, or had dementia in her final years. Any chance of our having dinner tonight?" she asked, trying to sound casual and not wanting to put pressure on him. But as soon as she said it, he groaned.

"Oh shit. It's Valentine's Day, isn't it? Or it was yesterday. Thanks for the chocolates, by the way," he said, glancing at the date on the newspaper on the table. "I'm sorry, Jane. I forgot. I have two papers due—there's no way I can do dinner. Will you accept a rain check for a couple of weeks from now?" He looked genuinely apologetic.

"Sure," she said easily. She had suspected as much—he was obsessed with school, and she understood. Her law school schedule and its demands on her had been grueling too, but her grades had always been stronger than his. "I figured. I just thought I'd ask." He leaned over and kissed her, and smiled when he noticed her red sweater. Holidays meant a lot to her, which he always teased her about. It was a corny side of her he thought was sweet, and blamed it on her growing up in the Midwest. His parents were in the film industry in L.A., and so were officially more sophisticated than hers.

Jane looked pretty in a short black skirt and high heels, with her long blond hair pulled back for her meeting at the bank. He loved her looks and enjoyed spending time with her when he didn't have two papers due, and his final project to work on. They had made no plans for the future and lived their relationship day to day, which suited them both. They were focused on their careers. She had no time or desire for marriage now, she wanted to establish herself first and so did he. They agreed on that.

"I'm going to be out all night with my study group," he said as she got up and put her coat on. She was wearing a red coat that day too, to mark the holiday, which he thought was a little silly, but it looked good on her. And the high heels she was wearing showed off her legs, which John always said were one of her best features. "We're meeting at Cara's house," he said vaguely, glancing at the newspaper she'd left on the kitchen table. He knew that Jane didn't like her. Cara looked like an underwear model, not a candidate for an MBA. John always said she was smart as a whip and admired her entrepreneurial skills. She had run and sold a business for a handsome sum of money before going back to school for her MBA, and at thirty-one was two years older than Jane. She was the most attractive single woman in the group, and John studying with her always made Jane uneasy. As far as she knew, he was faithful to her, and she expected that. But Cara always seemed like a threat to her. Her ample bosom was always a little too exposed, and she looked sexy in tight T-shirts and jeans, with lots of cleavage visible at all times.

"Will the other guys be there?" Jane asked, looking nervous, and John was immediately annoyed.

"Obviously. What difference does it make? It's not a sex therapy group. We're working on our papers for the end of the term, and Cara knows a lot more about running a small business than I do." It was always his excuse for being with her. They had done several projects together.

"I just wondered," Jane said softly.

"Jane, I don't need pressure from you. And if she helps me get my grades up, I'm damn glad to be working with her." He was in no mood for a jealous scene, but somehow the conversation degenerated, and within five minutes they were arguing about Cara. It had happened before. Jane always said that Cara flirted with him, which John vehemently denied, while Jane told him he was naïve. The conversation went nowhere, John stalked off to the bedroom looking irritated, and Jane left for work, feeling slightly sick.

They argued constantly these days about everything and nothing. They were experiencing a major slump in their relationship, and Jane knew it was only because of the pressure on both of them as they finished graduate school, and she tried to be patient with his moods, permanent exhaustion, and lack of sleep, and to not worry about his proximity to Cara. She trusted John, but he and Cara spent endless hours together, studying, alone and in their study group. It was obvious that Cara had the hots for him, and Jane didn't trust Cara for a minute. She hated nagging him about it, but her nerves were frayed too.

John was in the shower when Jane left the apartment, and she had that unsettled feeling one gets after an argument, where no one "wins," and she felt foolish now in her red sweater and coat for Valentine's Day, a day late. It was just another work day for her, and she wanted to look serious at the appointment, since it was only the second time she'd gone to do an inventory, and she wanted to be professional about it.

Hal Baker was waiting for her at the bank when

she got there, and shook her hand with a friendly smile and an appreciative glance as he took in the pretty face and graceful figure. She was not at all what he had expected from the surrogate's court. The clerks they sent were usually much older and very dour. Jane was a beautiful young woman with an interested, lively expression in her eyes. He led her downstairs to the safe deposit boxes, with the young female notary trailing behind them. Hal walked to the section with the largest boxes, used two keys to free the box, and carried it into a small private room, barely large enough to accommodate the three of them, and the notary brought in a third chair so she could sit down and observe the inventory, as they did it. Hal had Mrs. di San Pignelli's file in his hand, with the inventory he had taken two years before. He handed Jane a copy of it as soon as they walked into the room, and she took off her red coat. She read down the list of the box's contents, and when Hal opened the box, Jane looked inside.

She could see the individual jewelry boxes and the folders. He took out the papers first and set them on the desk, and then opened the folders one by one. Jane examined the one containing photographs first, and found herself looking at a beautiful woman with deep pensive eyes and a dazzling smile. It was obviously Mrs. di San Pignelli, since most of the images included her. There were some early photographs of her as a young woman, which were more serious, and many of her with a much older, very dashing-looking man. Jane turned each one over and noticed the date and his name, "Umberto," carefully written in an elegant handwriting on the back. Some were taken at parties, others on vacation, and there were several on yachts. Jane recognized some as having been taken in Venice, others in Rome. She also noticed pictures of them in Paris, and one of them skiing in the Alps at Cortina d'Ampezzo, a few on horseback, and one of them in a race car with Umberto in helmet and goggles. The older man appeared to be very protective of the beautiful young woman, and she looked happy at his side, and nestled in his arms. She saw several pictures of them taken at a château, and some in elaborate gardens with the château in the background. And there were faded clippings from Roman and Neapolitan newspapers that showed them at parties, and referred to them as Conte e Contessa di San Pignelli. And among the clippings, Jane noticed the count's obituary from a Neapolitan newspaper in 1965, indicating that he was seventy-nine at the time of his death. It was easy to calculate then that he had been thirty-eight years older than Marguerite, who was only forty-one when he died, and they had been married for twenty-three years.

It looked as though they had led a luxurious, golden life, and Jane was struck by how elegant they both were, and how stylishly dressed. Marguerite was wearing jewelry in the photos where she wore evening gowns. And in several of them, mostly the ones where she was alone, Jane noticed a deeply sad expression in her eyes, as though something terrible had happened to her. But she always appeared happy in the pictures taken with the older man. They were handsome together and seemed very much in love.

And at the very end of the file, there were a number of photographs of a little girl, tied with a faded pink ribbon. They had no name written on the back, but only the dates when they were taken, in a different, less sophisticated hand. She was a pretty little girl with a somewhat mischievous expression and laughing eyes. There was a vague resemblance to the countess, but not enough so as to be sure they were related. And Jane was struck with a sudden wave of sadness, looking through the memorabilia of a woman's life, who was no longer there and must have come to a lonely end, if she had died without a will and no known heirs.

She wondered what had happened to the little girl, who, judging by the dates on the back of the pictures, would be an old woman now as well. It was all a piece of history from the distant past, and it was unlikely that any of the people in the images were still alive.

Jane gently closed the folder with the photographs, as Hal handed her the next one, with assorted documents in it. There were several expired passports, which showed that Marguerite was a U.S. citizen, born in New York in 1924, and the stamps in her passport indicated that she had left the States, and entered Portugal, arriving by ship in Lisbon in 1942, at eighteen. Portugal was a neutral country, and the subsequent stamps in her passport showed that she traveled to England the day after she arrived in Portugal. And she had only returned to the States for a few weeks in 1949, seven years later. Further stamps in her passport showed that six weeks after she arrived in England in 1942, she had gone to Rome, with a "special visa." Jane couldn't help thinking that the count must have pulled some very high-up strings, or paid someone handsomely, to get his bride into Italy with the war on. There were Italian passports in the folder as well, and the first one was dated December 1942, and showed her name as di San Pignelli, so they were married by then, three months after she'd arrived in Europe, and she had acquired Italian citizenship with the marriage.

She came back into the States in 1960 on a U.S. passport that had been renewed at the American embassy in Rome. It was her first visit back to the States since her three-week trip in 1949—and in 1960, she only stayed for days, not weeks. The passport showed no trips to the U.S. after that, until she moved to New York in 1994, when she was seventy years old. All her American passports had been renewed at the U.S. embassy in Rome.

And she seemed to use her Italian one when traveling around Europe. She clearly had dual citizenship, and perhaps maintained her American one out of sentiment, since she had lived in Italy in the end for fifty-two years, the greater part of her lifetime, and all of her adult life till then. And she had not been to the States at all for thirty-four years, when she moved back for good in 1994.

Jane observed bank statements in the folder too, a record of her Social Security number, the rental papers for the safe deposit box, and a receipt for two rings she had sold in 1995 for four hundred thousand dollars. But nowhere among her papers could Jane find a will. There was nothing that referred to any heirs or next of kin, or anyone in fact. They found very little information in the folder. And other than that, there were only the two thick bundles of letters, written in fading ink, tied with a pale blue ribbon on one, and a pink one on the other. In one neatly tied stack, the letters were written in Italian, on heavy yellowed stationery, in brown ink, in an elegant handwriting that looked like a man's, and were written by her husband, Jane assumed. The second set of letters seemed to be written by a woman and were in English. Jane glanced at a few of them without untying the ribbon and saw that many of them began with "My Darling Angel." They seemed to be simple and direct outpourings of love, and were signed with the initial M. There was no will there. And the notary duly noted the two bundles of letters on her own inventory, as did Jane.

And then Jane carefully took out the twenty-two leather boxes, all of which looked like jeweler's boxes, and one by one, she opened them, and her eyes grew wide as she saw their contents.

In the first box, she found a large rectangular emerald ring in an emerald cut. Jane didn't know enough about jewelry to guess at its carat weight, but it was large, and the red leather box was marked "Cartier" in gold on the inside. She would have been tempted to try it on, but didn't want Hal to think her unprofessional. So she wrote down the description, closed the box, and moved it to the other side of the desk, so as not to confuse it with the others.

The next box yielded a large oval ruby ring with a triangular white diamond on either side, again from Cartier. And the ruby was a deep, almost bloodlike color. It was a magnificent piece. And in the third box was an enormous diamond ring, again with a rectangular emerald-cut stone, like the emerald. It was absolutely dazzling and this time Jane gasped. She had never seen a diamond so large, and she looked up at Hal Baker in astonishment.

"I didn't know diamonds came that size," she said in awe, and he smiled.

"Neither did I, until I saw that one." He hesitated and then smiled more broadly. "I won't tell if you try it on. You might never get the chance again." Feeling like a naughty child, she did as he suggested and slipped it on. It covered her finger to the joint and was absolutely spectacular. Jane was mesmerized by it, and could hardly bring herself to take it off.

"Wow," she said unceremoniously, and all three of them laughed to relieve the tension in the room. It was a strange and slightly eerie experience going through this woman's things, and it seemed so un-usual that a woman with such valuable possessions had no one to leave them to, or had failed to do so, and never reclaimed them herself, to keep, wear, or sell. Jane couldn't bear the thought of things as beautiful as this being sold for the benefit of the state, and not going to someone who would ap-preciate them, or had cared about her. This was just too sad.

The next box yielded an emerald and diamond brooch in a handsome design by an Italian jeweler. There was an invisibly set sapphire necklace from Van Cleef and Arpels, with matching earrings in a separate box, and an incredibly beautiful diamond bracelet that looked like lace. As she opened box after box, Jane found herself staring at one piece of jewelry more beautiful than another, and some of it, particularly the rings, set with very large stones. And there was a large round yellow diamond set in a ring by Cartier in the last box. It looked like a headlight, as Jane sat staring at the dazzling array in the now-open boxes. Hal Baker had said that Marguerite had some nice jewelry that might be of considerable value, but Jane had expected nothing like this. She hadn't seen anything of its kind since she'd gone to London with her parents at sixteen, and went to the Tower of London to see an exhibit of the queen's jewels. And some of these were prettier and more impressive than the queen's. Countess Marguerite di San Pignelli had owned some truly spectacular jewelry, and Jane could easily guess that what she had before her, in the elegant leather boxes from some of the finest jewelers in Europe, was worth a fortune. She wasn't quite sure what to do next.

"Maybe we should photograph it," Jane suggested, as Hal nodded agreement. "That way I can show my boss what's here."

She took out her cell phone and took photographs of each item. It would show the value and importance of the collection far better than her meticulous inventory. Among the pieces, there was also a pearl and diamond choker by Cartier, and a long string of very large perfect pearls in a creamy color. And she had also come across one box that contained a simple gold ring with a crest on it that looked like Marguerite might have worn it as a young girl, a gold chain with a heart-shaped locket on it with a tiny baby picture in it, and a plain gold wedding band. The items in the box were of very little value and looked completely unrelated to the expensive pieces in the other boxes, but the nature of them suggested that they must have had sentimental meaning to their owner.

Jane could only imagine that the countess must have led a very grand life at one time, and the locations of where the photographs were taken and the clothes she was wearing in them suggested that as well. She was wearing beautiful gowns and dresses, extravagant furs, and elegant hats in every photo. It made Jane curious now about who Marguerite di San Pignelli had been. All that she could tell from the contents of the box was that she had been a young American woman who had gone to live in Italy at eighteen, married the older man in the pictures within a few months, and he had died twenty-three years later. And years after that, she had moved back to the States and never left again after her return, until her death at ninety-one. Among all the passports in the safe deposit box, none were current. Her last one had expired two years after she moved back to New York, and she had never gone back to Italy again. All the information Jane could glean from photographs, newspapers, and documents were pieces of a puzzle, but so much about her was missing. When Marguerite died six months earlier, she had taken all the answers to their questions with her.

After Jane had finished taking the photographs

of each item, from several angles, she closed the jewelry boxes, and Hal put them back in the safe deposit box.

"I think we'd better leave them here for now," Jane said nervously. She had no intention of taking them on the subway with her, when she went back to work. The photographs were good enough to show Harriet what they were dealing with. They would have to call an auction house to dispose of them, and Jane was wondering which one Harriet would use. Sotheby's and Christie's were the obvious choices, and Jane had no idea if there were other venues for selling jewelry like this. She had no experience with items of this value and magnitude, and the kindly banker didn't either. Hal strode out of the little cubicle, and the notary and Jane observed him put the safe deposit box back where it belonged and lock it securely into place with both keys.

"You'll hear from me as soon as they tell me at the office what they want me to do. It sure is pretty stuff," Jane said dreamily. All three people in the tiny viewing room had been somewhat stunned by what they'd seen. They had never been exposed to jewelry like this before, and Jane suspected Harriet hadn't either, but she would undoubtedly know what to do.

Jane thanked Hal Baker and the notary when she left, and took the subway back to her office at the surrogate's court. The building itself was a beautiful example of Beaux-Arts architecture, built in 1907, and was landmarked. It was a handsome place to work, although not a happy job. When she got there, she found Harriet at her desk, going over some documents the probate court had sent over, and she looked up when she saw Jane standing in the doorway, hesitating to interrupt her.

"Nice coat," Harriet said, with a wintry smile. "What's up?"

"I just came back from verifying the inventory in the di San Pignelli case."

"I forgot you were doing that this morning," Harriet said, distracted, expecting it to have been routine. "How did it go?"

"Fine, I think," Jane said, worrying that she might have forgotten to do something official. "She had some beautiful things," she said softly, thinking of the contents of the jewelry boxes.

"Any sign of a will?"

"No, just photographs and letters, some newspaper clippings of parties and her husband's obituary, old passports from a long time ago, some irrelevant bank forms, and the jewelry."

"Anything we can sell?" Harriet asked, sounding official and matter-of-fact. She hadn't seen the photographs of the beautiful young woman with the dazzling smile and sad eyes.

"I think so." Jane pressed a button on her phone, and showed her the photographs of Marguerite di San Pignelli's jewelry, without comment. Harriet was silent for a minute after she finished looking at them, and then stared up at Jane in obvious amazement with wide-open eyes.

"You saw all this stuff today?" Harriet asked her in disbelief, and Jane nodded. "We need to call Christie's right away to get it into an auction." She jotted down a note to call Christie's on a scrap of paper and handed it to Jane, who took it from her, looking worried.

"Am I supposed to call them?"

Harriet nodded, with slight exasperation. "I don't have time." Their understaffing problem seemed to have gotten worse lately. "Just call Christie's and ask them to have someone from the jewelry department meet you at the bank, to have a look. We need an appraisal if any of the heirs shows up. And we'll need it for the court too." Jane confirmed to her then, in answer to Harriet's questions, that the contents of the box were mostly jewelry. There had been no cash, no stock certificates or bonds, and Hal had told her that the funds in her checking account had dwindled to under two thousand dollars at the time of her death. She hadn't written a check in years. The only money drawn out of her account was the automatic transfers to her nursing home in Queens every month, which she had set up when she moved there. But her jewelry was clearly worth a fortune.

Jane went back to her desk, took off the coat she had worn for Valentine's Day, and looked up the phone number for Christie's. When the number came up on her computer, she saw that their offices were at Rockefeller Center. Although by then it was nearly lunchtime, she called the number and asked for the jewelry department when they answered. The phone rang for a long time, and she was about to hang up, when a female voice finally picked up, and Jane asked to speak to someone about an appraisal to submit jewelry items for an upcoming sale, and they put her on hold, while she listened to an endless piece of music. It appeared that there was no one in the department, when a male voice said simply "Lawton" in a flat tone.

Jane explained that she was calling from the surrogate's court and needed an appraisal for a number of abandoned jewelry items they would be putting up for sale if no heirs showed up. There was a momentary silence, as Phillip Lawton sat staring out the window. He had been assigned to the jewelry department at the venerable auction house for the last two years, and felt like he was trapped. He had a master's in museum curating, with a specialty in Egyptian art and Impressionist paintings, and had waited forever for a job at the Metropolitan Museum. He had finally given up and taken a job at Christie's in the art department, and he had found it interesting for the three years he had worked there, until three vacancies came up in jewelry, when the head of the department moved to their London office, and the two people directly under him had quit. Phillip had then been transferred from art to jewelry, in which he had absolutely no interest. They had promised to move him back to the art department eventually, but it hadn't happened yet. And all his background and training was in art. His father had been a professor of art history at NYU until his death a few years before, and his mother was an artist. He had done an internship at the Uffizi in Florence after college, and had thought about moving to Paris or Rome, but came back to get a master's in the States instead. He had worked at an important gallery in New York for a while, and went to work at Christie's at twenty-nine, where he had been now for five years, the last two of them as a hostage in the jewelry department. He had recently promised himself that if they didn't move him back to the art department in the next six months, he'd quit.

Phillip Lawton objected to jewelry on principle. He thought the people who wore it were frivolous and vain, and he failed to see the beauty of it. Paintings and art in any form touched his soul and filled him with joy. Jewelry never had. To Phillip, only art was beauty—jewelry left him cold.

He sounded bored when he responded to Jane. He expected her call to be another request for a routine appraisal for the court. "Can you bring the pieces in?" he asked, in a disinterested tone. He had done appraisals for the surrogate's court before, and none of the items had been worthy of auctioning off at Christie's, with the exception of a minor recent piece that had qualified for their "fine jewels" auction, which hadn't been an important sale. And he thought it highly unlikely that these would be any different, or even as good. Most of what wound up in surrogate's court was of no interest to them.

"I'd rather not bring them in," Jane said honestly, thinking that he sounded as though he thought she was wasting his time, which annoyed her. She was calling him in an official capacity, not asking him for a favor. And she was trying to do her job. "There are twenty-two pieces, and I think they're too valuable for me to take them around the city."

"Where are they now?" he asked, still staring out his office window at the skyscrapers across the street. His office felt like prison to him, and his job a life sentence that would never end. He hated coming to work now.

"It's all in a safe deposit box at the Metropolitan Bank in Murray Hill. Would it be possible for you to meet me there to see the pieces?" Possible, he acknowledged silently, but not very appealing. But it was part of his job to do appraisals, mostly of estates for heirs who didn't want the old-fashioned jewelry they'd inherited, or greedy women who wanted to cash in on what they'd been given, after a divorce. Among their clients were often jewelers seeking to get rid of unsold pieces, since auction prices were usually somewhere between retail and wholesale, which was appealing to both sellers and buyers. "We need an appraisal," Jane explained, forcing herself to sound pleasant, "and unless an heir turns up soon, we'll be putting the items up for auction."

"I know how it works," he said brusquely, as Jane silently wished that someone else had taken her call. He didn't sound agreeable to deal with, or even interested in seeing the pieces. She smiled to herself, thinking that he was in for a surprise.

"Well, can you do it?" She felt as though she'd need an armed guard if she brought Mrs. di San Pignelli's jewelry to him, and the court would certainly not let her hire one. And she didn't want the responsibility of transporting all those jewels. So he would have to come to see them at the bank, or she'd call someone else, like Sotheby's, who were just as good, in spite of Harriet's preference.

"Yes, I'll do it," he said in a bored voice. "How about next Tuesday? Ten A.M.? I have to be back at noon for a sale." He had been trained as an auctioneer by then, and sometimes handled the bidding in minor sales. But he couldn't imagine that the jewelry the court wanted him to appraise would take that long, if they were small pieces, which he assumed. They always had been in the case of abandoned safe deposit boxes that he'd handled before.

"That will be fine," Jane said politely, after they agreed to meet at the bank the following week. She thanked him before hanging up, and was relieved he'd been willing to meet her. And then as an afterthought a moment later, she called him back.

"Sorry to bother you again," she apologized when he sounded busy when he answered. "I took some photographs of the pieces with my phone. Would you want to see them before we meet?" It might give him an idea of what was there, and spark his interest.

"Good idea," he said, sounding instantly more cheerful. If the pieces were as insignificant as he suspected they would be, he could refer her to a less important auction house, and spare himself the trouble of an appraisal. "Just send them to me." He gave her his email address. She sent the photos as soon as they hung up again, and pulled out one of the other files Harriet had assigned her to work on. The case was far less interesting and mysterious than Marguerite's. And Jane was surprised when her phone rang ten minutes later and it was Phillip Lawton at Christie's. The tone of his voice had completely changed from the first two calls, and he sounded excited, as he questioned Jane intently.

"What was the woman's name again? Was she well known?"

"I don't think so. Countess Marguerite di San Pignelli. She was a young American woman who moved to Italy at eighteen, during the war, from what I can deduce from her passports. She married an Italian count and lived there until the nineties.

He must have had money, given what's in the safe deposit box in terms of jewelry. It's all she had, as far as we know. She was down to her last two thousand dollars when she died. She was ninety-one." They were all the relevant details.

"If what she had is real, that's an extraordinary collection of jewelry." He sounded impressed finally, although the only pieces that had caught his interest in the past two years were jades he had seen at their sales in Hong Kong, which he thought had great romance and mystery to them, and required an expert's eye, which he was not, to understand them. The standard Western pieces never appealed to him, but even he had to admit that Marguerite di San Pignelli's jewelry was amazing.

"I have no reason to believe it's not real, and it's all in the original boxes," Jane said simply.

"I can't wait to see it," he said, with a tone of awe. Their appointment was five days away, and he was now planning to bring a camera to take better photographs than she had gotten with her cell phone.

"See you on Tuesday," he said, friendlier than he'd been before, and Jane smiled as she hung up. And as she sat at her desk afterward, she thought wistfully of the beautiful young woman who had moved to Italy and married a count, as in a fairy tale, and all the secrets of her life that had died with her.

When Jane got home that night, John was out,

as he had told her he would be. She thought about him with Cara, and his study group, and felt the same unease she always did when he was with her. But there was nothing she could do about it, and he had told her they would work straight through the night on their collective projects. She would have liked to tell him about the jewelry she had seen that day, and her conversation about it with Christie's. But it would have to wait until he had time and was less distracted. She took a bath and went to bed, still haunted by Marguerite di San Pignelli, the photographs of her and the count, and the jewelry he had given her. Without knowing the details, Jane sensed that it had been a great love story, despite the young woman's occasionally sad expression in the photographs. It was impossible not to think about who she had been, how the count had come into her life, and the exciting life they must have shared in a more glamorous era. It was hard to imagine a girl of eighteen receiving gifts like the ones Jane had seen. And Jane couldn't help wondering if the beautiful young woman had been truly happy.

# Chapter 3

The next morning John still hadn't come home when Jane left for work, and since he had warned her, it didn't surprise her. She knew she'd see him that night when she got home, and hopefully they'd spend some time together over the weekend, just to talk and relax and catch up on what they were doing. She missed their previously easygoing relationship, but felt sure it would return to normal after graduation, although he'd been particularly hard on her in the last few months. She was trying to be patient about it, and not make it worse by complaining.

And once at work, Jane decided to finish her due diligence in the pursuit of Marguerite di San Pignelli's lawful heirs. In an estate this size, now that the jewelry had surfaced, she wanted to leave no stone unturned, and she decided to go to Marguerite's last known address to see if someone knew something more about her there, if she had relatives or children. She might have had family who visited her but were unaware of the jewelry.

She consulted a map of Queens, and took the subway there later that morning. She discovered that the address that had appeared on her death certificate was a small nursing home, which was clean but depressing. When she checked with accounting, they confirmed that Mrs. Pignelli's monthly charges had been paid by automatic transfer from her bank account every month. They were unaware of how little she had left and that she would have run out of money shortly. They referred Jane to patient services, where their records showed that she had had no visitors in the three years she'd been there until her death, seven months before.

"She was a very sweet, kind woman," the patient services coordinator told Jane. "Her records show that she had dementia when she was admitted. Would you like to speak to one of her nurses?"

"Yes, I'd like that," Jane said quietly, after confirming again that there was no next of kin listed anywhere on her records. She appeared to have been entirely alone in the world, with no relatives or friends, which they said wasn't surprising. Many of their patients had no visitors, and no relatives listed, particularly if they were very old and had no children.

A few minutes later, a middle-aged Filipina woman walked into the room in a white nurse's uniform, and smiled as she looked at Jane. The patient coordinator introduced her as Alma, and said that she had been Marguerite's main nurse for her last two years, and Alma mentioned as well what a lovely woman Marguerite had been.

"She talked about her husband a lot at the end, and said she wanted to see him," Alma said with a gentle smile. "And a few times, she said she had some things she wanted to give me. A ring, I think, or a bracelet, I can't remember. A lot of our patients with dementia promise money or gifts that they don't have to give. It's their way of wanting to thank us." The pretty Filipina woman didn't seem surprised or disappointed by it, and Jane tried to imagine what it would have been like if Marguerite had given her the enormous diamond ring, the ruby one, or one of her brooches. There was no way to know what Alma would have done in that instance.

Alma said that in her final days, in a rare moment of lucidity, Marguerite had wanted to go to the bank to get some things, and write a will. She was in no condition to go out by then, and they had offered to call a notary for her, but Marguerite had rapidly forgotten about it, and had died by the end of the week, without writing the will. The nurse explained to Jane that Marguerite had died of a brief bout with pneumonia when she was suffering from the flu. She was bedridden by then, and had been for two years, rarely coherent, and none of it was surprising for a woman of almost ninety-two. Jane couldn't help wondering whom she would have left the jewelry to, had she been rational enough to write a will. To Alma at the nursing home? A distant relative she hadn't seen in years? There was no way to know. Alma said she had mentioned no one by name.

They seemed to be conscientious about their patients, although Jane found it grim with elderly people in wheelchairs sitting in the halls, looking vacant and not speaking. It seemed like such a sad way to end one's days on earth, and she hoped that Marguerite's dementia had made it easier for her, and prevented her from realizing where she was, with no one she loved to comfort her. And Marguerite's ultimate fate and final years seemed even sadder to Jane.

Jane felt melancholy thinking about it as she took the subway back to the city. And just for good measure, she stopped off at Marguerite's previous address listed by the bank, a few blocks from the branch, and she asked for the building manager when she got there. She didn't have to go to these lengths, but she wanted to. Something about the photographs she'd seen in the box, and the woman in them, had moved her deeply. And even the little she knew of her seemed very poignant. The manager remembered Marguerite clearly, and said that the workers in the building who had known her still missed her. He said she had been a very sweet woman, which was what they had said about her at the nursing home as well. He said that she had moved into a small one-bedroom apartment in the building in 1994, and had lived there for nearly twenty years, and had moved out roughly three and a half years before, when she moved into the nursing home, which corroborated what Jane already knew. She asked him if he recalled if she had children, family, or visitors, and he said that from what he knew from his own twenty years running the building, he had never seen anyone visit her, and he was sure she had no children. "She said her dogs were her children. She always had a little miniature poodle with her. I think her last one died a year or two before she moved out, and she said she was too old to get another dog. I think she missed it," he said sadly, remembering back to the days when Marguerite lived in the building.

The story seemed to be the same everywhere, she had no friends, no visitors, no relatives, no children. She lived alone, kept to herself, and seemed like the kind of person who led a quiet life, after an exciting one in the past, although at seventy when she moved into the building, by today's standards she wasn't ancient. But clearly her days of glory were already over, once she moved back to a small apartment in New York, twenty-nine years after her husband's death. Once back in New York, her world was far from all the glamour Jane had seen in the photos.

Jane thanked the building manager and left, and took the subway uptown to her own dingy apartment. She could hardly wait to move when they finished school and got decent jobs. She was tired of the grim building, and dark furnished apartment. The furniture was threadbare and ugly.

Jane set down her bag, took off her coat, sat down on the sagging faux leather couch, and put her feet on the coffee table. It had been a long and interesting week, and her search for Marguerite's heirs had been entirely fruitless so far. No one had responded to the ad. It really looked like there would be no one to claim her estate and her jewelry would be sold at Christie's for the state's benefit. It seemed such a shame and a waste, and she wondered what the man from Christie's would say about the pieces when he saw them on Tuesday.

She made herself a cup of tea, and was relaxing and reading a magazine, when John walked in an hour later. He looked in better spirits than he'd been in all week and announced that he'd finished one of his papers the night before, thanks to Cara, who had given him all the statistics and background research he needed.

"She was a godsend," he said, relieved, as Jane looked at him, always annoyed to hear about Cara, but she didn't comment. Everything about her set Jane's nerves on edge. "How was your day?"

"Busy. Poignant. I've been chasing down the heirs and details on the estate of that woman I was telling you about. It turns out she really had no one. It's so sad to think about someone's life ending like that, with no one to care about them."

"She was ninety-one when she died, from what you said, so don't get too worked up about it. It's just about her estate now, and who's going to get it. It's not as if you knew her." She could see that John thought her compassion for Marguerite was stupid.

"The state is going to get it," Jane said, looking down about it. "I'm meeting with a representative from Christie's next week to appraise it." She realized then that she hadn't seen John since she had done the inventory herself. "She had some amazing stuff, very important jewelry, like giant diamonds, bracelets, and brooches, even a tiara." Jane's eyes shone brightly, remembering the beauty of it.

"Was she some kind of royalty?" he asked, as he helped himself to a beer from the fridge in the small kitchen.

"She was American, but she married an Italian count at eighteen and lived pretty grandly in Italy, judging from the pictures. It looked like a very fancy life," she said, thinking of the race cars and château. "And it all ended in a nursing home in Queens, alone." With a safe deposit box full of fabulous jewelry, and no one to give it to. It all seemed so strange to Jane, and so incongruous. To John, it was just another story that didn't appear to move him, but he hadn't seen the photographs of her or gotten a sense of Marguerite as a person. Jane thought he was being insensitive about it, but the only thing that interested him lately were his own concerns. "Do you have time for dinner and a movie this weekend?" she asked hopefully. He shook his head ruefully in answer.

"I have to finish my second paper, and I just got assigned a new one. I think it's going to be pretty rough till May. I've got to stay focused."

"Let me guess, you're working with Cara again." She tried to keep the edge out of her voice as she said it, and didn't succeed. It was hard seeing so little of him, and knowing that she was always with him, whatever the reason.

"Get off my back. It's not going to change anything and just pisses me off." There was a strong warning in his eyes. Their last months before they graduated were turning out to be a real test of the relationship, and he wasn't getting high marks at it so far, and in his eyes neither was she. And her jealousy of Cara seemed unreasonable to him.

"Okay. Sorry," she said with a sigh. "I've got some reading to do this weekend anyway." She tried to sound easy about it and she wanted to see a friend for lunch, and needed to work on her own paper. She could tell that she was about to spend another weekend on her own. And she knew he was right, her getting wound up about Cara wouldn't do them any good.

John went to the gym to work out that night, before he went back to the research for his paper, and Jane did laundry and paid bills. It felt good to catch up, although they barely exchanged five words with each other, and by the time John went to bed, she was asleep, and he was already gone the next morning when she woke up. He had left her a note on the kitchen table that he would be at the library all day. But at least he wasn't at Cara's, she thought to herself. There was just something about her that always made Jane jealous, probably how sexy she looked, and she was smart too, a winning combination. She was the kind of woman men flocked to. And Cara took full advantage of it. All her friends were men. Women never liked her.

Jane called her friend Alex, and they agreed to meet at the Museum of Modern Art for lunch. Alex had graduated from law school the year before, and had landed a job in a Wall Street firm. She said they were working her like a slave, but she was making decent money and she liked it. Her specialty was intellectual property law, which was interesting and fun. Alex was hoping for an eventual junior partnership in the firm, in a few years.

"So how's Prince Charming?" Alex asked with a broad smile. She was small with dark hair and green eyes, and appeared younger than her thirty-two years. In jeans, a fisherman's sweater, and ballet flats with her hair in a braid down her back, she looked like a kid. The two women were an interesting contrast, with Jane's long, lean blond good looks, and Alex's dark pixie quality, which was her personality too. They had shared some good laughs and lively times together.

"Not so charming these days," Jane said about John with a sigh, as they finished lunch in the museum cafeteria. They both wanted to see a Calder exhibit that had just opened. He was a favorite of Jane's. "He's in such a shit mood, finishing up his papers and final projects. That's all he thinks about now. I haven't had dinner with him in a month."

"I don't know what it is about guys, they can never multitask. It's all one thing or another, with no room for anything else." Alex had broken up with her last boyfriend a year before, and had just started dating a junior partner in the firm. And her parents had been nagging her about getting married for the past two years, since she turned thirty. Jane's parents were more relaxed about it, for now. Her mother had started making comments about John, and questioning their plans for the future but marriage just wasn't on her radar screen for now. Alex was a little more concerned in recent months, and had started talking about wanting kids. "Is the old magic still there?" she asked Jane, who thought about it for a moment before she answered.

"To be honest, I don't know. I'm not sure we ever

had 'magic.' We like each other a lot, we like doing the same things. It was easy, and we get along, or at least we used to. I guess if you put a gun to our heads, we'd say we love each other, but I don't think either of us are passionate people. Maybe we're too interested in our careers." Jane thought about it at times, but she had no real complaints about John either, except lately, with his intense study habits and no time for her, and her mild concerns about Cara, and women who looked like her. Jane was wholesome and natural, she wasn't a sexy type or a femme fatale like Cara. John liked to talk about "hot women." Cara definitely was one. And their sex life had fallen off too, which also put distance between them. He was never in the mood now, he was too tired, or not at home when Jane was.

"Maybe he's not the right guy," Alex threw out as a possibility. She had never been crazy about him, and thought he had a big ego, which didn't seem to bother Jane, but it annoyed Alex. "Maybe you'd feel more passionate about a different guy," she said cautiously, not wanting to offend Jane.

"I don't think so. I had a hot romance like that in college. It was awful. I cried all the time, and lost fifteen pounds."

"That's not all bad," Alex grinned. "Except the crying part. Sometimes John reminds me of the guy I used to go out with before law school. I liked him and we got along, but it was never really right. And once we started arguing about everything, it was all wrong. I think we just ran out of gas, and then it went sour. If I'd stayed with him, we would have wound up hating each other. We broke up before that happened. Some relationships aren't meant to last forever. Maybe this is one of those." Jane didn't want to admit it to her, but she had wondered about that too. And their constant arguments now depressed her. She didn't want to fight with him. But she was still hoping it would get better again. They were at each other's throats whenever they were together.

"I don't think we can figure anything out or make any decisions until after we graduate in June," Jane said calmly. "We've never had any major problems until now. He's just in a shit mood and at maximum stress levels all the time trying to finish everything before graduation. It's not a lot of fun for either of us, and I snap at him too." About Cara.

"Doesn't sound like fun to me," Alex agreed. They walked in the museum garden then, and Jane told her about Marguerite, and her search for heirs to the estate. She told her about the jewelry and trying on the enormous diamond ring. "Wow! It's hard to imagine romances and people like that. They're part of another century. Can you imagine any guy we know giving someone that kind of jewelry, riding around in a race car, or living in a château? Sounds like a fairy tale, or an old movie."

"It is," Jane agreed with her. "And it's sad to think how the story ends up. Alone, with dementia, in a nursing home in Queens. That sounds like a nightmare to me."

"Yeah, me too," Alex said as they walked into the Calder show and spent a pleasant afternoon, talking about nothing in particular and enjoying each other's company. At four o'clock, they said their good-byes and Jane took the subway back uptown, and Alex went to the West Village, where she lived in the meat-packing district. She had rented an apartment in a good building in a trendy neighborhood as soon as she got her new job, and she was loving it. And she had a date that night with her new guy to go to the theater.

Jane found herself envying her when she went back to the empty apartment, and worked on her paper that night. John called her around nine o'clock and had been at the library all day. They were on separate paths for now. And she tried not to think about what Alex had said at lunch, that John might be the wrong guy. She wasn't ready to believe that yet. And she thought about what she'd said, that some relationships just played themselves out and ended. She hoped that hadn't happened. But the stress on both of them had clearly taken a toll.

On Sunday morning, Jane woke up to find John in bed with her, which was beginning to seem like a miracle, and they made love for the first time in a month. She felt better about them after that, and they managed to have brunch at a nearby deli before he went back to the library for the rest of the day and night, but at least the morning had gotten off to a good start, and she felt connected to him again.

She went to a movie alone on Sunday night, a French art film she'd been wanting to see, which wasn't as interesting as she hoped, and that night she went to sleep and dreamed of Marguerite. She was trying to say something to Jane, and explain something to her, but through the entire troubled night, Jane never figured out what it was. John didn't come home again on Sunday night and had texted her he'd slept on someone's couch. She got up Monday morning, feeling drained and frustrated, and got ready for another week in surrogate's court. At least she had the Christie's appraisal to look forward to the next day. It was a welcome change. And with all that spectacular jewelry, Marguerite's estate was anything but boring. It was the only excitement and bright spot in her life for now.

# Chapter 4

Phillip Lawton left his apartment in Chelsea at the crack of dawn on Saturday morning, as he did every week, to rendezvous with the love of his life. Her name was **Sweet Sallie,** she was an old wooden sailboat he had owned for eight years, and he kept her in a small harbor on Long Island. He spent every weekend on her, no matter what the weather, and when it was decent, he spent all his time sanding, cleaning, painting. She was immaculate, and no woman had ever given him as much joy. He was fiercely proud of her, and he usually spent Saturday night on her, and Friday night too whenever possible. It was a prerequisite that the women he went out with also loved **Sweet Sallie.** Some did more than others. Most women got tired of the boat after a while, and Phillip's passion for

her. She was the possession he was most proud of.
He had loved sailing since he was a boy, even more
than he loved art. He was a good sailor, and would
often take her out in rough seas or summer storms.
But at those times, he went alone and didn't expect
anyone to go with him.

At thirty-four, he had been involved in numer-
ous relationships over the past years, but none
either serious or long-term. A few had lasted a year,
but most of them ran their course in a few months,
and by then he or the woman or both had figured
out that it was going nowhere and never would.
Phillip had high ideals about what he wanted in a
long-term relationship, and particularly a wife, and
his role model was his parents' marriage, which had
seemed perfect to him. He compared all relationships to theirs and wanted nothing less for the long
haul. His parents had been crazy about each other,
until his father's death three years before. They had
been the ideal complement to each other, and fit
together seamlessly. The whole relationship had always been characterized by humor, kindness, compassion, tenderness, a profound love for each other,
and deep mutual respect. Phillip had no sense of
how rare that was in today's world and thought it
was normal. His father was ten years his mother's
senior. They had met when she took one of his art
history classes at NYU. His mother was a serious
artist, for whose work his father had the greatest
admiration.

They had been unable to have children for the first fifteen years of their marriage, despite many attempts and several miscarriages, and had finally given up and decided that their relationship was so strong and meaningful to both of them that perhaps they would be happier without children, and had finally accepted their inability to have them. And six months later, when his mother turned forty, and his father fifty, she had gotten pregnant with Phillip, and this time the pregnancy went effortlessly to a successful end. They called him their miracle child, doted on him, and included him in the magic circle of their deep affection for each other. He had grown up bathed in the warmth of their love and approval, and every relationship he had as an adult fell short of the generosity of spirit and sheer joy he had seen between his parents, and he wasn't willing to accept less. And unless he had a relationship like theirs, he had no desire to settle down, and was comfortable alone. Maybe too comfortable.

His mother had been concerned, for several years now, that his standards were so high, and his idealistic vision of them so strong, that he would wind up alone when no one measured up to his parents' marriage. He didn't seem worried about remaining a bachelor and often said that he would prefer to be alone than with a woman who was less than what he wanted. And his mother had suggested to him that he was looking for a female with a halo and wings, which was certainly not who she was. But it was how Phillip viewed her, and he stubbornly refused to tolerate any woman's flaws. And by now, he liked his own habits. Adjusting to someone else was not his strong suit. As a result, he spent a lot of time alone on his boat, working diligently on it during the weekends. For now, **Sweet Sallie** was enough for him, or so he claimed. And solitude didn't scare him. He liked it.

On Sunday afternoon, after two good days of sailing in bright sun and strong winds, he drove into the city, to have dinner with his mother at her apartment, as he often did on Sunday nights, when neither of them had other plans. She liked to stay busy. She readily admitted that she was a terrible cook, and reminded him regularly of one of her many human failings that he chose to overlook. When he came to the apartment to have dinner, she would go to a nearby delicatessen and buy all the things he liked, and they would sit at her kitchen table, talk about her current work, her next gallery show, his discontent with Christie's, or anything else of interest to him. She was more like a friend than a mother to him now, was seldom critical of him, made intelligent suggestions, and at seventy-four was the most youthful person he knew, with an open mind, a deep knowledge of art she had always shared with him, and fascinating creative ideas. She was never afraid to tackle difficult or controversial subjects, and sometimes preferred them. Valerie had always encouraged her son to think outside the box and explore new concepts and ideas. She hoped that he would meet a woman who would challenge him, enough to conquer his own fears of winding up with the wrong woman, but so far he never had. She thought his expectations of a woman were unrealistic, but she hadn't lost hope for him yet, and hoped the right one would come along and shake him up a little. And he was young enough that there was no rush. But she was also well aware that he had gotten set in his ways, and enjoyed his own company too much. Lately, he had gotten lazy about dating. And his obsession with his boat didn't appeal to many women, as she pointed out to him.

"Why don't you go skiing, or take up some sport where you'll meet women?" she prodded him occasionally, and he just laughed at her. She didn't like interfering in his life, but was sorry to see him alone, and didn't want him to stay that way forever.

"I'm not trying to meet women, Mother. I meet women every day." The kind who sold the gifts men had given them when the marriage or affair ended, and had little respect or affection for the sentiment behind the gifts. They were only interested in the money they would get from selling them at auction. Or he met women who worked in the other departments at Christie's, who were sometimes a little too serious for him. He had gone out with one who was extremely knowledgeable about gothic and medieval art, and his mother had thought she seemed like a member of the Addams family when she met her, but didn't comment. Phillip had come to that conclusion too and stopped seeing her shortly after. He had been without a relationship for a year now, since the last one. And most of his friends were married by now and having first or second children. He preferred women his own age to younger ones, and many of them were married.

In the meantime, he had Sunday-night dinner with his mother whenever she wasn't too busy to see him. He enjoyed her company, and they often laughed at the same things. And he always relaxed in the comfortable chaos of her apartment. All her life, she'd had the ability to turn her surroundings into a magical world. She and Phillip's father never had a lot of money but were comfortable enough and had never lacked for anything; nor had their son. They were satisfied with what they had. Her circumstances had altered considerably three years before, from the insurance policy her husband had left her that she had known nothing about. It had dramatically changed her bank account, but not her life. She still enjoyed doing all the same things, and had never felt deprived by their lack of fortune. She intended to leave most of the insurance money to Phillip one day. She was careful and responsible with it, and hoped it would be useful for him, perhaps to start an art consulting business or a gallery of his own. She had mentioned it to him several times, but he wanted his mother to benefit from the money first. He thought she should travel, enjoy herself, and see the world. But she was too busy painting, and still studying, to venture far from home. "I'm having too much fun to go anywhere!" she would say, laughing at him, with her big bright blue eyes, and nearly unlined face.

She was still energetic, lively, and beautiful at her age. She was blessed with a youthful look and spirit. It was easy to see why her husband had been in love with her till the end. She was an enchanting woman full of mischief and charm, with a mane of once pale blond hair that was now snow white, and she often wore it loose down her back, as she had all her life.

By contrast, her older sister by four years, Winnie, was her opposite in every way. They were the yin and yang of life, but best friends nonetheless. While Valerie had never been concerned with the absence of luxury in her life, Edwina, Winnie, had thought of nothing else, and, like their parents, had worried about money and the possible lack of it, since she was a young girl. Born the year after Pearl Harbor, Valerie came into the world on the cusp of a more prosperous time. Winnie was born in 1938, nine years after their family had lost everything in the stock market crash, and she was a child in the years of the Depression and remembered their parents' constant discussions about money. Their family had had a considerable fortune, and both their parents came from aristocratic ancestors, but lost almost everything they had. Winnie's answer to their financial insecurity was to marry a young man from a wealthy family, and she had lived in extremely comfortable circumstances all her adult life. And when her husband died ten years before, he had left her a considerable fortune, and she still worried. Valerie had simply never cared about money, and always thought that whatever they had was enough.

Winnie and Valerie both remembered their father as a kind, though serious and somewhat chilly and austere man. He was a banker and was conservative about money. Losing their fortune had sobered him, and Valerie's recollection of him was of his being at the office most of the time. And her memories of their mother were of an ice-cold woman, whose approval she could never win, no matter what she did. They had had an older sister who died of influenza in Europe at nineteen, whom Valerie didn't remember, as she had died a year after Valerie's birth. Winnie, on the other hand, insisted that she had some vague memories of her, and made excuses for their mother's coldness by saying she had never recovered from their sister's death. She would never speak of her first daughter as the younger girls were growing up, and they had rapidly understood that the subject was taboo, it was just too painful for her.

Winnie had been born when her older sister was fourteen, and her arrival had come as an awkward surprise to her parents, which her mother had grudgingly adjusted to. But Valerie's birth four years later was simply too much for their mother. She was forty-five years old and seemed embarrassed to have a baby at that age, rather than pleased. Valerie had felt unwelcome in their midst all her life, until she married Lawrence and escaped the family she had nothing in common with. But Winnie was just like them, serious, austere, nervous, humorless, critical, and most of the time cold. She was a dignified woman, always concerned with doing the right thing, but never a warm one. There was nothing spontaneous about her, and she had grown up to be just like her mother. Valerie loved her sister anyway, and had managed to forge a strong bond with her. Valerie spoke to Winnie almost every day, and listened to her complain, often about her daughter Penny, who was more like Valerie than her own mother.

Penny was an attorney, with three children of her own, who Winnie thought were rude, unruly, and undisciplined, and she had never liked her son-in-law either. Winnie needed an orderly, peaceful life, unlike her younger sister Valerie, who was open to all possibilities and led what Winnie considered a bohemian life, as their mother had said about her too. But Winnie was more tolerant of her than their mother had been. Valerie had never been able to scale the walls her mother built around her, and eventually gave up, long before she died. She had never approved of her youngest daughter and made that clear. And with a husband and child she adored, Valerie had stopped caring about her mother's disapproval years before. She didn't miss her when she died, although Winnie had mourned her for years, and spoke of their mother as if she had been a saint. And Valerie understood even less, when she had her own child, how her mother hadn't been able to view her arrival as an unexpected blessing rather than a curse.

Valerie's family had been a mystery to her all her life, even Winnie, of whom she forgave much even now, and she often made jokes about having been switched at birth at the hospital with some other family. The greatest difference between them was that Valerie was a warm, loving person, and her parents and even her sister were ice cold. She thought of it as unfortunate for them, and was grateful that her son had inherited none of their traits. Nor had her niece Penny, who was a very sweet girl and a very successful lawyer. She was ten years older than her cousin Phillip, and they were good friends, more like sister and brother since both were only children, and she often called her aunt Valerie for advice, rather than dealing with

Winnie, which was always a no-win for her, in the face of her mother's criticism of everything she did, including a law degree from Harvard, which her mother thought was inappropriately ambitious for a woman. Penny was a better mother than Winnie claimed. Her philosophies about childrearing were similar to her aunt's. Winnie was hopelessly old-fashioned in her outlook, whereas Valerie was full of life and always willing to embrace anything new.

When Phillip arrived for dinner on Sunday night, Valerie was cleaning her brushes and had just finished painting. She was working on a portrait of a woman that had a mystical quality to it, and Phillip stood staring at it for a long time. Valerie had real talent as a painter, her gallery shows got good reviews, and all her pieces sold. She was represented by a respected gallery near her apartment in SoHo. They had lived there for as long as Phillip remembered, long before it became fashionable. And she enjoyed how lively it had become, and all the young people who lived there. She compared it to the Left Bank in Paris.

"I like your new painting, Mom," he said admiringly. It was a subtle change from her previous work. She was always pushing herself to grow as an artist, and studying new techniques.

"I'm not sure where I'm going with it. I had a dream about it the other night. The woman in it has been haunting me. It's driving me crazy," she said with a broad smile, looking happy and untroubled. The smell of her paints was heavy in the apartment, it was a familiar part of the artistic ambiance around her, along with the bright fabrics and interesting pieces she and his father had collected over the years, some pre-Columbian, others European antiques, some from India, and a number of paintings and sculptures by her artist friends. His father had thrived on the eclectic people she drew to them, and had enjoyed meeting most of them. He had called it a "modern-day salon," like those in Paris in the twenties and thirties, or the entourage around Picasso, Matisse, Cocteau, and Hemingway or Sartre. She also collected playwrights and writers, anyone who was steeped in the arts, or creative in some way.

"I'm sure you'll solve it," he said, referring to the painting. She always did. She put a great deal of thought into her work. They chatted easily while she spread out all his favorite food on the kitchen table. One of her greatest joys in life was spoiling him, in whatever way she could, even with a simple dinner in her kitchen. He was touched by the effort she made.

He complained about the jewelry department at Christie's again, and she reminded him that it was up to him to make a change, and not just sit there stagnating, waiting for fate to take a hand.

And then he told her about the collection of jewels he was going to see that week, and how impressive they appeared to be from the photographs he had seen.

"Who did they belong to?" she asked with an interested look.

"Some countess who died penniless with a fortune in jewels, and no heirs," he said, summing it up for her from the little he knew himself.

"How sad for her," Valerie said, sympathetic for a woman she didn't know, as she pushed her mane of white hair back with a graceful hand, and they sat down to dinner together. And eventually she got around to asking him if he was dating anyone special at the moment. He shook his head.

"Not since the last one I broke up with almost a year ago. I've just had casual dates since then. She hated my boat. I think she was jealous of it." His mother grinned at what he said.

"I think I would be too. You spend more time on that boat than with anyone you've gone out with. Women are funny about things like that—they expect you to spend time with them too."

"Oh, that," Phillip said, and laughed. "I will spend more time when I meet the right one." His mother gave him a cynical glance, and he looked sheepish for a minute. "What's wrong with spending weekends on a sailboat on Long Island Sound?"

"A lot, in freezing weather in the winter. You

have to do other things too, or you'll wind up alone on that boat forever. I was talking to your aunt Winnie about going to Europe together next summer, by the way," she said, as she handed him a platter of tomatoes and mozzarella with fresh basil leaves on it. "But she's not an easy person to travel with," Valerie said about her older sister.

"Are you going?" Phillip was curious.

"I don't know. I love Winnie, but she worries about everything and complains all the time. And everything is scheduled down to the last second. I like trips to be more free form, and make decisions as I go along. That drives Winnie nuts, and makes her anxious. We have to stick to her schedule at all times. It's a bit like enlisting in the army. I think I'm getting too old for that," she said, smiling.

"Or too young. I wouldn't enjoy that either. I don't know how she doesn't drive you insane." Phillip had kept his distance from his dour old aunt for years.

"I love her. That helps make her more tolerable. But traveling in Europe with her might be too much to ask." She had done it before, but always swore she wouldn't do it again, and then she did, mostly out of pity for Winnie, who had no one else to travel with. Both women were widowed, but Valerie had a much larger circle of friends, many of them artists, and in a wide variety of ages. Some of her friends were Phillip's age, and others were even older than she was. Valerie didn't care about their age as long as they were interesting, intelligent, and fun.

Phillip left shortly after dinner, and went back to his apartment to catch up on some work. His mother hugged him warmly, and he had a feeling she was going back to work on the painting of the mysterious woman after he left, and he wasn't wrong. Mother and son knew each other well.

"And good luck with that woman's estate this week," she said to him as he was leaving. "It sounds like her jewels would make an impressive auction, particularly if you tell something about her story in the catalog." She was right, of course, along with using photographs of the countess wearing some of the pieces, if they had any. It would certainly be more interesting than the heading that the jewelry was being sold by the surrogate's court of New York, which they would have to say too.

"Property of a Noblewoman," he said to his mother, quoting a typical catalog description, and she smiled.

"I like the sound of it already. Good luck," she said, and kissed him.

"Thanks, Mom. I'll call you, thanks for dinner."

"Any time," she said, and hugged him again, and a moment later he left. And just as he had suspected, the moment the door closed behind him, she went back to work. She was determined to get further insight into the woman she was painting.

Maybe the subject of her canvas was a noblewoman too, she thought to herself, and smiled again. Her work always had a certain mystery to it, and told a story, but sometimes it took her a while to figure out what it was.

# Chapter 5

Jane arrived at the bank before Phillip on Tuesday morning. It was pouring rain, her umbrella had turned inside out as soon as she left the subway, and she was soaked. She felt like a drowned rat. He looked no better when he arrived. He had forgotten his umbrella in the cab he had taken from Christie's, and he was ten minutes late. Traffic had been awful.

She saw him glancing around the lobby of the bank when he got there, trying to figure out who she was. She was talking to Hal Baker, and had spotted Phillip immediately in a dark suit and a Burberry raincoat. She noticed how tall he was and how businesslike he appeared. He looked more like a banker than an auctioneer. She had forgotten that he would be doing an auction immediately after. She was wearing boots and a down coat that had soaked the water up like a sponge, and black jeans and a heavy sweater. It was windy and cold outside despite the rain. Spring seemed like it was an eternity away, and New York was chilly, wet, and gray.

"Miss Willoughby?" Phillip asked, looking uncertain as she smiled and nodded, shook his hand, and then introduced him to Hal Baker. Phillip seemed personable and polite, as the two men greeted each other.

"Sorry to bring you out in such awful weather," Jane said apologetically. "I think it might be worth your while, though. The pieces are really beautiful," she said as they followed Hal downstairs to the safe deposit boxes. They didn't need the notary this time, as all the official work had been done, and the inventory had been notarized and was complete. Now all they had to do was make a decision about how to dispose of it. They had stopped running the notices that week, and no heirs had appeared. Jane thought it was really a shame that no one had surfaced.

Hal unlocked the box as he had before, and they followed him into the same cubicle where Jane had first seen the pieces and the other contents of the box. He set the box down on the table, and left them there alone. Jane took out the jewelry boxes one by one and set them on the table. Phillip began opening them. The first box he opened held a diamond and sapphire brooch from Van Cleef, and he looked visibly impressed. He saw the ruby ring next. He took a jeweler's loupe out of his pocket, and held it to his eye.

"This is a 'pigeon's blood' Burmese ruby," he said to Jane as he looked at it. "It's the finest quality and color there is." He took the loupe from his eye then and gazed seriously at her. "I'd say it's about twenty-five or thirty carats, at a guess. It is incredibly rare to find a ruby of this quality in that size. It's a knockout, and would sell for a fortune." He examined the emerald ring after that, which he guessed was about the same size as the ruby, or slightly larger, and declared it to be first rate as well. He placed it back in its box with great care, and opened the box with the diamond ring next, which was even larger, and this time he smiled. "Wow!" he said, sounding like a kid, and she laughed.

"That's what I said when I saw it," she admitted, and then looked sheepish. "I tried it on," she confessed, and he grinned as he imagined it.

"How did it look?" he teased her a little. This was suddenly fun. The jewels were fabulous, and if the surrogate's court sold them with Christie's, it was going to be a fantastic sale.

"It looked pretty good. It's the closest I'll ever get to a rock this size," she said, smiling back at him. "How big is it?"

"Probably about forty carats, depending on how deep it is. That's just a guess." But he had gotten good at estimating size and quality of stones during his two years in the jewelry department, and had taken a basic gemology class to educate himself. These were the finest pieces he'd seen so far.

He studied the invisibly set sapphire necklace and earrings from Van Cleef, and the pearls, which he said were natural, which made them incredibly valuable too, and the tiara, the pearl and diamond antique choker from Cartier, and the pieces from Bulgari in Rome. He went through all of it in under an hour, and looked at Jane when he was finished, deeply impressed.

"Until I saw the photographs, I figured all you had here was junk. And once I saw the pictures, I knew it would be good stuff, but I didn't expect quality like this. And no heirs have come forward at all?"

"None," she said sadly. "Would you like to see the photographs of the countess? She was a beautiful young woman." She took them out, and they went through them together. He pointed out where she was wearing the jewelry—there were several photos. And what struck Jane again was how happy she looked with the handsome count, and how much he seemed to love her as he gazed at her adoringly.

"He appears to be old enough to be her father," Phillip commented.

"He was thirty-eight years older," Jane responded. She had figured it out from his obituary and her passports.

"What were their names again?"

"He was Count Umberto Vicenzo Alessandro di San Pignelli. And her maiden name was Marguerite Wallace Pearson—di San Pignelli, once they married. She was eighteen then, and he was fifty-six." Jane looked wistful as they stared at the photographs together, and Phillip glanced at Jane in surprise.

"It's a fairly common name, but my mother's maiden name was Pearson too. Maybe they were distantly related, cousins or something, although it's probably just a coincidence. There was no Marguerite that I know of. I'll have to tell my mom. I'm not suggesting that she's an heir," he said, looking embarrassed, "it's just an odd coincidence of name. She's never mentioned a relative who married an Italian count, and the countess was a generation older than my mom. Maybe she was a distant cousin of her father's, or more likely no relation at all." But the name had sparked his interest, though not as much as the jewels, and the fabulous auction and buzz they would create. He hadn't seen jewels like that in all the time he'd been there, and they had sold some beautiful things in the past two years. "Who should I speak to about an auction?" he asked Jane directly.

"My boss, Harriet Fine. I'm just a temporary clerk. I'm finishing law school in June."

"NYU?" he asked with interest.

"Columbia. I had to do an internship or clerk for a court to finish. Surrogate's court hasn't been too entertaining till now," she admitted to him as Hal Baker came back and locked up the safe deposit box again, and they followed him out. "All the clerkships I wanted were taken, family court and criminal, so I got this. I took it instead of probate, which would have been worse." She smiled ruefully, and so did he in answer.

"The jewelry department at Christie's isn't much better. They transferred me from the art department two years ago, which felt like a prison sentence, although I have to admit, this auction would be spectacular. Are they talking to any other auction houses?" he asked, and she shook her head.

"No. Just you. Christie's was my boss's first choice. She told me to call you, so I did. I'm glad you like Countess di San Pignelli's things. I think they're beautiful too."

"They're better than beautiful. They are all of the finest quality. It's rare to see pieces of that caliber, with such important stones. The count and countess must have led quite a life."

"It looks like it from the photographs," Jane said quietly.

"I wonder what happened after that," he said,

curious. It was impossible not to wonder about her and the count.

"I wish I knew too. They look so happy together, although she had sad eyes."

"Did she?" Phillip was surprised. "I didn't notice. I was too distracted by the stones." He smiled, thinking that Jane was an interesting woman. He had expected to meet some boring humdrum clerk. She was a vast improvement over that.

"What happens now?" Jane asked him when they were standing in the lobby of the bank again, and Hal had left them to go back to his desk.

"My boss speaks to yours," Phillip explained. "We make a bid to sell the pieces, negotiate our fee, and discuss the catalog with them. If they like what we have to say, they consign the pieces to us, and we put them in our next Magnificent Jewel sale, probably in May, September, or December, right before the holidays. We would do a whole section about her with some of the photographs, and try to make it sound romantic and appealing, and then we sell them, take our portion of the hammer price from the seller and the buyer, and turn the rest over to the state. It's pretty straightforward, unless an heir shows up of course, but it doesn't sound like that's going to happen, from what you've said." She had told him about going to the nursing home and the countess's old apartment building in the city, while he was photographing the jewelry for his files, so he could show his boss what kind of story they could build in the catalog, even though she wasn't well known. But a "Countess" had some magic to it, and the jewels spoke for themselves. He didn't need to make a hard sell.

"None of it will probably happen before I go back to school," she said quietly, thinking about it. "I'll have to keep an eye out for the auction, or maybe someone could let me know." She had taken a personal interest in this, and he could see it.

"You should come to the auction. A sale like this will be very exciting."

"Will you be the auctioneer?" She was curious about him.

"I doubt it. This sale will be too important. It will be part of a bigger sale, but it will certainly be one of the highlights. Important jewelers and collectors will be bidding from all over the world on the phone, and some of them will be in the room. It would be quite an experience for you to see it." And opportunities like this wouldn't come her way often.

She was pensive before she answered. "I think it might make me too sad." He was touched by what she said. She really cared about this woman, although she had never known her. "It seems so heartbreaking that she died alone, with no family around her." Phillip nodded, not sure what to say, as they left the bank together. The rain had finally stopped.

"Can I give you a lift?" he offered as he hailed a cab.

"No, thanks. I'll take the subway back to the office. I'll tell my boss that Christie's would be interested in selling the pieces at auction. I'm sure she'll call you."

"If she doesn't, I'll call her. I might anyway. We wouldn't want this sale to get away from us," he said, as he opened the door of the cab.

"Thank you for coming," she said politely, and he smiled as he closed the door and waved as they drove off. He had been bowled over by everything he'd seen that morning—the jewels, and the girl.

# Chapter 6

When Phillip got back to the office, he had to get ready for the jewelry sale they were doing at noon, and he only had half an hour to prepare. It was not an important sale, and was listed under the heading "Fine Jewels," which was a far cry from the "Magnificent Jewels" he had just seen, in a whole other category. And he realized he would have to discuss them with his superiors after the noon auction. He didn't have time now to do them justice, and he wanted to show them the photographs he'd taken.

The sale he ran at noon went smoothly, but took longer than expected, and it was four-thirty before he walked into the office of the head of the jewelry department. Ed Barlowe was looking over a list of the hammer prices from that afternoon and seemed pleased. He glanced up at Phillip.

"Nice sale," he commented, as he set the list down on his desk. "What's up?" he asked, pointing to a chair and inviting Phillip to sit down.

"I looked at an abandoned estate today with a clerk of the surrogate's court. It's a collection of extraordinary pieces, all by major jewelers," he said quietly, as he handed Ed the photographs he had just printed out, and he watched Ed's face as he sifted through them, examining each one. He looked startled when he glanced back at Phillip.

"Are these pieces as good as they look?"

"Better. The photographs don't do them justice," Phillip said calmly. It was the first time he'd enjoyed working in the department in two years. This was like discovering oil, or finding gold. Even if they weren't his, it was exciting to be part of it, and hopefully have a role to play in the sale.

"Do we know the provenance?" his boss asked him.

"We have a name, and some photographs. She was a young American girl who was married to an Italian count from 1942 till 1965. Probably a young heiress. She died without money or heirs. All she had were the jewels, which the bank discovered when they drilled open the box."

"Is everything in order?" Ed asked with concern. "Were all the time restrictions respected?"

"Diligently. The box was abandoned three years

ago, the bank drilled it open after thirteen months and sent a registered letter in the right time frame. They waited two years after that, notified the surrogate's court, and they've placed ads to locate the heirs. None have turned up. I saw all the records myself."

"Good." Ed seemed pleased, as he sat behind his desk, an enormous antique partner's desk that Christie's had purchased years before. "I don't want slip-ups with pieces like this. Why don't you call the clerk of the court and discuss our fees with them, just so everything is clear? I'd like to schedule it for the May sale. There's still time to photograph them. We can just squeak under the wire, and get these into the catalog. Make sure you call her right away."

"I'll take care of it first thing tomorrow morning," Phillip assured him, and left Ed's office with the Pignelli file in his hand. It was too late to call them today, it was after five, and as a government office, he knew they'd be closed.

He was tempted to call Jane to tell her, but it would be improper to discuss it with her before they came to an agreement with Harriet, so it would have to wait, although he hoped their paths would cross again.

And the next day, as he had promised Ed he would, he called Harriet, per Jane's suggestion, had a frank discussion with her, said they were interested in selling the pieces, and quoted their fees of ten percent from the seller on the hammer price, with the rest of the proceeds going to the state. And the cost of photography for the catalog would have to be paid for by the surrogate's court, which didn't surprise Harriet, she was used to it, since they put items up for auction all the time. He told her they would want to use some of the photographs of the countess in the catalog, to help hype the sale, if Harriet didn't mind. She didn't care, it was fine with her. And she promised to get back to him with a decision by the end of the week. He told her that they were a little pressed for time, to get the items into the catalog for the May sale. She said she'd see what she could do, and Phillip wondered if she'd shop it around and get quotes from Sotheby's too, but Jane had said it would be unlikely, since Harriet had suggested Christie's herself. So all he could do now was wait for their answer, and hope the surrogate's court placed the items with them. They'd be a fabulous addition to any sale.

He still hadn't heard from them on Friday, but didn't want to push, and he decided to wait until Monday to call Harriet again, although Ed inquired about it on Friday afternoon.

Phillip spent the weekend on his boat, as usual, and dropped by his mother's apartment on Sunday afternoon on his way home. He wasn't staying for dinner, since Valerie had told him she was going to dinner with friends. Someone else had invited her to the ballet, and she'd declined.

She poured tea for both of them, and they spent a few minutes together before she had to leave. She was already dressed for the evening, and looked very nice in jeans and a heavy black sweater, with heels, and she was wearing makeup.

"How did your week go?" she asked him with interest, and he told her about the jewelry he had seen, and Christie's wanting to include it in a sale. He told her he hadn't had an answer from the clerk of the surrogate's court yet, but was planning to pursue it again the next day.

"The jewelry must be impressive if Christie's wants to sell it," Valerie said, finishing her tea. And then he remembered the coincidence of names.

"The woman's maiden name is the same as yours, by the way," he said with amusement, "though I doubt we're related to this woman," he added, and she nodded.

"It's a pretty common name. I'm afraid we don't have any relatives who'd own that kind of jewelry, although it would be nice if we did." She smiled at him, but they both knew that she wasn't dazzled by it, and money was never a strong motivating force to her, particularly other people's. His mother had never been a greedy woman, and had always been satisfied with what she had.

"I think the prices on this sale will go through

the roof. The pieces are incredibly beautiful, with big stones of high quality. It's going to be an exciting sale, if the court lets us have it."

"I'm sure they will. Why wouldn't they?" Valerie said reassuringly as she stood up. "Now I have to go."

"You never know. They might get a better deal from another auction house."

"I hope not," she said loyally.

He thought for a second about telling her about meeting Jane, but he felt stupid doing it. He'd probably never see Jane again. So he stood up, hugged his mother and kissed her good-bye, and promised to call her soon.

"Have fun tonight," he said as she closed the door and he got in the elevator.

The next morning he called Harriet Fine again. She apologized for not getting back to him. She had been waiting for clearance from her own supervisors to proceed with the sale, and she had just gotten it an hour before.

"It's a go," she said quietly. "They've accepted your terms for the sale."

"That's fantastic!" Phillip said, sounding excited. "I'd like to pick up the pieces in the next few days, so we can photograph them for the catalog. May I have your authorization for the bank?"

"I'll take care of it right away," Harriet assured him. "I'll notify the bank. Will you pick them up yourself?"

"Yes. I'll probably bring a security guard with me, with a town car. After that, should I keep them in our safe at Christie's pending the sale, or do you want them returned to the court?" It all sounded like a headache she didn't want or need, and this was much bigger than any sale she'd dealt with before. And Christie's was certainly reliable and trustworthy to keep the jewels in their vault until the sale.

"I'd prefer that you keep them until the auction. I'll send a clerk over to ensure that the transfer goes smoothly the day you pick them up. Just let me know when you plan to do it." He thought about it for a moment and checked his calendar before he spoke. The following morning was clear.

"Would tomorrow be too soon?" he asked hesitantly. "I could be there when the bank opens at nine." And with luck, he could get them to the photographer by ten, so they could get started.

"That will be fine. I'll have the clerk bring all the documents and photographs back to us, but the jewelry is yours." He knew Ed Barlowe would be pleased.

"I'll want to reproduce some of those old photographs," he reminded her.

"That's fine," she said simply. There were no family members to object, and it seemed all right to her, if it would help the sale. This was all about business now, for the state. She was always diligent about defending their interests. "I'll have my clerk at the bank at nine," she confirmed, and a moment later she walked into Jane's office, and told her she had to be at the bank the next morning, to collect the documents from the safe deposit box, and observe the transfer of the jewels to the representative from Christie's. Jane wondered if it would be Phillip again—she wasn't sure and didn't want to ask. She had liked talking to him, and examining Marguerite's jewels and photographs with him, and she liked the idea of seeing him again, if it worked out that way. If not, that was all right too. And from what Harriet had said, she gathered that the Christie's sale was moving forward.

She mentioned it to John that night. He had finished another paper, and had a hamburger with her at a nearby diner, before going back to the library to do some more work. She felt like they hadn't had a decent conversation or dinner together in weeks. Instead of catching up on each other's news at dinner, she had the sense that they had become disconnected. It was an unhappy feeling, and all she could hope now was that their relationship would come back to life in June. It was the light at the end of the tunnel, and until then, she was trying to be patient and supportive. He was like a phantom roommate.

But in three and a half months it would be over. She could hardly wait for their life to pick up where it had left off. He was beginning to seem like a stranger. And he didn't seem interested when she told him the jewels she had been mentioning were being put up for auction at Christie's. They were just too far from anything he cared about, and not on his radar screen at all. He went back to the library after dinner, and she went home, wishing that their relationship was still the same as it had been six months before, but it just wasn't. He seemed less and less connected to her every day.

He was still sleeping soundly when Jane left the apartment and took the subway downtown the next morning. She got to the bank just as Phillip Lawton got out of a town car with a driver. She noticed that there was a security guard in the front seat. Phillip was wearing a blazer and slacks, a crisp blue shirt, and a good-looking dark blue Hermès tie, under a well-cut navy overcoat, and he seemed pleased to see her. They stood chatting outside the bank for a few minutes, waiting for the doors to open. They had both arrived five minutes early.

"It sounds like everything's on track for the sale at Christie's," Jane said as she smiled at him. She was wearing a short gray skirt and a pea coat, and she was fresh and bright in the morning sun, as her neatly brushed hair hung past her shoulders. And he noticed that she was wearing small gold earrings.

The doors of the bank opened, and Phillip motioned to the Christie's security guard to join them. He had brought two large leather cases to put the jewels in, and the guard from Christie's followed them inside and down to the safe deposit boxes.

Jane had to sign several sets of papers to take responsibility for emptying the box, on behalf of the surrogate's court. And then Phillip had to sign another set to her, acknowledging receipt of the twenty-two pieces of jewelry he would take with him to consign to Christie's. It took several minutes to get all the papers in order, and then Jane took out the jewelry boxes and handed them to Phillip one by one. He had signed a copy of the inventory as well. Jane then put all the documents in a large manila envelope she had brought with her, with the seal of the surrogate's court on it. She put the letters, passports, and bank statements in it. And then she and Phillip sifted through the photographs. He selected half a dozen that he thought would reproduce well. One of the count and countess in front of the château. Another of them in evening clothes, where she was wearing the sapphire necklace and earrings. A beautiful one of Marguerite alone, also in an evening gown. Another of them on horseback, and one skiing. And a sweet one of her in the tiara, looking very young. The photographs established them as a golden couple, and had all the elegance and glamour of a bygone era. And then Jane sat looking at the photographs of the little girl.

"I wonder who she was," Jane said softly.

"Maybe a younger sister," Phillip suggested.

"Or a child who died. Maybe that's why Marguerite looked so sad," Jane guessed about the countess, frustrated that they would never know. There was so much they didn't know about the woman who had owned the jewels. Why had she left the States during the war, and gone to Italy? How had she gotten there, since her entry point into Europe had been England via Lisbon, according to the stamp in her passport? How had she met the count, and when had they fallen in love, and what had she done between 1965 when the count died, and 1994 when she moved back to New York? And what had made her come back? The address on her documents had been a Roman one after 1974, so what had happened to the château? Jane wished that there was someone who could tell them and explain it all. Marguerite had left no trace of her past except the photographs, two sets of letters, her addresses at different times, and the jewels.

"I guess some questions are never answered, and some mysteries are never solved," Phillip said thoughtfully, as he watched Jane put the photographs of the little girl into the envelope of documents and photographs he wasn't borrowing. Jane sealed the envelope carefully so nothing would fall out, and she had written Marguerite's full name on it, to turn over to Harriet when she got back, as her documents had to be preserved for seven years, in case relatives eventually turned up. Jane didn't know what would happen to them after that, if they would be archived or destroyed. It made her sad again to think about it. And she had all the releases Phillip had signed to give to Harriet as well. And as they stood up in the now familiar cubicle, the security guard from Christie's picked up one of the leather bags. Phillip picked up the other one, and Jane followed them out. The empty safe deposit box was sitting on the desk. Hal came to say good-bye to them as they left. He almost seemed like a friend now, in this unusual adventure they had embarked on, to auction off Mrs. Pignelli's jewels.

Phillip offered Jane a ride again, and she declined. He promised to call her when they had reproduced the photographs, and return them to her at the court. They drove away a moment later as Jane headed toward the subway, with the thick envelope in her arms. She was feeling pensive, as she thought about the documents in her possession, and the jewelry Phillip had just taken. The last remnants of Marguerite di San Pignelli's life were about to be sold. It was a somber thought as she hurried down the subway steps to go back to the court.

# Chapter 7

On Thursday, Phillip's mother called and asked if he wanted to go to a black tie event with her at the Metropolitan Museum that evening. It was an elegant dinner that the Costume Institute gave every year, and she was on the board. Her sister was supposed to go with her, but she canceled at the last minute, with a bad cold. Winnie was a hypochondriac, and always had some minor ailment or other, and she didn't like to go out when she was sick.

"I'm sorry to ask you so late," his mother apologized. "But I have the tickets, and I hate to go alone." He thought about it for a minute and then agreed. It was nice to be able to do something for her. Valerie was very independent, led a busy life, and rarely asked anything of her son. And she told him she thought he'd enjoy it. He had been to the same dinner with her once a few years before, right after his father died. It was an impressive event, and he knew that the tickets cost a fortune. It was one of the nice things she could do with the money she got from her husband's insurance. Now she went every year, and treated her sister to the ticket. His aunt Winnie would never have spent the money, although she could afford to, far more so than his mother.

He picked Valerie up at her apartment that night, and she was wearing a simple black evening gown, which showed off her still trim figure, and a silver fox jacket that she had had for years and it still looked glamorous on her. Seeing her, he was suddenly reminded of the photographs of the countess that he had picked up from the photographer that afternoon. His mother looked nothing like her, but they had the same aristocratic elegance of another time. And he was proud to be with her, as she took his arm and followed him to the town car he had hired for the evening.

"Darling, you spoiled me!" she said, smiling at him like a delighted child. "I thought we'd take a cab."

"Certainly not," he said, as he slipped onto the backseat beside her. He was wearing a well-cut tuxedo he'd had made on Savile Row in London, the last time he'd been there for an auction.

"You look very handsome," she commented, as they headed uptown to the Met, and when they arrived, he saw that the cream of New York was there in full regalia, including the governor and the mayor, and it was in fact the glittering event she had promised.

They were seated at a table that included one of the curators of the Costume Institute, a well-known fashion designer, and a famous artist, and the conversation was lively. Phillip was next to a young woman who had produced a successful play on Broadway, and they talked about theater and art all evening. He would have been interested in her, and she was very attractive, but he was disappointed to discover that she was there with her husband, who was a writer, and had just published his first book. It reminded him of how active his mother was, and the crowd she moved in. She was a very unassuming woman, but she had a natural grace that was timeless and ageless, and he had noticed more than one man admiring her that evening. They were among the last to leave, and talked animatedly about the party on the way home.

"I had a terrific time," he said, and meant it. "The woman I sat next to was great, and I thought the man you sat next to was very nice."

"It's always a fun night," she said, still lively and full of energy. "I didn't even have a chance to ask you what you've been up to. How are you doing with the sale of that woman's jewelry? The one married to the Italian count," she asked him with a warm smile.

"The surrogate's court consigned the pieces to us on Tuesday. We've been photographing them all week. I don't know what it is, but there is something about that woman that is so haunting. Maybe because we know so little about her. It's fertile ground for one's imagination. Are you sure you're not related to her? It's so odd that you both have the same maiden name."

"Along with about ten million other people with Anglo-Saxon origins. I'm sure the New York phone book has ten pages of Pearsons, not to mention Boston. But if I claim her as a relative, do I get some of her jewelry?" She grinned at her son mischievously.

"All of it," he said happily.

"What was her first name?" Valerie asked casually. She didn't have even the remotest thought that they were related. Just as she said, it was a very common name, and she had no relatives who had gone to Italy and married a count around that time. It was the sort of thing she would have known. No one in her family had ever lived in Europe. They were all firmly planted in New York, and had been for generations.

"It was Marguerite," Phillip answered as they drove downtown, and Valerie looked surprised.

"Now that is a coincidence," she said brightly,

but still unimpressed. "There were dozens of them in our family. It was my oldest sister's name, and my grandmother's and great-grandmother's. It was a popular name in those days, at the beginning of the twentieth century. And I think Pearson is almost as common as Smith. What a shame." She laughed as she looked at Phillip, who was surprised as well. He had only heard his great-grandmother referred to as Maggie, and never knew his great-great-grandmother's first name. "You'll have to show me the catalog when you have it. I'd love to see her jewels," his mother said wistfully.

"I'll give you a catalog when I have them. She was very beautiful, and the count was very dashing. I wish we knew more about them, but we just don't. I have to research the jewelry now. Cartier keeps records on every piece they ever made. I'm going to ask them to check their archives to see if they have any information that might help the sale. I have to go to Paris next month, and I was planning to go and see them myself, to look for the working drawings in their archives."

"Now, that sounds very exciting," his mother commented as the car stopped in front of her building. The doorman opened the door for her, and she kissed Phillip, thanked him for joining her, and disappeared into the building. And on the drive uptown, he thought of Marguerite again, and the email he wanted to send to Cartier, and then his mind drifted to Jane. He was going to return the original photographs to her the next day. He wondered if it was an adequate excuse to invite her to lunch. He wanted to see her again. He still hadn't mentioned her to his mother, but there was nothing to say except that she was a temporary clerk at the surrogate's court. He knew nothing else about her except that she was graduating from law school. But she seemed intelligent and pleasant to talk to, and he wanted to know more.

He was sitting at his desk the next day, thinking about Jane, with the photographs of Marguerite in front of him, when he decided to call her, and use that as an excuse. He had nothing to lose, and maybe something to gain if she agreed to lunch.

He called the phone number he had for her at the surrogate's court, and Jane answered on the first ring.

"Jane Willoughby," she said in a smooth, even voice, and for a fraction of an instant, he didn't know what to say, and then told her he'd called to tell her the photographs were ready to send back to her.

"I could messenger them over to you today. Or if you like," he said, trying to sound calm, "I could give them to you at lunch." He suddenly felt foolish for asking and was sure she'd refuse. "Or does that sound ridiculous?" he asked, with the odd sensation of being fourteen years old. He hadn't been on a date in three months, and it seemed awkward. Why would she accept?

"That sounds very nice." Jane seemed surprised. "I could pick the photographs up," she said, feeling strange too. But she was sure it was innocent, and only business. Phillip was just being cordial, after their common interest in Marguerite.

"I'll give them to you at lunch," he said, since she hadn't rebuffed him, hung up, or laughed into the phone, which he had almost expected her to do. He wished he were free that day, but he wasn't. He had to attend a department meeting at one o'clock, to discuss upcoming sales. "What about Monday? Does that work for you?"

"Yes, it does," she said pleasantly, reminding herself not to assume that he meant anything by it. It was just lunch.

"If you meet me at the office, there's a nice little restaurant nearby. I'll keep the photographs in the safe till then."

"That would be fine," she said with a lilt in her voice, and then added, "Have a nice weekend," after he told her to come to Christie's at noon.

"Thank you—you too."

They hung up a moment later, and Phillip sat staring out the window, thinking about her, wondering what she'd be doing until he saw her on Monday, and if she had a boyfriend or was unattached.

The next day Jane was still feeling slightly awkward about their lunch date, and mentioned it casually to Alex when they met for lunch at

Balthazar, and were going to a movie afterward. John was with his study group in the Hamptons for the weekend. It didn't sit well with Jane, but she hadn't complained about it, knowing it would only heighten the tension between them. He was paying for a share of the house but never invited Jane to join him. He said it was exclusively for the use of the study group.

"I think I may have done something stupid yesterday," Jane confessed as they finished burgers that were sinfully good.

"Like what? Slept with your boss?" Alex looked amused.

"My boss is a woman, and she's hell on wheels. Sometimes I think she hates me," Jane said about Harriet, and was thinking about Phillip's invitation to lunch. "No, I met a guy over this case I've been working on. He works at Christie's, in the jewelry department, and we consigned some jewelry to him to sell for the state. I've only met him twice, and he invited me to lunch."

"And you turned him down?" Alex was instantly disappointed.

"No, I accepted. I'm having lunch with him on Monday. But he's not some fusty old guy from an auction house. I hope he didn't mean it as a date."

"Are you kidding? Is he young, single, and attractive?" Jane nodded with a smile on her face.

"He's young, and attractive. I don't know if he's single but I assume he is. He acts like it."

"Then why the hell not have lunch with him? Why wouldn't you? Just go to lunch," Alex said with a determined look. "You're not going to have sex with him at a restaurant. You need some distraction at least, and male attention. What's he like?" Alex was curious about him, and pleased for her friend. Her relationship with John was such a wasteland at the moment. She felt that an opportunity like that was long overdue. Alex thought she needed to meet other men, and John had been miserable to be with for months.

"He's good-looking, intelligent, well dressed. His background is in art, but he wound up in jewelry at Christie's, and he doesn't like it, but he seems to know a lot about it. He's just a nice guy." Jane looked ill at ease as she said it, still worried that she'd done the wrong thing, by accepting lunch with him. She was living with John, after all. But Phillip hadn't invited her to dinner, just lunch.

"Can I come too?" Alex teased her. "And if this guy is interested in you, don't tell John when he comes home on Sunday night, just because you feel guilty. You have nothing to feel guilty about. As far as you know, it's just a business lunch." And whatever it was, Jane was looking forward to it, even if she was nervous.

"Maybe I should cancel," Jane said as they left the restaurant, still uneasy about the lunch. "Maybe my boss wouldn't like me having lunch with a guy from Christie's."

"If you cancel, I'll kill you. Go. He sounds nice. And it's none of your boss's business who you have lunch with. It'll be good for your ego." John certainly wasn't, Alex thought, but didn't say. He had been ignoring Jane most of the time for months, and took her for granted, and that wasn't new. Alex didn't like the way he spoke to Jane at times, although she never seemed to notice. Alex thought he was arrogant and dismissive and full of himself. And Jane seemed to think that was okay. "You're not doing anything wrong," she reminded Jane again. "Have some fun for a change."

"Yeah, maybe," Jane said, unconvinced, but she was going. She liked him and was flattered by the invitation, whatever his motivation. "He probably just wants to talk about the sale," she said to reassure herself.

"Exactly," Alex said, trying to encourage her so she wouldn't feel so guilty. "Just remember, it's a business lunch. Then it won't seem scary."

"He wouldn't ask me otherwise," Jane said, sure of it now. He probably just wanted to discuss some aspect of the sale.

"Of course not. You're ugly, stupid, and boring. He probably feels sorry for you," her friend said, teasing her, and they both laughed as they got to the movie and bought tickets and then popcorn and Cokes. It was a nice way to spend a Saturday afternoon, and now that she'd talked to Alex about it, Jane felt better. Alex didn't tell her that she was beginning to suspect John was sleeping with Cara, from what Jane had said. He was spending way too much time with her and the group, at the library and coming home at four in the morning or later, and weekends in the Hamptons without Jane. She didn't want to panic Jane about him, but she was happy Jane was going to lunch with Phillip. It was exactly what she needed. A little male attention in her life from someone new, even if it was just business. And they both forgot about it, as they watched the movie. Alex couldn't wait to hear how lunch turned out on Monday, and made Jane promise to call her that afternoon.

While Alex and Jane watched the movie, Valerie went to visit her sister. Winnie's cold had turned into a sinus infection and bronchitis, and she was miserable. Valerie had promised to buy some groceries for her, and turned up with chicken soup from a nearby deli, and a bag full of fresh fruit, and oranges she was going to squeeze for her.

Winnie lived on Seventy-ninth Street and Park Avenue, which was a long way from Valerie's cozy apartment in SoHo. Winnie had lived in the same apartment for thirty years. It was somber looking, filled with dark English antiques, and Valerie always wanted to pull the curtains back to let in the sunlight when she went there, but the tomblike atmosphere suited her sister. She was feeling terrible, and Valerie went to the kitchen to squeeze the oranges for her, and handed her a glass of fresh juice a few minutes later. Winnie had a maid during the week, but no help on the weekends, and she was completely unable to fend for herself. Valerie put the groceries in the fridge, and told her to heat the soup in the microwave later, as Winnie looked at her mournfully. The doctor had given her antibiotics, but she said they weren't working.

"Maybe it's pneumonia. I should get an X-ray next week," Winnie said nervously.

"I think you'll be fine," Valerie said calmly, and handed her some magazines she'd brought her to distract her.

"I had a flu shot before Christmas, and a pneumonia shot. I don't think they worked," Winnie said, looking panicked. She was going to be seventy-nine on her next birthday, nearly eighty she often said, which frightened her. She was terrified of dying, and went to the doctor all the time.

She drank the orange juice, and then took a swig of Maalox in case it gave her heartburn. She took a dozen different vitamins every day, and still got sick. Valerie tried not to make fun of her or tease her about it. Winnie took her health very seriously, although her daughter Penny said she was strong as an ox and would outlive them all.

"So what have you been up to this week?" Valerie asked her, trying to get her mind off her health.

"Nothing. I've been sick," she said, as they sat

down in the little sitting room where Winnie watched TV alone at night. She didn't go out as often as her sister, had few friends, and no activities that interested her, except playing bridge, twice a week. She was good at it. Valerie thought it was incredibly boring, but didn't say so. At least it gave her something to do that involved other people.

"We missed you at the museum party on Thursday night. We had a good table. I took Phillip." Valerie knew that if she'd gone with Winnie, her sister would have insisted on leaving right after dinner. She hated staying out late, and said she needed her sleep. "Have you talked to Penny?"

"She never calls me," Winnie said sourly. Her relationship with her daughter had been strained for years, and she complained that her grandchildren never came to visit. They loved visiting Valerie and exploring her studio, but she never told her older sister, nor the fact that she and Penny had lunch occasionally so she could vent about her mother. Penny's complaints about her mother were similar to what Valerie had felt about her own. Winnie and their mother were cold women, who always saw the glass as half empty and never half full.

"Phillip is working on an estate at the moment," Valerie said to distract her. It was hard coming up with subjects Winnie wouldn't say something unpleasant about. She was constantly annoyed at something—taxes, or the fees charged by the bank, her losses in the stock market, her rude grandchildren, a neighbor she was feuding with. There was always something. But Phillip's estate sale seemed like a neutral subject. "The surrogate's court had him appraise the contents of an abandoned safe deposit box, and they found jewelry in it worth millions. The woman it belonged to died intestate, and no heirs have turned up, so they're selling it all at Christie's, for the benefit of the state."

"As high as our taxes are, the state doesn't need millions in jewelry," Winnie said sourly. "If she had all that jewelry, why didn't she leave a will?" It seemed stupid to her.

"Who knows? Maybe she had no one to leave it to. Or maybe she was sick or confused. She was American and had married an Italian count during the war. It's sort of a romantic story, and a coincidence—her maiden name was Pearson, like ours. And even more so, her first name was Marguerite. Phillip asked if we might be related to her, if she was a cousin or something, but I don't know of anyone in our family who lived in Italy or married an Italian count. She died seven months ago at ninety-one. Actually," Valerie said, suddenly looking pensive, "that's the same age our sister would have been. That's even weirder." And as she said it, she felt as though puzzle pieces were slipping into place or cogs in a machine. "I've never thought of it, but what if Marguerite didn't die when we were kids, but moved to Italy and married an Italian count? It would have been just like our parents to disapprove of it, and pretend she had died. Wouldn't that be amazing?" Valerie said thoughtfully, turning the idea around in her mind, as her older sister looked at her, horrified by what she was saying.

"Are you insane? Mother never got over her death. She mourned Marguerite, our Marguerite, our sister who died, for the rest of her life. She couldn't even bear to see a photograph of her, she was so heartbroken, and Daddy forbade us to talk about her." Valerie remembered it too.

"She might have been just as heartbroken over her marrying an Italian count. Can you see our parents ever accepting that?" And Valerie had thought it odd that when their mother died, they had found not a single picture of their older sister among their mother's things. Valerie had always assumed that photographs of her had been put away, but if they were, they had never found them. They had no photographs of their older sister, even as a child, although Winnie claimed she remembered what she looked like, which Valerie seriously doubted. And the idea she had just come up with was fascinating to her, but Winnie looked at her in strong disapproval.

"Are you trying to convince me or yourself that you're an heir to that jewelry worth millions that Christie's is selling? Are you that desperate for money? I thought you still had most of Lawrence's insurance," although it certainly wasn't worth as much as the jewelry that was going to be auctioned. Valerie looked at her as though that was ridiculous, and not simply rude.

"Of course not. I'm not interested in the money. But the story is intriguing. What was Marguerite's middle name?"

"I'm not sure," Winnie said fiercely, "Mother and Daddy never talked about it."

"Was it Wallace? I think that's the name Phillip mentioned when he asked me."

"I've never heard that name, and I think you're getting senile," Winnie said angrily. She suddenly reminded Valerie more than ever of their mother. There had always been subjects they weren't allowed to ask about or mention, and their older sister was one of them. They'd been told all the years that they were growing up that their older sister's death at nineteen was a tragedy that their mother had never recovered from, and they weren't allowed to bring it up, or anything relating to her. Eventually, it was as though she had never existed. And she'd been so much older than they were that they never knew her. It was as though Marguerite had been their real child, and Winnie and Valerie were the interlopers, unwelcome visitors in their parents' house, and Valerie even more so than Winnie, since she had been so different from them all her life, just as she was from Winnie now. "How dare you come up with a theory like that, to besmirch our sister's memory, and dishonor our parents? They were kind, good, loving people, no matter what you choose to say about them now."

"I don't know who your parents were," Valerie said coolly, looking straight at her. "My parents had ice in their veins, and stone hearts, Dad and particularly our mother, and you know it. She liked you better because you were more like her. You even look like her. But she couldn't stand me, and you know that too. Dad even apologized to me for it before he died, and said she'd had a hard time 'accepting' me, because she was so much older when I was born, which is a poor excuse for the way she treated me. I was forty when Phillip was born, and it was the happiest day of my life, and still is."

"Mother was older, and she went through a difficult change of life. She was probably suffering from some form of depression," Winnie said, always willing to make excuses for her, which Valerie had stopped doing years before. Their mother was a mean woman, and had been a terrible mother, to Valerie certainly, and she was only slightly warmer to Winnie, which Winnie had decided was acceptable. But it wasn't, by any means, to her younger sister. In fact, although she had been cold to Winnie, which was her style, she had been downright cruel to Valerie at times, in ways she wasn't to Winnie.

"She was depressed for my entire life?" Valerie said cynically. "I don't think so, although it's a good story. And I think there are some very strange coincidences here. The age of the woman who left the jewelry, the fact that our sister was a forbidden subject, and this woman who became a countess went to Italy around the same time our sister left and died a year later. And what was she doing in Italy during the war? They never told us, and we were never allowed to ask. Don't you want to know more? What if she'd been alive for all these years, and only died recently? How many Marguerite Pearsons of that age can there be in the world? What if she's related to us, Winnie? Don't you want to know?" Valerie suddenly couldn't tear her mind away from the possibilities, and she wanted answers, but all she could do was guess.

"You want the jewelry and the money," Winnie accused her, and Valerie stood up, disgusted with her.

"If you really think that, you truly don't know me. But you know me better than that. You're just afraid to find out what they may have hidden from us. Why? What good are all those taboo subjects now? Who are you protecting? Them or yourself? Are you so frightened that you don't want to know the truth?"

"We know the truth. Our sister died of influenza at nineteen while traveling in Italy, and it broke our mother's heart. What more do you need to know?"

"There was a war on then, Winnie. What was

she doing there? Visiting Mussolini?" It had always seemed odd to Valerie in later years that their sister had been in Italy during the war, with no explanation for why she'd been there. But there was no one left to ask.

"I don't know, and I don't care. She's been dead for seventy-three years. Why would you even think of digging all that up now? And dishonoring our parents? The only reason I can think of is that you want to claim you're the heir to the jewelry being sold at Christie's. Did Phillip put you up to this? Is he in on it too?" Winnie said accusingly.

"Of course not. I told him we weren't related to her. But suddenly I'm wondering if that's true. Maybe we are. Maybe she isn't even a cousin. Maybe that was our sister who married the Italian count. We may never know the truth, but at least at our age, we're allowed to ask."

"And who's going to tell you the truth? Mother and Father are gone. We have no photographs of her. No one else would know. And I don't want to know. We have a sister, who, we were told with absolute certainty by our parents, died in 1943. That's good enough for me. And if you're not after this money or jewelry that doesn't belong to us, just let it go."

"It's not about money or jewels. It's about the truth. We have a right to that. We always did. Our parents cheated us out of love and affection and kindness while we were growing up. And maybe they cheated us out of our sister as well. If she were alive, we could have gone to find her, and met her when we grew up. Maybe she was alive for all that time. And if so, I want to know that now."

"You're always demonizing our parents, and they don't deserve that. Let their memories rest in peace. What did they ever do to you to deserve this kind of disrespect? They can't defend themselves now," Winnie said in a fury.

"They didn't love me, Winnie, and you know it. I'm not even sure they loved you, or were capable of it. But I know they didn't love me. I felt it every day of my life until I left and married Lawrence." She said it quietly and with enormous strength. It was the core truth of her life.

"What you're saying is a lie," Winnie said, standing to face her and shaking with rage. "Get out of my house!" she shouted at her younger sister, and what Valerie could see in her eyes was fear, raw terror, of a ghost she couldn't face and everything she didn't want to know. Valerie nodded, picked up her coat and bag, and walked out without a word. But the voice of truth she was seeking couldn't be silenced anymore.

## Chapter 8

Phillip spent the weekend on his boat, as he always did. Valerie had plans on Sunday night. She had said she was dining with friends, and he knew she had the occasional suitor, men her age who admired her, usually widowers. But she was never interested in them romantically and treated them as friends. Valerie had made it clear to him several times that the only man she had ever loved, or would love, was his father, which was easy to believe, given how happy they'd been together. Valerie went out with friends, but not on dates.

Phillip wanted to do some work at home, but he stopped in to see her on the way to his apartment. He called first, and she was back from dinner. She made tea for them after he declined a drink, and she seemed subdued to him, and he asked her if anything was wrong.

"No, no, I'm fine," she said quickly, but he wasn't convinced.

"What did you do this weekend?" He was always concerned about her, and something in her eyes seemed sad.

"I went to see Winnie yesterday."

"How was that?" He knew how difficult, and aggravating, his aunt could be. He was his cousin Penny's confidant too. His mother smiled with a small wintry look before she answered.

"She was Winnie. She's sick, and she wasn't in a great mood." And she'd been in an even worse one when Valerie suggested that their mother had never loved them, and might have lied to them about Marguerite.

"You're a saint," Phillip said with feeling. He avoided his aunt whenever he could. He had given up trying to have a real or decent relationship with her years before.

They talked about an exhibit of South American artists Valerie had been to during the weekend that she had enjoyed, and another show was coming to the Met that she wanted to see. And then she doubled back to what was on her mind. She didn't want to say too much about it to him, and tried to sound casual when she brought it up.

"I was thinking about your big jewelry sale again,

the one of the contents of the abandoned safe deposit box. It probably sounds ridiculous, but I'd love to see the photographs you have of Marguerite—in fact, all of them. You said you were going to use a few in the catalog, but I'd really like to see them. You never know how it might inspire me—maybe I'll get a painting out of it. The story is haunting, and the fact that she wound up so alone, from what must have been a very glamorous life when she was young, and married to the count." She tried to make it sound artistic and historical, rather than personal, and he looked pensive when she asked.

"I've only got a few of them myself, and I was going to return them to the clerk of the court at lunch tomorrow. I'm sure she's not supposed to pass around those photographs, the surrogate's court is responsible for them, and any papers, correspondence, or documents. But the clerk I've been dealing with is a very nice woman, she's a law student, and she might be willing to make copies for you if I ask her. I'll ask when I return the ones I have tomorrow." The way he had said it instantly caught Valerie's attention, although Phillip thought he had sounded very neutral about it. She knew him better.

"Do I sense some kind of interest there, other than returning photographs to the court?" He was stunned by what she said. It was always as though she could look into his soul. It had seemed almost eerie to him when he was a boy. She always knew what he was up to, as though she could read his mind.

"Of course not. She's been very helpful. I've only seen her twice at the bank," he said, brushing his mother off, but she had an odd feeling that she was on to something.

"Sometimes that's enough." She smiled directly at him, not wanting to tell him her own suspicions about her parents lying about Marguerite. "Anyway, see what she'd be willing to let you have. I'd like to see all the photographs if I could." She was very definite about it, which made him curious. He knew her well too.

"Is there some deeper reason?" he asked candidly.

"No. I just have strong feelings about this woman, of sympathy and compassion. She must have been so lonely, and it's amazing that she held on to the jewelry for all this time. It must have meant a great deal to her, or the man who gave it to her. It seems like a powerful love story somehow."

"I hadn't thought about it that way. The jewels are just very beautiful, and worth a great deal of money," Phillip said honestly.

"I'll bet that's not why she hung on to them, or she would have sold them long ago, particularly if she needed money." Her circumstances sounded so sad when Phillip had told his mother about her. And now, like him and Jane, Valerie was haunted by her. That much made sense to him.

"Are you at all intrigued by the coincidence of your maiden names?" It wasn't a loaded question, just a direct one.

"Not really, although I suppose that could be some kind of bond." She looked vague as she said it, and then got up to take their teacups into the kitchen, and turned the conversation to something else. She hoped that her request would be fruitful and the young clerk he had mentioned would give him copies of the photographs. She didn't dare bring it up again, or alert him to what she wanted to know. She wasn't even certain what she was looking for, since she had never seen a picture of her oldest sister, but she hoped there might be some kind of clue, if they were related somehow. You never knew. And she had felt compelled to ask. She had thought of nothing else since the day before. And Winnie's vehement denial of the possibilities she had proposed to her only made her want to know more. She wanted to actually see Marguerite di San Pignelli now, in the only way she could, in the contents of the safe deposit box.

The next morning, before meeting Jane for lunch, Phillip sent an email to Cartier in Paris, to inquire about their archives. He knew that they saved working drawings of all the pieces they made, particularly the ones for important people, or unusually beautiful orders that had been placed. Cartier prided themselves on their archives. And he explained that Christie's would be selling several of their more important pieces from the 1940s and 1950s, which had belonged to the Countess di San Pignelli. He gave them Umberto's name as well, and said he believed that they had lived in Naples and Rome between 1942 and 1965, from when Marguerite had arrived in Europe until her husband died. He doubted that any of the pieces had been commissioned after that. And he said he wanted to know everything about them, who they had been commissioned by, when, and for what reason. The original prices would have been interesting to know too, although they would bear no relation to their current value. And the origin of the stones would be helpful to them too. Anything that Cartier could provide would enhance the catalog and create further interest in the sale. He asked them to email any available information, and said he would also be in Paris in late March for an important jewelry sale being run out of Christie's Paris office. He said he would be happy to meet with the director of their archives at that time.

He sent a similar email to Van Cleef and Arpels, and had enough time to return a few calls, before Jane arrived. He was finishing his last call, to make an appointment for an appraisal, just as Jane was walking through the impressive lobby, with three-story ceilings and a huge mural, and getting in the elevator to meet him in the jewelry department on the sixth floor. She was a little awestruck when she arrived. She had expected it to be an ordinary office building, and Rockefeller Center was anything but that. It had been home to Christie's for eighteen years. A young woman in a simple black suit and a string of pearls called Phillip in his office and told him that there was a Miss Willoughby waiting for him in the reception area. Phillip smiled and left his desk instantly.

He came out to meet her, happy to see her, and escorted her back to his office, which was handsome and had an enormous desk.

"So this is where you organize all those important jewelry sales," Jane said with a soft smile. It made it all seem very real suddenly being there.

"Some of them. I don't make the decisions here, I just implement them. And we have offices all over the world." He told her about the upcoming Paris sale then. Some of Marie-Antoinette's jewelry was going to be auctioned off by a family that had owned it since the Revolution. They had offered to sell it to a museum, but they wouldn't pay enough, so it was going to a public auction, along with other important pieces, many of them historical. Paris had seemed like the right venue for the sale. There were often equally important sales in London, and some in Geneva, but New York was the venue for most of their important sales. He explained to Jane that whatever the location, there would be people bidding on the phone, and in the room, from around the world.

"It's very exciting, especially when the bidding gets hot, and there are several active bidders determined to get the same item. That's when the price goes sky high. It all depends on how badly someone wants it. Jewelry is very emotional, but the really big prices are in art. That's not just about passion, it's about business and investment. Art is perceived as a better investment than jewels. But things can get pretty heated at our jewelry auctions too. The Elizabeth Taylor sale in 2011 went right through the roof. It was the highest total for any collection we've ever achieved before or after. There was a lot of mystique to the woman and her jewels. There are only a handful of people who create that kind of excitement and demand, like the Duchess of Windsor. You could sell one of her handkerchiefs and make a fortune." He smiled at Jane as he explained. "I had just started here, and was still in the art department during the Elizabeth Taylor sale. We sold a number of her paintings too. She had some fabulous art, most of it given to her by Richard Burton. It was a tumultuous relationship, but he was very generous with her. She was the kind of woman who inspired that. Even the sale of her clothing brought in a huge amount, as though women felt that if they could wear some item of her wardrobe, they could 'be' her, or inspire the same kind of love and passion she did. It's all part of the magic of an auction, which is why we want to make Marguerite di San Pignelli's sale as personal as we can. The provenance, and who owned it previously, is very important to a lot of buyers." Jane was riveted by what he had said. He made auctions sound almost magical. It was all new to her.

"I'd love to come to the sale," she said softly, as he led her out of his office.

"I told you, you can sit in the room if you like, or with me at the phones and hear what's happening with the bidding. It can get pretty crazy, especially at these big prices." They were still working on the estimates they were going to put on the pieces, but the final results were always hard to predict—it all depended on how much a buyer wanted a piece, or better yet two or several buyers, determined to get an item at any price, to create a bidding war. The seller and the auction house always hoped for that, and the bidder who ultimately prevailed, no matter what the cost. Phillip would love Marguerite's pieces to draw that kind of interest, and the more they could put in the catalog to add to the excitement, mystique, and hype, the better it would be for the sale. And even though the sale was only to benefit the state of New York, Phillip's innate professionalism made him want the results to be exceptional. The pieces they were selling deserved it.

He explained all of it to Jane as they went through the lobby, left the building, and walked two blocks to the restaurant. It was a tiny place, but cozy, pretty, and warm. He had asked for a quiet table, and Jane settled back against the banquette and smiled at him. Everything he had told her had been interesting, and had helped to put her at ease with him. This was obviously not a date, and Alex had been right, she had nothing to feel guilty about. This was all about the upcoming sale that they were both involved in. She felt foolish now for having been worried about it.

"So how did you spend your weekend?" he asked.

"I went to the movies with a friend," Jane said benignly. "And did some review work for the bar exam, and worked on my final paper."

"That doesn't sound like fun," he said, looking sympathetic. She seemed like a serious person, and he admired her for what she was doing, and had done very well, with the Pignelli estate. "What kind of law do you want to go into?" he asked with interest.

"Family law. Child advocacy. While parents are battling in a divorce, sometimes people forget what's best for the child. All these tug-of-war arrangements, joint custody where a child switches homes on alternate nights, or every few days, or flip-flops week by week so both parents feel they're 'winning,' can screw the kids over in the end.

I want to start there, in a family law firm, and see where it takes me after that. Foster care, working with indigent kids. There are a lot of possibilities."

"So you're not interested in estate or tax law?" he asked, smiling at her.

"Hell, no!" she said, and laughed. "I can't think of anything worse. This case has been really interesting, but everything else I did at the surrogate's court has been tedious and depressing." After she ordered cheese soufflé, and he ordered confit de canard, Jane asked, "What about you? What did you do this weekend?"

"I spent the weekend with my mistress," he said matter-of-factly, and Jane looked startled.

"That's nice," she said, trying to be open-minded about it, but it confirmed that this was definitely not a date. So much for Alex, and what she'd thought. And he looked innocent as he smiled across the table at Jane.

"She's a thirty-foot, classic forty-year-old sailboat I keep on Long Island. She eats up all my money, and takes all my energy and concentration, and I spend every weekend taking care of her. I think that's pretty much what a mistress does. And being with her is pure joy. I can't stay away from her, much to the dismay of every woman I've ever gone out with. Her name is **Sallie.** Maybe you'd like to meet her sometime, when the weather gets warmer. It's a little chilly on Long Island Sound right now." Not that he cared. He went out on her no matter what the weather, winter or summer. Jane could see the love in his eyes, and she laughed.

"A boat is stiff competition for most women, more so than any mistress. My father keeps a sailboat on Lake Michigan. My mother says it's the only rival she's ever had. I used to sail with him every weekend when I was a kid." She didn't tell him that her father's boat was three times the size of his. "His boat is the love of his life."

"**Sweet Sallie** is mine," Phillip confessed proudly, without apology or shame. He thought it best to be honest right from the first.

"I'd love to see her sometime," Jane said easily. "I went to sailing camp for three summers in Maine when I was a kid. I was kind of a tomboy since I have no siblings and my father taught me to sail. Then I discovered high heels and makeup in high school and kind of lost interest in sailing. But I still go out on the boat with him sometimes when I go home. My mother hates it, so he always wants me to sail with him."

"**Sallie** has broken up most of my relationships," he said with a slightly sheepish look. "How has your parents' marriage survived? Or are they divorced?" He was learning about her, and he liked what he'd heard so far.

"No, they're together. I think they came to a compromise years ago. My father doesn't ask her to sail with him anymore, and she doesn't expect him to go skiing with her. My mom was a champion ski racer in college, and won a bronze in the Olympics, downhill racing. She still loves it, and he hates skiing, so they each do what they like to do. And they expected me to learn both, but I'm not in my mom's league on the slopes. She skis the French Alps and goes helicopter skiing in Canada every year."

"My mother is an artist, and she's pretty good, very good, in fact. I can't draw a straight line. My father was an art history professor, so I take after him. I've always been passionate about art, and boats." He smiled.

"I feel that way about the law," she said as they ate their lunch, "and championing the cause of the underdog. And I'm passionate about protecting kids. I worked for a legal coalition for inner-city kids in Detroit during the summers when I was in college, and I was a paralegal at the ACLU before I went to law school. I finally decided to stop horsing around and get my degree. It's been a rugged three years. The surrogate's court has been pretty uneventful compared to all that, until now. All you get to do is dispose of the belongings of people who had no one to leave them to, never thought about it, or didn't care, and settle disputes between greedy relatives who weren't interested in the person when they were alive. It's not very happy work. I couldn't do this for the rest of my life. I barely made it through the last three months. And I have kind of an unfriendly boss. I guess you get cynical and sour dealing with this kind of thing all the time, and I think she has an unhappy life. She's never been married, and she lives with her sick mom. I think she's a very lonely woman. She's been nicer to me lately, but we got off to a bad start." Harriet seemed to have more confidence in her since the Pignelli estate, but Jane could never imagine their being friends, or even having lunch together at work. Harriet kept her distance at all times and remained aloof. Jane had the feeling that Harriet had no life, other than work, and caring for her mother, at night and on the weekends.

"As I told you, I've been unhappy, assigned to the jewelry department," Phillip said. "All I wanted was to get back to art. But I have to admit, this sale has made it more interesting for me. Something about it touched me." So did meeting her, which he didn't say. He didn't want to sound stupid or soft, or scare her off. But Jane was very real and genuine, which appealed to him, almost as much as Marguerite's estate and the woman who had owned the jewels, and he liked talking to her.

They chatted easily during lunch, exchanging experiences in their respective fields, and personal views on a variety of subjects, including relationships, travel, and sports. He told her how much he had enjoyed his trips to Hong Kong for work, and that now, as superficial as he had found jewelry in the beginning, and the people who bought and sold it, he had become intrigued by all things jade. It represented infinite mystery to him, and he said it was an area of expertise that few people understood and did well. And then he remembered his mother's request.

"This probably sounds silly, but my mother has become totally enthralled by and wrapped up in what I've told her about Marguerite, and the sale. Maybe she feels some tie to her because they had the same maiden name, although they're not related. But as an artist, she has a very creative mind, and is always interested in the hidden aspects of things. She has an amazing imagination, and a kind heart. She asked if she could see copies of all the photographs in the safe deposit box, just to get a feeling for her. She thought it might inspire a painting, not necessarily of Marguerite herself, but maybe someone like her. It's hard to understand how artists work sometimes. She wanted to see the photographs not just of her, but also of Umberto, and even the ones of them at parties, all the pictures that we looked at." It didn't sound outlandish to Jane, and she thought his mother sounded like an interesting woman.

"Do you think she'd want to see the pictures of

the little girl?" They still didn't know who she was, or what relation she'd been to Marguerite, if any, and they didn't know her name.

"Why not? It's part of the mystery surrounding her," he said simply, and Jane nodded, thinking about how to fulfill his request. "Do you want me to return the ones I have, and then you can send me the complete file, or should I get these copied and give them back to you another time?"

"Why don't I take these now? I have to ask my boss about giving you copies," she said, pensive for a minute. "Would it be all right if I told her you wanted to see them all again for the sale, for a last, comprehensive look? I think if I say it's for your mother, she would balk, but if they're for you, the sale, or the catalog, she won't hesitate, and then I can send you the entire file, and you can copy them for your mom. I don't see anything wrong with that." He nodded and agreed with her, pleased. "I'll ask her when I go back to the office. I have all of them on my computer, I just want to ask her permission to send them to you, so I don't get in trouble later. She's been giving me a free hand with it. But I've been doing it according to the rules."

"If you send them to me in an email, I can print them up for my mother. She's not a computer person. It would probably take a year for her to open the files." They both smiled and she said her own mother wasn't good with computers either, as he gave her back the photographs he had. Computer skills were not of their parents' generation, particularly his mother who was considerably older than her parents, and old enough to be her grandmother, or even his, since she had been so much older when he was born. But he said that she was younger in spirit and had more energy than anyone he knew of his own age. "She has a sister who's only four years older and acts like she's a hundred. It's hard to believe she's almost the same age as my mom—they seem generations apart. I guess it's all in your outlook on life, and how connected you stay to the world. I don't think my aunt Winnie ever was. My mother says their parents were like that too, stuffy and old-fashioned and rigidly stuck in their ways and antiquated points of view. My mother is entirely different, fortunately. I never knew my grandparents, but I take her word for it, if they were anything like my aunt. My maternal grandmother died before I was born, and my grandfather when I was a year old." And then he startled Jane by saying that he'd like to see her again sometime, maybe for dinner. He said he'd had a great time at lunch with her, and she said that she had too.

"Dinner might not be such a good idea," she said regretfully, looking at him across the table, and wishing that she could. "I've been living with someone for the past few years. We've hit kind of a rough patch lately. He's getting his MBA in June.

It's all he thinks about. I hardly see him, and our time together is pretty much a disaster at the moment." She didn't tell him that the relationship was too, which would have seemed disloyal to John. She didn't want to give Phillip the impression that she was more available than she really was. She was still living with John. "I have lots of free time on my hands, since he's either at the library or with his study group, but I figure things will get normal again when we graduate. I don't think it would really be fair for me to go to dinner with someone else right now." Phillip admired her for her honesty and the fact that she didn't want to sneak around behind John's back, which was clearly not her style. She was smart, attractive, and straightforward. She seemed to have it all, and he felt like it was just his luck that she was involved with someone else. The good ones always were.

"Maybe a movie sometime," he said hopefully, "just as friends. Or you could come out on the boat some weekend in the warm weather, while he's studying."

"I'd love that," she said, her eyes shining. She was grateful that he understood, and a little disappointed too that she wasn't free, but she was glad she'd been honest with him. Now he knew. And it didn't seem to discourage him from wanting to see her away from work. Maybe they could wind up friends. She'd had a wonderful time with him at lunch.

They left the restaurant, and he walked her to the subway. She promised to ask Harriet about sending him copies of all the photographs, and he knew she would. She was a woman of her word, and had done everything so far that she'd promised to do.

"Thank you again for lunch," she said warmly, as he smiled down at her as they stood next to the subway stairs.

"Let's do a movie soon. And I want to introduce you to **Sallie,** as soon as she's presentable. I'm going to paint her hull in a few weeks." There was always some part of her that he was working on, just like Jane's father with his boat. She had spent a lot of weekends scraping, sanding, varnishing, and painting to help him when she was young. She knew all about men with boats, and smiled at what he said.

She went down the subway stairs then and disappeared, as Phillip walked back to work, thinking about her, and looking forward to seeing her again. He was disappointed that she had a boyfriend, but there was always the possibility, however remote, that things wouldn't work out with them, even after graduation in June. He was willing to wait and see.

Alex called Jane as soon as she got off the subway and was walking to work.

"So how was lunch?" She had been itching to call her for the past two hours and couldn't wait for Jane to call her.

"It was great. He's such a nice guy. I told him about John, and he understood."

"Why did you do that?" Alex was instantly annoyed. Clearly Jane was not destined to be a femme fatale.

"I had to. He asked me to dinner, and I told him I couldn't. But he suggested we go to a movie sometime, and he has a boat. He invited me to go out on it with him this spring." She was happy at the prospect, and it all sounded hopeful to Alex. She was pleased for her friend.

"That's perfect. Don't write him off yet. You never know what will happen with John, and this one sounds like a good man."

"He is. His mother is an artist, his father was a professor, and he's very knowledgeable about art. I might go to the Christie's sale with him."

"He seems interested in seeing you again. Today was a perfect first move." Alex was treating it like a chess game or a battle plan to catch him, which wasn't Jane's style either. She had never done anything premeditated or conniving to catch a man. Things either happened or they didn't, and Phillip seemed that way too. Alex liked to give destiny a hand to get what she wanted, which didn't always work for her. Some men figured it out and ran like hell, and the ones who fell into her well-laid traps often turned out to be stupid and bored her.

When Jane got back to work, she had a stack

of messages on her desk, of people she had to call, and two new folders of cases that had been referred to the court, all small estates. She didn't see Harriet till four o'clock when she brought one of the completed folders back to her, after determining that the person listed was in fact deceased, just as she had done with Marguerite in the beginning. She handed the file to Harriet across her desk, and Harriet thanked her. She appeared tired and discouraged, and Jane almost felt sorry for her.

"Everything okay?" she asked hesitantly. Harriet looked as though she might have been crying, which was unusual for her. There was a vulnerability to her that Jane had never seen before or even suspected.

"More or less. Thanks for asking," she said with tears shining in her eyes. "I had to admit my mom to the hospital last night. She has advanced MS, and she's getting worse. She was having trouble swallowing and breathing. I may have to put her in a nursing facility now, and she's going to hate it if that happens." There was no way to reverse the disease, and Harriet had been caring for her at home for seven years with the help of visiting nurses. "We knew it would come to this sooner or later. She's just not ready to face it, and I'm not sure I am either. It's challenging, but I'd rather keep her at home with me."

"I'm sorry," Jane said gently. She had always

suspected that Harriet had a sad life, and she had heard that her mother was sick, but she didn't know it was as bad as this. And the genuine pain and sadness on the older woman's face tore at Jane's heart. Some people had such hard lives, and Harriet Fine was one of them, and her mother. She had given up her own life to take care of her invalid mother, and it was all she had now. It seemed too late for her to marry, and have kids. And when her mother died, she would be all alone. It almost made Jane cry when she answered. "Is there anything I can do?"

"No, but you're kind to offer." She didn't tell Jane how jealous she had been of her at first. She was young and free and alive, with a whole life and career ahead of her. For Harriet, it was more than half over, and everything she could see ahead of her was a dead end. But she had made her own choices, for better or worse, along the way. What one forgot while doing so, however good one's motives, was that you don't get the time back in the end. And one day, the game is over. Jane's youth and opportunities were what Harriet resented, although it wasn't Jane's fault. And she had come to like her, in spite of it. Harriet thought she would make a good lawyer one day. Harriet had nothing bad to say about her, and had grown to like Jane, with her gentle, sunny ways.

"By the way." Jane remembered Phillip's mother then. "The jewelry rep at Christie's asked if I could send him digital copies of all the photographs we have in the Pignelli case, from the safe deposit box. I think he wants to check them again for the catalog. Is it all right if I send them to him?" It sounded as innocent as it was, and Harriet didn't need to know they were for his mother.

"Of course," Harriet answered, and didn't ask any questions. Jane went back to her office then, wrote a short email to Phillip, thanking him for a delightful lunch, and told him she had gotten permission to send the images. She sent him all of them in a separate email a minute later, even the ones of the unidentified child, so the selection was complete.

He saw the email come through, smiled as he read her short note, and printed the photographs for his mother, and another set for himself, just to have them if he wanted to refer to them again. He put both sets in confidential envelopes, and sent one set to his mother by messenger. Jane had made it easy to fulfill his mother's request, and then he went back to work. He had been in a good mood all afternoon after his lunch with Jane. It made him even sorrier that she had a boyfriend, but he was determined to see her again anyway, even in the guise of friendship.

Jane thought about Phillip too, as she took the subway home that night. She was hoping to see

John, since he had sent her a text that he'd be back
from the library early. She didn't feel guilty about
Phillip, since she'd been honest with him, and
she had decided to follow Alex's advice, and not
say anything about it to John. Things were tense
enough between them at the moment, without
adding fuel to the fire.

She was pleased that John was home when she
walked into the apartment. He was sprawled out
on the couch, with papers all around him, his computer on the table, and he was reading something.
He seemed happy to see her, and she leaned over to
kiss him as he lay there.

"What a pleasure that you're here for a change,"
she said sincerely.

"What's that supposed to mean?" he asked, instantly irritated. He had dark circles under his eyes,
as he'd had for months. Learning to become a successful entrepreneur wasn't easy, and seemed a lot
harder to her than becoming a lawyer.

"It means I'm happy you're home," she said
simply. His temper was always short these days,
he was sleep deprived, and he obviously felt guilty
for the time he wasn't spending with her. "Should
I make something for dinner?" she offered. "Have
you eaten?"

"I don't have time. We're meeting at Cara's in
an hour. I have to get going." He got up off the
couch, and Jane looked disappointed. And it didn't

go unnoticed that Cara seemed to have become house mother to the group.

"Are you going to the Hamptons this weekend?" Jane asked, as she sat down on the couch where he'd been lying. She looked worried as she asked him, wondering if it was going to be another lonely weekend.

The Hamptons were deserted in winter. They walked on the beach when they took breaks, even when there was snow on the ground. The walks were healthy and invigorating, and John said the air cleared their heads. And they all pitched in doing the cooking, and none of them brought their significant others, so Jane had never been invited.

"I need to," he said to justify it. "I think I'm going to be out there every weekend now till June." He looked almost belligerent as he said it, which was pure guilt. He was ready for a fight, but she wouldn't give it to him. She tried to be understanding, and not rock the boat unduly. They were on very thin ice these days.

"How do people manage to graduate who don't have a house in the Hamptons?" she asked him in a more acerbic tone than she usually used when they discussed it. But hearing that he was going to be at Cara's with the others every weekend for the next four months was not good news to her. It wasn't even about jealousy now, although some of it was; it was about respecting their relationship and trying to maintain it through this dry spell, and he really wasn't trying. He was doing whatever worked for him, and forgetting about her. It was tough to live with.

"You don't need to be a bitch about it, Jane." His comment was particularly unfair since she hadn't been and had made a real effort not to press him about it, or complain.

"I'm not, but you're gone all the time. How many nights do you think you've slept here in the last month? Ten? Five? And now you're gone every weekend. What am I supposed to think about us?"

"You're supposed to think that that's the deal if you live with a guy getting an MBA in four months," he said in a nasty tone.

"I have a hard time believing that the other MBA candidates are sleeping with their study groups, and spending every weekend in the Hamptons. Some people even manage to maintain relationships and marriages." She paused for a moment then, and suddenly decided to confront him. "Are you sleeping with Cara, John? Maybe we should just be honest with each other. Is it over with us? If it is, I'll move out."

"Is that what you want? You want out?" he said, moving his face close to hers. It didn't frighten her, or even intimidate her—it just broke her heart. She could hear sucking sounds as she watched their relationship slide down the drain like an aspic. He was no longer the kind, funny, easygoing man she had fallen in love with three years before, and loved to be with. He was a stranger, with or without an MBA.

"I don't want out. But I want you in this relationship with me if you still want it. I'm here all by myself." And he hadn't answered her question. And maybe because she'd had lunch with another man that day and had had a nice time and been treated well, she decided to press it. "What about Cara?" Her eyes never left his, and then he turned and walked away.

"What about her?" he said angrily.

"Are you having an affair with her?"

"Of course not," he said, but didn't sound convincing. "I don't have time to sleep with her or anyone else."

"You have the opportunity. You spend a lot more time with her than you do with me now."

"I spend more time with Jake, Bob, and Tom too, and I'm not fucking them either, or are you accusing me of that too?" He tried to make her seem ridiculous for worrying about Cara, but that only made him seem more guilty. And she had serious concerns about their relationship and the amount of time he was spending with Cara and not with her. "Look, this is the deal now. You know how hard I've been working." He tried to speak to her more calmly but barely succeeded. "If you can hold out till June without going crazy and driving me nuts with jealous bullshit, we can make it. If you're going to bust my chops about it all the time, I can't take it. So figure out what you want to do. You need to keep yourself busy until I'm done. Until then, I have no time to give you, and I don't want to hear about it every time I see you." Listening to him, she wondered if she should move out. He had absolutely no interest in her needs or feelings, only his own. It was what Alex had never liked about him. Even at his best, she had thought he was a totally selfish guy, and he was proving her right.

Jane didn't say a word to him, as he strode around the apartment gathering things up to put in his backpack and computer bag. She saw a clean sweatshirt, socks, and underwear go into the back-pack and knew it meant he wasn't coming home.

"I take it you're staying out tonight?" she said tersely.

"You're not my mother, Jane. I'll come home when I want to and when I can." She didn't know exactly when it had happened, but he had clearly lost respect for her. Completely. She didn't answer him. She didn't want to dignify his insults with a response, or lose her temper at him. She had to come to her own conclusions, and she was begin-ning to realize what they were. She knew in her heart of hearts that this would never be a healthy relationship again.

He didn't say good-bye when he left the apart-ment, nor did she. She was too ashamed to call

Alex and tell her what had happened, or what he had said to her. She just sat on the couch, thinking about it, her heart aching, and burst into tears. No matter how long it took her to deal with it, it was over, and she knew it. Now it was a matter of self-respect. Whatever he had been in the beginning, he no longer was. And all he could see in his future was Cara, not her. It was time to move on.

# Chapter 9

When Valerie got the copies of the photographs that Phillip had printed out for her,
she spread them on her dining room table carefully, and stared at them intently. She thought
there was a faint family resemblance somewhere
around Marguerite's eyes, although she wasn't sure
to whom. Maybe to her mother, or to herself, but
it was so faint that it could have been her imagination, or something she wanted to see that wasn't
there. And she was struck in several photographs
by the poignant expression in Marguerite's eyes,
despite the wide smile. She was haunted by the
images of her with Umberto, and the tangible love
that jumped from the pictures and that they obviously shared. He looked as though he adored her,
and she seemed happy with him. Marguerite was

so young in the early photographs that it touched Valerie's heart.

But she couldn't honestly say that she was certain they were related. Marguerite had a very different look and style, and was very much herself. She had a very distinctive appearance and was a beautiful girl. And although Valerie didn't resemble Winnie and her parents, she didn't bear a strong similarity to Marguerite either. There was no reason to think that they shared anything more than a fairly common name. Valerie herself didn't know why she was so intent on establishing a bond between them. It wasn't about the jewelry, it was something more. It was about history and blood, if that proved to be the case. She felt closer to the woman than ever after staring at her photographs for two days. And finally, late the second night, she spread out the pictures of the unknown child. She looked like a sweet little girl, and the photographs documented her two or three times a year. At first she was only a baby, then a toddler, and a little girl.

But it was a photograph of the child at around the age of five that nearly stopped Valerie's heart. She picked it up and stared at it, looked at it under a bright light, and stared into the little girl's eyes. She'd had dresses like that as a child, and worn the same haircut. So had half the children she knew at the time. But it was the face that was familiar to her, and the eyes. She was certain of it. She sat for hours looking at it, went away, and came back to it. She examined all the pictures more closely, and in two or three she was almost sure. Not totally certain, because most of them were from a little distance, and they weren't in perfect focus, but she grew more mesmerized by them by the hour. She looked at them in daylight the next day, gathered them up and put them in her purse, and called Winnie, who was finally recovering from her cold.

"Can I come over?"

"You'll have to come this morning," Winnie said tersely, "I'm playing bridge at noon."

"I won't stay long."

Valerie hailed a cab in front of her building, and was at Winnie's apartment in twenty minutes, which was record time from downtown. Winnie was still eating breakfast when she arrived, with all her pills lined up in front of her. And she nearly groaned when she saw Valerie's face. She could see that she was on another crusade.

"What now?" she asked, sipping her coffee, while the maid asked Valerie if she'd like tea. Valerie smiled at her and declined, and focused on Winnie, and then took the photographs out of her bag, and held them in her hand. It was almost as though she could feel a connection to the little girl through the images on the paper.

"I don't know if Marguerite di San Pignelli was any relation to us, and she probably wasn't. And

I have no idea who this child was in relation to her . . . but I am absolutely certain," she said as she handed the pictures to her sister, "that that child is me. I have no clue as to why there would be photographs of me in that safe deposit box, but Winnie, look at her. It's me." Valerie appeared thunderstruck as she said it, and had been since the night before. Her sister was unimpressed. She glanced at the photographs and shrugged.

"All children look alike," she said, not willing to agree.

"That's a ridiculous thing to say. We don't have any photographs of our sister, thanks to our parents throwing them all away, God knows why."

"Because they made our mother sad," Winnie said fiercely, defending them again.

"We have none of her at any age, so we don't know what she looked like. But we have a few of me. You can't deny it. This child looks just like me as a little girl. I even had a dress like that."

"So did every child I knew. In those days, everyone dressed their children alike. We all had the same haircuts, either bowl cuts or braids. We all wore little smocked dresses. I can't even tell you from me in half the photographs we have, and we look nothing alike."

"No, we don't," Valerie agreed with her, "but I looked just like this child." Valerie was dogged about it.

"So you should get the money and jewels be-

cause you think you look like this child? She probably wasn't even related to Marguerite, the one
who owned the jewels, not our sister."

"So why did she keep photographs of her in her
safe deposit box and hang on to them for more
than seventy years?"

"Why are you driving yourself crazy? This has
been settled. It's all about the money for you, isn't
it? You're possessed," Winnie said, distressed again.
Valerie was disturbing her peace of mind. Winnie
liked an orderly life with all the loose ends tied up,
and they always had been. And now Valerie was
trying to make a mess of everyone's life, past and
present.

"It has nothing to do with the money," Valerie
insisted, took a breath, and tried to explain. "Winnie, all my life I felt like an outcast in my own family, a stranger among all of you. You and Mother
looked alike and got along. Father protected both
of you. I was the ugly duckling, the strange one,
the one who was always different, who never
looked or thought like any of you. I never, ever fit
in, and they hated me for it. All I want now is to
find out who I am, who I was, and why I didn't
fit. I think the answer is here, somewhere in these
photographs, and I don't know why, but I think
this woman knew. Maybe she wasn't our older sister, or maybe she was. Maybe she was an outcast
too. They wiped our Marguerite off the slate of
our lives, as though she didn't exist. She disap-

peared out of our family history, and they would have done the same to me if they could. And now I want to know why. If she was our sister, what did she do? What happened to her? And was I too much like her? Was it acceptable in our family only to be carbon copies of them? Was it a crime to be different? Punishable by death or banishment? They didn't mourn her, they erased her completely. **Why?**"

"They didn't kill our sister," Winnie said with a furious look. "Or banish her. She **died.** And they never did anything to you."

"Except hate me, and ignore me, and treat me like I didn't belong to them, and should never have happened. Did they do that to her too?"

"Let her rest in peace," Winnie said desperately. She didn't know the answers either, but she didn't want to. Valerie did. She was starving for answers she had waited all her life to hear, and refused to be silenced again.

"I can't let her go," Valerie said miserably. "And I don't know why, but the child has the answers. I know she does. I can feel it in my bones. And I want to know those answers now too, about why they never loved me and I never fit in. Look how different we are. We're sisters, and we're night and day. If the woman in the photographs was our sister, maybe she and I were more alike."

"You're trying to exhume an ally," Winnie said angrily, "who's been dead for seventy-three years.

You have to make your own peace with who you are, and why you never fit."

"I can't. I don't know why, but I just can't," Valerie said as tears slid down her face. For years, as an adult, Valerie had accepted the fact that her parents didn't love her, and had a good life anyway. She'd had a great marriage, and loved her husband and son, but now something jarring had happened, and she needed to know what it was. It had brought back all the unhappy memories of her childhood, and her parents' constant rejection of her and either inability or refusal to love her. And she had to know why and if the answers were somehow linked to the photographs she believed were of her as a child. She felt she had a right to know.

"You won't find the answers here," Winnie said coldly, "or by maligning our parents, or by turning our sister into someone she never was. The woman who married the Italian count was no relation to us, no matter how badly you want her money. Valerie, this is all about greed. And that child in the photographs looks like any other child at the time, not just you."

"No!" Valerie said, her eyes blazing. "She's me! I know it, no matter how you want to deny it. Winnie, that child is me, and I want to know why."

"A dead woman won't tell you, no matter how rich she was. If any of what you say is true, and I don't believe it, she took her secret to the grave. And she wasn't our sister," Winnie said in a tone of fury. "Our sister died seventy-three years ago," she repeated. "Let her be!" Winnie said and stood up, glaring at her sister. "I have better things to do than listen to this insanity. I think you're losing your mind. I would worry about that if I were you." What she said was like a slap across Valerie's face, and she left a few minutes after a terse goodbye between the two sisters. Winnie's hands were shaking when she got dressed to go out for her bridge game.

And when Valerie got back to her apartment, she sat down and cried, and then stared at the photographs of the little girl again. But however adamantly Winnie was denying it, Valerie knew she was right, that it was her. And then she remembered something she had gotten the year before, and had almost forgotten since. She went looking for it in some of her files, and couldn't find it. She tore a whole file cabinet apart where she kept correspondence, and it wasn't there. She knew she had kept it, out of sentiment, but had no idea where she'd put it. Obviously in some unusual place. It was a Christmas card from their old nanny, who had come to work for the Pearsons when Winnie was two, two years before Valerie was born, and had stayed until Valerie was ten, a span of twelve years. Fiona had been a young Irish girl of eighteen when she came to work for them, which made her ninety-four now. She had married and moved to New Hampshire, where she was in a nursing home, but her mind was still clear. Her handwriting on the Christmas card was shaky, but she was still lucid despite her age. Valerie hadn't visited her in nearly twenty years, since Phillip was fifteen, although they stayed in touch and Valerie wrote to her. She had loved her passionately and been devastated when she left, and Fiona sent her Christmas cards every year. Valerie just hoped she hadn't died since the previous Christmas, but she thought her children would have let her know. It was two in the morning when Valerie found the card, along with some others she had saved and put in her desk drawer. It was the last place she had looked. She had kept the envelope too, with the address of the nursing home. She was in southern New Hampshire, where she had lived for more than sixty years. It was a six-hour drive from New York.

Valerie lay awake in her bed all night after she found the card, and she called the nursing home at eight in the morning. They told her that Fiona McCarthy was very much alive and doing well. They said she was bedridden now from her arthritis, but she was clear as a bell, "and still feisty," the nurse who answered said laughing. "She keeps us on our toes."

An hour later Valerie was at the garage where she kept the car she owned but seldom used. She liked to have it if she ever needed it, and talked about selling it occasionally. She was on the road by nine-fifteen, and crossed through Connecticut and Massachusetts and into New Hampshire. There was still snow on the ground, although it was March, but there was very little, and there was no sign of spring yet.

It was almost three o'clock when she reached the tiny town that had been Fiona's home for so many years. And the nursing home looked warm and inviting. It was white and freshly painted with a picket fence around it, a front garden, and rocking chairs on the porch the residents used in warm weather, but it was still too cold at this time of year.

Valerie walked up the front steps with trepidation, wondering if Fiona would remember her, or even recognize her, and what would she say about the photographs? Valerie was an old woman now and looked very different than Fiona's memories of her even after twenty years.

She spoke to a nurse's aide at the front desk, who smiled and asked her to sign in, which she did. She said that Fiona had just woken up from a nap and it was a good time to visit. She said her children had been there that morning, and she was alone and would enjoy the visit. Valerie thanked her and walked to the room. She peeked in and saw a wizened old woman with a face full of wrinkles tucked into the bed, with a bright handmade quilt on it. Her hair was wispy and white, but her eyes were the same. They were a brilliant blue that burned right through Valerie as the old woman looked at her. She smiled as Valerie stood in the doorway.

"Are you going to stand there like a statue forever, or come in?" she said, grinning. She knew instantly who Valerie was.

"Hello, Fiona. I don't know if you know who I am." She started to explain, and Fiona laughed.

"And why wouldn't I? You haven't changed, except for the blond hair going white. How's your boy?" She remembered Phillip—her mind really was clear. Phillip had loved her when they met, and she had told him tales of his mother that made him laugh and brought tears of memory to Valerie's eyes.

"All grown up," Valerie answered. "He's a good man."

"He was a fine boy when I met him." She pointed to a chair, and Valerie sat down, wondering where to start, after all this time, but Fiona did it for her.

"You took a long time getting here. I've been waiting for so many years," she said cryptically. "I thought maybe after your last visit, you'd come back with some questions, but you didn't. Why now?" She looked interested in what Valerie had to say, and she was wide awake and alert.

"Some strange things have happened. None of it may mean anything, but it's been driving me crazy. Some photographs have turned up, in an unclaimed estate my son has been working on. And there's a coincidence of name. The woman who left the estate had the maiden name of Pearson. And the same first name as my sister, the one who died, Marguerite. We're probably not related, but there are some photographs of a child . . ." Her voice drifted off as Fiona watched her intently. "Winnie says I'm insane, and maybe I am, but I thought you would know." Valerie delved into her handbag then, and brought out the photographs of Marguerite, before she showed her the ones of the little girl with no name. "I've come up with some very odd theories in the past few days. Maybe there's no connection with this woman, but there are no pictures of my sister. My mother destroyed them all. Winnie and I don't know what she looked like." She handed the photographs to Fiona, who examined them through her bifocals one by one, and nodded, as Valerie held her breath. Her whole body was trembling, as though something terrible was about to happen. Or maybe something very good that would set her on a path to freedom, from a family that had never understood nor wanted her. All her life she had felt obligated to them, and had been respectful, while they had reciprocated none of it.

Fiona finished going through the pictures and looked at her with a solemn expression. "What do you want to know?"

"I know it sounds crazy," Valerie said in barely more than a whisper. "But is that woman my sister Marguerite, who died in Europe at nineteen?" Fiona didn't hesitate before she answered, and she looked certain.

"No, it isn't." Valerie's heart sank at the words. She had hoped it was. Fiona reached out a gnarled hand then and patted Valerie's hand with a tender look. "The woman in the photographs is not your sister. She's your mother," she said gently. "Marguerite was your mother, child." Valerie felt like one as she listened in sudden shock. "And she didn't die in Europe. She got married."

"When I was born?" Suddenly it was all so confusing, and everything had been a lie, just as she had thought, and Winnie denied. But this was even more complicated than she could have imagined.

"You were born before she left. She was eighteen. I always thought they would tell you one day, but they never did. She was just a girl, and madly in love with a boy called Tommy Babcock, and the worst happened. She got pregnant. They wanted to get married, and her parents wouldn't let them, and neither would his. The poor things were like Romeo and Juliet. Your mother," Fiona corrected herself, "her mother said she would never forgive her for the disgrace. A few days later, they shipped her off to a home for wayward girls in Maine. It was right before Thanksgiving in 1941, she was just seventeen, and Tommy was the same age, but turning eighteen. I don't think anyone knew about what had happened. And in those days pregnancy was such a disgrace. They sent her off very quickly, and told everyone they were sending her to finishing school in Europe for a year, in Switzerland, I think. The war had already started in Europe, but Switzerland was safe. But she wasn't there. She was in Maine, writing me letters about how miserable she was. Winnie was only four then, and didn't know what was going on. But she cried when Marguerite left. Marguerite was such a sunny little thing, everyone loved her. The house became a tomb without her. And her mother had murder in her eyes. Her mother was going to put the baby up for adoption. They were forcing her to give it up.

"She had been there about two weeks when the Japanese bombed Pearl Harbor, and everyone was in a panic. And the next thing I heard, Tommy had been drafted and was in boot camp in New Jersey. I think he was sent to California right before Christmas. I don't know if Marguerite ever saw him again, I doubt it, but I don't know that for sure. Maybe he went to Maine to say good-bye, and if he did, he probably promised he'd be back for her. I think he'd been in California for a month when he was killed in a training accident. Marguerite wrote to me that he was dead at the end of January. Your mother had a strong will and a strong mind, and after he died, I think she told her parents she wouldn't give up his child. The next thing I knew your mother, or grandmother, told everyone she was expecting, and they were going to the country so she could rest. They rented a house in Bangor, Maine, and I used to visit your mother at the home for girls. The poor thing was heartbroken over Tommy. Your grandparents had agreed not to put the baby up for adoption, and to say it was theirs. You were born in June, a big beautiful baby, and your mother had a hard time of it, she was so young. We spent the summer in Maine, and in September, we went back to New York, your grandparents, as they were rightfully, with 'their' new baby. And two weeks after we got back to New York, they sent Marguerite away. And they claimed you as their own. I've never seen anyone cry in my life like your mother the night before she sailed for Europe. They booked her passage on a Swedish ship called the **Gripsholm.** It was sailing to Lisbon with other civilians on it, because Portugal wasn't in the war. And she was planning to go to England after they docked. They sent her to Europe with a war on. The ship could have been torpedoed, and they didn't care." Tears ran down Fiona's cheeks as she told the story. "I went to see her off. They gave her no choice, they wanted her gone. She held you all night, the night before she left, and she swore she'd come back for you one day. And in the morning, she left. I promised to send her pictures of you whenever I could, and I did, for as long as I was there. Your parents never wanted her to come back. She told me they were going to make her stay in Europe, even with the war on.

"She met the count very quickly after she got to England. I don't remember, but she might have met him on the trip over. She said he was a kind man, and wonderful to her, but she always missed you and said her life wasn't complete without you. She was meant to stay in England when she got there, but she went to Italy with him instead. He got her into the country with an Italian passport after he married her in London. I know she tried to get you back at one point, I think you were about seven. She came for two weeks with her husband to see lawyers about taking you to Italy with them. The war was over. She met with your grandparents, and she told me they wouldn't give you up. I'm not sure what they did to convince her, but she and her husband left without you. I never saw her again after that. Your grandmother was livid and threatened to expose Marguerite, disgrace her, and cause a scandal. I think she and her husband tried to get you back through the courts after that, but it didn't work, and she eventually gave up. Her parents fought too hard. Your grandmother never had any maternal feelings for you and she left you to me to take care of, but they were trapped in a lie and the story they had made up, that you were their child, and they wouldn't return you to your rightful mother. They had forced her to let them adopt you. Marguerite never had any other children, she didn't want any. All she wanted was you, and they kept you from her. It was cruel, but at least she had a kind husband who doted on her and took care of her. She was still young when he died, but she stayed in Italy afterward. She had nothing here. Your grandparents saw to that." Fiona looked angry as she said it.

"She never wanted to see her parents again, and they didn't want to see her either. Once she left, the following year they told a story that she had died of influenza in Europe. She was nineteen then, and they put a black wreath on the door. I would have been heartbroken, except she wrote to me. She was very much alive, and she didn't know what they'd said until I told her. They wanted to be sure she could never come back. I heard your grandmother tell your grandfather they had destroyed all her photographs. It was unnatural. Decent people don't do things like that. They stole you from her, and buried their own daughter alive in everyone's minds. I could never think of them as your parents, and they didn't act like parents to you. They treated you like a stranger someone had left on their doorstep. I always hoped they would tell you one day, about your mother, and what they'd done, but they didn't. And no one else ever knew, except the doctors at the home in Maine and their lawyers. You had a proper birth certificate that named them as your parents. I saw it once. It was all a lie, and they broke their own daughter's heart. I was very glad she met the count and he loved her so much, or she would have been alone in the world. She loved you, Valerie, very dearly, and she would never have left you if she had a choice. She's not still alive, is she?" Fiona wanted to know now, as Valerie shook her head, with tears running down her cheeks. Now she knew for sure.

"She died seven months ago. She'd been back in New York for twenty-two years. I could have met her if I'd known." It shocked her too to realize that Fiona was only two years older than her mother and was still alive. Her mother hadn't been as lucky, but had had a hard life, and didn't have loving children to care for her, like Fiona did.

"I'm sure she would have looked for you if she'd dared." Valerie couldn't help wondering why she hadn't. Or maybe it was too painful to explain her return from the dead. "You were a grown woman. She must have thought it was too late." Valerie would have loved to meet her real mother at any age. And it was shocking now to realize that she'd been right about all of it, that her grandparents masquerading as her parents had hated and resented her, and probably thought of her as a constant reminder of her mother's shame. And they had kept her mother away from her for an entire lifetime, until her mother's death, long after their own. The only mother love Valerie had ever known had been from Fiona, until she was ten. And she looked gratefully at her now.

"Thank you for telling me the truth," Valerie said in a hushed tone.

"I always wanted to. I thought you would suspect something or find out in some way. I never expected it to take this long." It had taken seventy-four years to find out who her mother was, and she suddenly felt like the orphan she had been all her life, but at least she knew now that her mother had loved her. She was shaken too to realize that it was only a strange quirk of fate that had brought Phillip into the appraisal of the abandoned safe deposit box. Otherwise she would never have known. She was grateful for all of it now. "Tommy's parents were Muriel and Fred Babcock, by the way, if you ever want to look for them. I hear you can find people on the Internet. My son tried to give me a computer but I'm too old to learn. But they're your family too." It hadn't even occurred to Valerie to do that, and she wanted to think about it. She had so much to absorb and try to understand first. She had just gained a mother who loved her, and lost her, all in the same day.

Fiona was tired after the long story she'd told Valerie, which had taken two hours with all the details.

"I'm ready for a nap," she said as she closed her eyes, and Valerie leaned over and gently kissed her cheek. Her eyes fluttered open, and she smiled.

"Thank you, Fionie. I love you," she said, just as she had as a child.

"I love you too," Fiona said, patting her hand again. "Just know that she loved you, and she's an angel watching over you now." It was a sweet thought, and Valerie tiptoed out of the room as Fiona fell asleep. It had been the most emotional day of Valerie's life.

Valerie got back in her car then, and thinking of everything Fiona had said, she drove back to New York. She stopped for coffee once at a truck stop on the way, and sat staring into space, thinking of her mother and everything that had happened to her, and the terrible parents she'd had. They had done all they could to ruin their eldest child's life, as punishment for a youthful mistake and an illegitimate child. It made Valerie furious thinking of it, and as the anger subsided, she was overwhelmingly sad, and filled with compassion for the mother she had never known, who had wanted to come back to her and never did.

She got back to New York at midnight, and lay awake for most of the night. She had a lot to think about. She had no idea what to do now. She wasn't ready to tell Phillip yet, although she planned to, but first she had to make peace with it herself, with all its implications and ramifications. She wasn't who she thought she'd been all her life. The only one she wanted to tell was Winnie, to vindicate herself. She wasn't crazy after all. And she had never felt saner or clearer in her life. She propped a photograph of Marguerite on her night table as she got into bed. She had finally found the mother she'd never had.

"Goodnight, Mama," Valerie said softly, and drifted off into a deep sleep.

# Chapter 10

All Valerie knew when she woke up the next morning was that she had to take what had happened one step at a time. A bomb had hit her life the day before, and she wanted to control the damage as much as possible. She was planning to move slowly, and think it all out carefully before she did. The one thing she knew was that Fiona had given her an incredible gift: the truth about herself. It explained so much, why she had always felt like a stranger in their midst. And she had been her parents' grandchild, not their child. It made a big difference to her now. And the only person she wanted to tell at this early stage was her sister Winnie. Everything and everyone else could wait, even her son. She didn't want to share the story with him yet. She needed to try to understand it first.

She called Winnie again that morning, and told her she was going to drop by shortly. She didn't ask her this time, and she didn't care if it was convenient or not. What she wanted to say had waited seventy-four years, and she didn't want to wait any longer.

Winnie was fully dressed in a navy blue Chanel suit when Valerie arrived, and she'd had her hair done the day before. She looked like the wealthy, aristocratic Park Avenue matron she was. Valerie was wearing jeans, a sweater, and ballet flats, and her snow-white hair in a braid down her back. Her eyes were bright, and she looked rested. She felt better than she had in years, and suddenly free of the burdens and disappointments of the past.

"I won't take long," Valerie said calmly as she sat down, and Winnie looked instantly worried. She had a feeling she wouldn't like whatever it was that Valerie was going to say. She was much too calm, and she was almost euphoric.

"Did something happen?"

"Yes," Valerie answered, "I visited Fiona yesterday, our old nanny."

"She's still alive?" Winnie looked surprised. She had never corresponded with her or stayed in touch. Only Valerie had, and Fiona with her Christmas cards to her every year.

"She is."

"She must be a hundred years old," Winnie said, dismissing her.

"Ninety-four, and clear as a bell. I drove to New Hampshire to see her. I figured she might have the answers that you and I don't. We were too young when Marguerite left. And I was right. I didn't get the answers I expected. I showed her a photograph, and I thought she was going to tell me that Marguerite Pearson di San Pignelli was our sister. I was dead certain of it, but I was wrong." Winnie ruffled up her feathers and looked self-satisfied and triumphant as Valerie admitted her mistake.

"I told you she wasn't. You were just trying to make trouble for Mother and Dad."

"All I wanted was the truth," Valerie said quietly, "no matter what it was. And that's what I got. The woman who left the safe deposit box full of jewels, and was married to the Italian count, was in fact your sister, but not mine. She was my mother," Valerie said softly, with tears in her eyes. "She got pregnant at seventeen, by a boy she was in love with. They wanted to get married and their parents wouldn't let them. They separated them immediately, and your parents, my grandparents, sent Marguerite to a home for wayward girls in Maine, and told her she had to give up the baby for adoption. They gave her no other choice, since it was considered scandalous to have a child out of wedlock at the time." Winnie's eyes had opened wide, and she looked shocked by what Valerie was saying, but she said not a word, which made Valerie wonder if she had suspected it, but there was no way she could have known.

"That was November 1941. And two weeks later, the Japanese bombed Pearl Harbor, and the boy who was my father was drafted or enlisted in the army and went to boot camp. He was sent to California for further training. And he was killed in a matter of weeks in a training accident. And apparently my mother refused to give the baby up after that. So your mother and father, not mine," Valerie said pointedly again, "moved to Maine, pretending that your mother was pregnant. They returned to New York in September, claiming me as their own child. They forced Marguerite to let them adopt me. And days later, they put Marguerite on a ship to Europe, with a war on, banished from their home, and risked her life, on a ship to Lisbon, and from there she went to England. Essentially they forced her to give me up to them, even though they didn't like me or want me or approve of me. And a year after she left, they told everyone that Marguerite was dead, depriving me of my mother, and her of her child. They kept me as their own child to avoid any scandal and broke her heart, and then pretended to all of us she was dead. Apparently, she married very shortly after she got to London, to a man who loved her dearly, thank God. Fiona says she tried to get me back, but they fought her tooth and nail, and threatened her with scandal and she eventually gave up. She never had other children, and I never had a mother who loved me, thanks to them. You may think they were good people, but I don't. They perpetuated a terrible lie for most of my life. And all evidence points to the fact that my mother, your older sister, led a lonely life once she was widowed at forty-one, and for the next fifty years I could have known her and loved her if I'd known she was alive. Your parents, my grandparents, robbed you of a sister, me of a mother, and her of her only child.

"I haven't digested it yet, and I don't know what I'm going to do about it. There's nothing I can do. No one can undo what's been done, and what they did. But I wanted you to know before anyone else. I'm not crazy or senile or delusional, as you suggested. I was right, more so than I ever knew. I thought Marguerite di San Pignelli was our sister. I never suspected for an instant that she was my mother. And whatever happens, I thought you should know. I can't imagine ever forgiving them for what they did. We were both innocent victims, you and I, we were lied to all our lives." Valerie fell silent and looked at Winnie, who must have believed her. No sound came out of her mouth, and there were tears rolling down her cheeks. It still didn't seem possible to her, but everything Valerie said was so clear and so cohesive that however much Winnie hated it, it had the ring of truth. And as she listened, all her illusions about their family were shattered. Just as Valerie had said. Winnie was shocked, and she felt her safe, orderly little world crumbling around her. It was hard to imagine how Valerie felt, having never met the mother she had lost.

"I think they did love you, though," Winnie insisted in a hoarse, shaking voice, as Valerie looked at her, stone-faced. "They probably thought they were doing it for the best." She was always loyal to them, even now.

"They ruined my mother's life, your sister. And made my childhood a living hell. Fiona was the only loving adult in my life, and God knows how my mother must have felt, being robbed of her only child. It doesn't bear thinking. And she died alone, while you and I went on with our lives." It was a horrifying thought, and Winnie continued to cry silent tears as the two women faced each other, and Valerie stood up. "I'm sorry I sound so harsh about it. I just wanted you to know." Winnie nodded but made no move toward her. She wasn't sure if Valerie was angry at her by association or not, and she looked afraid.

Valerie hugged her on the way out, and turned at the front door, with a wry smile. "And by the way," she said with an ironic look at her very proper sister, "you're not my sister anymore, you're my aunt." She laughed and softly closed the door.

And then she went back to her own apartment in SoHo, to decide what to do next. The whole configuration of her life had shifted in the past twenty hours. The map of her world would never be the same again.

# Chapter 11

Jane had been thinking of moving out all week. She knew the relationship had gone from bad to worse in recent months, and appeared to be unsalvageable. John was in the Hamptons again this weekend, and she was going to tell him when he got home later that night. She had been packing all day and a truck was coming for her boxes on Monday to put into storage. She was moving in with Alex for a few weeks until she found her own place. She hadn't told her parents yet—she was embarrassed to admit that she was breaking up with John. She had finished packing the cartons of books, papers, memorabilia, and sports equipment, and was about to start packing her clothes, when John got home.

The weather had been nice all weekend, and he'd

gotten some sun, lying on the beach, even though it was cold. He looked relaxed. It still shocked her that he had left her to fend for herself every weekend, and was hanging out with his friends. Even if they were studying, they managed to have fun and had a barbecue the night before. It was a huge slap in the face. But she had finally realized that there was no point fighting the inevitable. It was over. She couldn't hide from it anymore.

He looked startled when he saw the boxes in the front hall. "What's all this?"

"My stuff. I'm moving out," she said simply, avoiding his eyes.

"Just like that? We don't discuss it?" He didn't seem sad or upset, just annoyed.

"You didn't discuss it with me when you rented the house in the Hamptons with your pals. You haven't invited me out there once." She looked hurt as she said it.

"We study all weekend. No one brings their partners out there. It's just us guys." He looked innocent as he explained.

"Cara and Michele are not guys," she said coldly, to mask the hurt she felt. He had turned out to be a huge disappointment and a waste of three years of her life.

"They're in my study group," he said, and moved to put his arms around her. "What's the big deal?"

"I never see you anymore. We have no life together. Our relationship is a disaster. It's over. It's been over for months." Tears stung her eyes as she said it, but she refused to cry and look pathetic to him.

"You can't sit it out till June?" He went to the fridge, helped himself to a beer, and stared at her.

"And then what? This isn't working anymore. We used to like each other. We did things together." She had the feeling that they weren't talking about the real issues. "Are you sleeping with Cara?" They were back to that again, but now she wanted to know. School was no longer an adequate excuse for the disintegration of their relationship in the last six months. There was nothing left.

"Oh, for chrissake. Are you cheating on me? Is that it? Are you projecting?" He was very clever at deflecting and not responding, and she got angry as she watched him. He wasn't even upset.

"Answer the question," she said harshly.

"Sorry, counselor. Maybe it's none of your business what I'm doing, if you're moving out." He was being an asshole again and playing with her, it was a game of cat and mouse.

"Do you care about this relationship?" she asked him bluntly.

"Of course I do. But I can't sit here with you all day and night while I'm trying to graduate."

"You don't need to study in the Hamptons every weekend, or I could come with you sometimes." It was obvious he didn't want that, and she suspected why. Someone was texting him frantically while they were talking, and she could guess who. She grabbed his cell phone off the table, while he took a sip of beer, and her heart stopped when she read it. It was too late for him to stop her. The message read, "Is the bitch home? Can I come over?" And it was signed "C." Jane had her answer. He looked shocked, and pulled his phone out of her hand. "What's that about?" Jane asked in an icy tone.

"Mind your own fucking business," he said, stormed into the bedroom, and slammed the door.

She went back to packing her clothes from the hall closet, and he came out of the bedroom a few minutes later. She was shaking, but he couldn't see it.

"Look, we're both under a lot of pressure. Things get crazy sometimes. Whatever happens with her doesn't mean anything. You and I have been together for three years."

"You seem to have forgotten that. I'm leaving. This isn't good for either of us. It hasn't been for months." She turned to face him then. "I thought we were honest with each other, and faithful. Apparently I was wrong."

"So who are you doing? The Christie's guy? You seem to like him a lot."

"Yes, I do. And I'm not 'doing' him. I told him about you. I don't 'do' people. I live with you, and I thought we loved each other, whatever that means to you."

"I'm moving back to L.A.," he said, looking sheepish. "She's going back too. I know you want to stay here and get a job with a fancy New York firm." He was finally being honest with her. Way too late.

"So you just cheat on me and get your next romance going? That's how you tell me?"

"I've had a great opportunity. Her father is going to give us seed money to start a business. It's a start-up. This could be a big deal for me."

"Great. It would have been nice if you ended it with me first. Why keep up the charade? Why bother? What's wrong with you?" What he had done was hopelessly sloppy. She had been sitting at home, waiting for him, while he slept with Cara, and her father gave them money for a business.

"We don't want the same things," he said, sounding lame.

"I thought we did. My mistake. You should have explained it to me when you figured it out. And Cara does want the same things?"

"We're both from L.A. It was her idea to go back."

"Terrific," Jane said, as tears stung her eyes while she packed. She didn't want to look at him.

"You're from Michigan. That's different." He thought he was cool, and instead he was just a jerk. He had completely changed, or finally exposed who he'd always been. It no longer mattered which.

"Yeah, we're stupid, boring people, who tell the truth. That must have sucked for you."

"You're too wholesome for me," he said honestly. "Cara is a 'dirty girl.' That's who I am right now." He sounded proud of it, and he had gone from denying that he was sleeping with her to tacitly admitting it and bragging about it.

"Whoever you are, or think you've become, why don't you just let me pack in peace. I'll stay somewhere else tonight, and you can tell her 'the bitch is gone.'"

"Come on, babe, don't be like that. Let's not end it like this after three years."

"You already did," she said quietly, went into the bedroom, took out her suitcases, and dumped whatever was left into them. All she wanted to do now was get out. She felt ridiculous being there while he told her she was too wholesome and made fun of her. She felt as though he had ripped her heart out through her throat. And he had obviously been cheating on her for months, and laughing at her. She had been a total fool. It was hard to remember what she'd ever loved about him while she listened to him now.

He sat on the couch, drinking beer and watching TV while she packed the rest of her things. Half an hour later, there were four suitcases in the hall full of her clothes; the rest was in the boxes she had packed that afternoon that she was going to send to storage until she got her own place. She was leaving him everything she'd bought for the kitchen and didn't care. Cara could use it if she cooked for him. Her skills seemed more appropriate to the bedroom than the kitchen.

Jane put her coat on and picked up one of her bags. The apartment already looked barren. She could see that he was half drunk, and he looked stunned.

"That's it? You're really leaving?"

"Yes, I am."

"What happened to talking about it and working it out?"

"You can work it out with Cara. I heard enough." And what was the point, if he was moving back to L.A. with her? Jane pulled open the door to the apartment then, and carried her bags into the hall. He got up to help, and she put up a hand. "Don't. I can do it myself."

"Like everything else you do so perfectly. Not everyone is as smart as you are, with your perfect grades and scores. Life hands everything to you. Some of us have to hustle for it. You never do." She realized then that he was jealous of her and maybe always had been. There was no love in his eyes when he looked at her, and hadn't been in months. She understood it now. And Cara was part of the hustle for him. She would help him set up a business, and her father would pay for it. Jane had nothing like that to offer him. So they were through.

"Good luck in L.A." The bags were heavy for her, but she didn't want his help. It disgusted her to look at him. She got all four bags into the hall and from there into the elevator, and then went back into the apartment. "I'm having someone pick my boxes up tomorrow, and then I'll send you the keys. You can tell her the coast is clear."

"This isn't about her," he said, slightly disoriented from the beer. She wondered if he'd been drinking all day.

"No, it isn't," Jane agreed, "it's about us. You and me. I should have left months ago. Or maybe we should never have started." She was still convinced he had changed, but it didn't matter now. "Goodbye," she said quietly, looking at him for a last time.

"I love you, babe," he said, trying to put his arms around her, and she pushed him away. He didn't know the meaning of the word. "Maybe we should try and work this out." As far as Jane was concerned, it was way, way, way too late for that, and she was sure that Cara would be in their bed that night. It was what she had always wanted, and apparently so did he. They were kindred spirits. They were two users, who were using each other and had lied to her.

Jane didn't say another word—she just walked

out and closed the door to the apartment, got in the elevator with her suitcases, and went downstairs. She dragged them through the lobby and across the sidewalk and hailed a cab. The driver put her bags in the trunk and on the front seat, and she gave him Alex's address. Jane had told her she'd be there that night.

And as the cab sped downtown on the West Side Highway, she got a text from John. He was just drunk enough to have sent it to the wrong person. She was sure the message was meant for Cara, but he had sent it to her instead. All it said was, "She's gone. Come on over. J." He was pathetic and she was tempted to send him a reply that said "Fuck you." But she didn't. She erased his message, and stared out the window as they drove downtown. She felt empty and numb, stupid and used. Three years of her life had just gone up in smoke.

Phillip and Valerie were having dinner that night at a Thai restaurant she liked, and he found her strangely subdued.

"Are you feeling all right?" he asked, concerned.

"Of course. I'm fine." She smiled at him, but there was something melancholy in her eyes that he had never seen before.

"You're very quiet," he said, worried about her.

"I'm just tired. I drove to New Hampshire and back yesterday."

"You did? Why?" It made no sense to him.

"I went to see my old nanny, Fiona McCarthy. Do you remember her? You met her when you were about fifteen."

"Yes, I do. She was funny. She's still alive?"

"Very much so, at ninety-four. But I thought I should visit her before too long, at her age."

"Why didn't you spend the night?"

"I wanted to come home."

"You're crazy, Mom. I didn't even know you were gone."

"I was fine," she said, smiling at him, and seemed more like herself again.

"Have you looked at those photographs, by the way?" He was referring to the ones Jane had emailed him, of Marguerite.

"Yes, I have," she said quietly.

"Recognize anyone you know? Or some family traits?" He was teasing her, and she didn't comment. She was definitely more serious than usual.

"Not really," she said, and changed the subject. "She was such a pretty woman. I can't wait to see the jewels at the exhibition for the show."

"You can come in and look at them anytime you want. I have them in the safe. We're trying to work out the estimates now. I think the prices are going to go through the roof." She nodded, but didn't say anything.

They talked about his upcoming trip to Paris then, for a big Christie's sale. And he told her he was planning to go to Cartier and Van Cleef, to get more information about the pieces, when they'd been purchased, and for what occasions. It had taken three days to hear back from Cartier's archive department in Paris, in answer to his inquiry. They were looking for the files on the pieces he had inquired about, and promised to get back to him in the next two weeks, and would be ready to show him their archives when he got to Paris. They were extremely gracious and assured him that they were making every effort to find the records and working drawings of the pieces he was interested in. And Van Cleef had said the same.

"Having the working drawings in the catalog will give life to the show," he explained to her.

"How long will you be gone?" she asked him quietly.

"A week. I have to go to London too, and maybe Rome." He wanted to trace the Pignelli pieces at Bulgari. He wanted to do as thorough a job of it as he could. Even if jewelry wasn't his preference, he gave the sales his all, particularly this one, which he had developed a personal interest in. And clearly, his mother had too.

After dinner, he walked her back to the building, and she went upstairs. She hadn't told Phillip any of what she had discovered from Fiona. She wanted time to digest it, and she wasn't ready to talk about it. She had no idea what would happen when she did, or how it would affect the sale. She didn't want to upset the apple cart yet, although in time she'd have to if she was Marguerite's heir.

He took a cab back to Chelsea, and when he got back to his apartment, he thought about Jane. He still wanted to see her, but didn't know when. He didn't want to be a pest since she had a boyfriend. He had no way of knowing that at that exact moment she was sitting in her friend Alex's apartment, telling her what had happened with John. The whole thing seemed sordid and humiliating and she wanted to put it behind her. She was surprised that she wasn't sad, just angry and relieved for now. Maybe disappointment and loneliness would come later, but not yet.

"Now you can go out with the guy from Christie's," Alex said after they brushed their teeth and climbed into bed. Jane's bags were standing in the hall, still packed.

"Not yet," Jane said, thoughtfully. "I need some time to sort this out and get over it."

"Don't wait too long," Alex cautioned her and Jane laughed. "Good guys don't stay on the market. They get snatched up fast."

"I'm fine without a man," she said as much to herself as her friend. She could do anything she wanted now. And the best part of it was that she was free. And she knew she had done the right thing, leaving John. It was the best decision she'd made in years and long overdue.

# Chapter 12

When Jane went to work on Monday morning, she noticed that Harriet looked exhausted and had circles under her eyes. She looked as though she'd had a rough weekend, and Jane cautiously inquired about her mother later that morning, and Harriet looked touched. As much as she had resented Jane in the beginning, and assumed she was a spoiled rich girl, she had come to discover what a kind person and hard worker she was, and was growing increasingly fond of her. She had discovered that she could count on her to go the extra mile at work, and realized that she would miss her when she left. There was a freshness and energy to her that their regular employees just didn't have. She looked up at Jane with a bleak smile.

"My mom had a setback this weekend, her MS seems to be getting worse at a rapid rate. I don't know if I'll be able to bring her home, and it'll kill her if I have to put her in a nursing home." Worse, Harriet had come to understand how dependent she was herself on having her mother there, and having someone to take care of. They had always been very close, and the prospect of coming home to an empty apartment, living alone, and visiting her in the nursing home in the coming years depressed Harriet profoundly, and Jane could see it in her eyes.

"I'm so sorry," Jane said softly, and meant it. Her own troubles and upsets seemed insignificant compared to Harriet's, and she felt foolish for being disappointed in John. A broken romance didn't compare to a slowly deteriorating mother, whom Harriet obviously loved.

"You look a little rocky too," Harriet commented, having noticed Jane looking less put together than usual. She hadn't unpacked at Alex's, and had come to work in jeans, which was rare for her.

"My boyfriend and I broke up this weekend, I moved out," she admitted, feeling sheepish about it, as though somehow it were indicative of a failure on her part for not realizing what a loser he was while he cheated on her and set up his business plan with Cara, financed by her dad. It made her feel stupid as much as hurt. And she'd had the same feeling when she told her mother about it the night before, who had told her she should have figured it out sooner, and she had always known the relationship wouldn't go anywhere. Jane's mother thought all relationships should lead to marriage, and told Jane that this was what she could expect if she was avoiding long-term commitment, living with men, and focusing only on her career. So she wound up with John, who only cared about his career too. But despite what her mother said, Jane didn't feel ready for marriage, and wasn't going to be shamed or rushed into it. And Alex was right. He was the wrong guy for her. It had taken him three years to show his true colors, but now she knew.

"Are you heartbroken?" Harriet asked her gently, with a sympathetic expression Jane had never seen before, and she slowly shook her head.

"Not really. Disappointed. And I feel kind of stupid. Sometimes my mother is the master of 'I told you so.' I guess she was right."

"Then he wasn't the right guy."

"No, he wasn't," Jane agreed, and it was hard to admit. It was a rare exchange between them, and she could see that Harriet felt sorry for her.

"I have a project for you." Harriet changed the subject then, as a relief for both of them. "I thought about it this weekend, I just want to make sure we've been completely thorough in the Pignelli case. I know we didn't find a will among her documents, but I was thinking about the letters. The ones in Italian appear to have been written by someone else, but the ones in English may have been written by her. I'd like you to copy them, and read through them, just to make sure we haven't missed something, the name of a relative or an heir, a letter of intent to leave the jewelry to someone, even a friend. Sometimes things turn up in old correspondence like that. Will you give them a quick read just to be sure we checked everything?" Jane was surprised at the request and hadn't thought of it herself. She nodded agreement, and Harriet gave her a permission slip to get the letters out of the vault where the documents were being kept.

"I think that's a really good idea," Jane said enthusiastically. For all of Harriet's appearances of being bored by her job, she was good at what she did, and conscientious about it.

"There's probably nothing in them, but you never know. Stranger things have happened."

Jane went straight from Harriet's office to the vault for documents being stored, handed the slip to the woman in charge, and was given the bundle of letters a few minutes later. She went to the copy machine, and made copies of all of them, and then returned the original letters to the vault. It was a thick stack of letters, written in a small, old-fashioned handwriting, and she took the copies back to her desk, poured herself a cup of coffee

at the office machine, and settled down to begin
reading. She flipped through them before she
started, to see who they were addressed to, and saw
that all of the salutations were similar and began
with "My Beloved Angel," "My Darling Girl,"
or "My Darling Child." There was no name at
the beginning of any of the letters. And when she
checked the signature at the end, in most cases
they were signed with the initial "M," and only a
few were signed "your loving mother." It was impossible to say, before she read them, if they were
written by Marguerite, or to her by her mother.
And they had few examples of Marguerite's handwriting to compare them to. But instinctively Jane
had the feeling that they were written by her. Not
all of them had dates, but most did, and the first
one was dated September 30, 1942, and beneath
the date, the author of the letters had written
"London." The first letter was addressed to "My
Beloved Angel."

"I still can't believe that I have left you. Unthinkable, unbearable, the most agonizing of all possible
events. A tragedy for me. They took you from me,
and now I am here, in London, living at a small
hotel. I need to find an apartment. But where will
I live? How will I live without you? How could this
happen? How could they do it? I don't know if I
will send you these letters one day, but if so, I must
let you know how much I love you and miss you,

and tell you of the agonizing hole in my heart that happened the day I left you.

"I have met a very nice man, who has been so kind to me. He is here by special permission, on a diplomatic passport from Italy, and will only be here for a few weeks, and then he will return to Naples, where he lives. I met him the day after I arrived, when I tripped and fell in the street and he picked me up and dusted me off and then insisted on taking me to dinner at a very nice restaurant. He acted like a father to me, and I told him about you. I think only of you now, and wonder what you are doing, how you look, if you are healthy, and if they are being good to you. I know that Fiona will be loving to you, even if my parents are not. Please know that if they had let me stay with you, I would have. They gave me no choice." The letter went on to describe what she had done with the Italian man—dinners, lunches, a drive to visit a friend at a manor house outside London. She wrote constantly about how kind he was to her. They had gone to the library, and in the next letter, he had found her a better place to stay and bought her a warm coat. There was something very young and innocent about the letters, as Jane read them, one after the other. Sometimes the dates were very close together, sometimes there was a gap of weeks or even a few months.

At the end of October, she said the kind man

was going back to Italy and had invited her to go with him. She also said that he had asked for her hand in marriage, and she had accepted, and they were to be married shortly as soon as it was arranged. Jane couldn't tell from what she'd written, somewhat demurely, if she was truly in love with him, or clinging to her only friend and protector in London. There was a war on, American and British soldiers were everywhere in London, and she was totally alone. She had mentioned in the first letter that her parents had given her money to live on, so she was not without means, at least for some time, but she had been set adrift in an unfamiliar world, with no contacts, friends, family, or protection at eighteen, and the Italian man she referred to was kind and loving, and she felt safe with him. She said that they would be married before they left for Italy, and he was taking care of everything. He was traveling on a diplomatic passport, and they would live in Naples when they went back to his home.

She wrote again after the fact, spoke in somewhat vague terms about the Germans in Italy, and that her new husband had been able, with high connections, to obtain an Italian passport for her, since they were married, which she had to use now, instead of her American one, since Italy and America were at war. She mentioned traveling through Switzerland on a diplomatic train to Rome, and then to Naples. "So now I am Italian and a countess," she said almost playfully in another letter that had begun with "My Darling Angel." She said that she was happy with her new husband, who was wonderful to her. She mentioned their supplies being rationed, how much she loved his home, and that the German **Oberführer** for the area came to visit them from time to time, and her husband felt it was wisest for them to be polite and entertain him, although they didn't agree with his point of view or his politics.

In July of the following year, the Allies were bombing Rome, and she wrote how frightening that must have been for the residents of the city. And Umberto wouldn't take her to Rome anymore. A week later, in the same letter, which she continued on a different day, she spoke of the Italian government falling, and of their surrender to the Allies in September, the Germans occupying Rome again three days later. And in October, the Allies entered Naples, and the Italians joined the Allied Forces. And they had entertained the American commanding officer in their home. She said that he had been surprised to discover that the countess was an American. She mentioned various events of the war, and bombings that continued into the following year, which was 1944. She had been in Europe and married for almost two years by then.

As she continued to read, it was clear to Jane that the letters had in fact been written by Marguerite.

And through each letter was woven the thread of how much she loved her husband, and she spoke of how much she loved and missed her "darling angel." The count had promised her that after the war, they would go to New York and reclaim her. She seemed to believe it was a certainty that that would happen, and she could not wait until that day.

There was a heartbreaking letter several years after that, written in 1949, which made it clear that they had gone to New York, consulted a lawyer, and attempted to reclaim the child—and had been fiercely rebuffed and attacked by Marguerite's parents. The birth certificate they had manipulated falsely for her child in 1942 when she was born would have proved difficult to discredit. They had threatened to claim that Marguerite and Umberto were Nazi sympathizers, which would not have gone well in court. And in another heart-wrenching letter, Marguerite lamented not even being able to see her when they were in New York. The lawyer they had consulted had advised them that they had no hope of reclaiming the child, or even seeing her, and suggested they contact her directly when she reached eighteen. There was nothing more he or anyone could do. Marguerite's parents had blocked them at every turn. They had told her that everyone thought she was dead and they wanted it to stay that way. They had buried her alive and kept her child from her.

And a letter farther down the stack, written in the summer of 1960, indicated that Marguerite had tried to follow the attorney's advice, or intended to. She had gone to New York to see her daughter and tell her the real story of her birth, and who her mother really was. Marguerite had followed her on the street unseen, for several days, bowled over by how beautiful she was, and how happy she looked. And she realized with an aching, broken heart that to tell her the truth would rob her of the only identity she knew, and the legitimacy she believed was hers, and would have replaced it with scandal, shame, and confusion. All Marguerite had to offer her was illegitimacy and disgrace. And in the end, Marguerite had gone back to Italy without contacting her, or making herself known to her daughter. It felt wrong to her to shatter the peaceful, secure world she lived in, the respectable identity she believed was hers, and force herself on her, a mother she never knew was her own. The letters Marguerite had written after that were deeply depressed, for a long time. She had lived for the opportunity to see her daughter, and make contact with her, waiting patiently to do so for many years, when she turned eighteen, only to realize that what would have been a joy for her might be a shocking tragedy to her daughter.

Five years later she wrote of her husband's sudden death of a heart attack while he played racquetball, which left Marguerite alone in the world again, without the pillar of comfort and protection she had relied on for twenty-three years since she was a young girl herself. She had explained again and again over the years that having another child would have seemed like a betrayal to her, having been forced to relinquish her first one. She always said that Umberto wanted children, and had none of his own, but Marguerite felt she couldn't do it. It was unthinkable to have another child while she still mourned her firstborn. And at forty-one, she found herself without child or husband.

After that, she spoke of the difficulties of maintaining their estate after his death, the money they had spent in the years before. She spoke of his extreme generosity to her, and for the first time mentioned the many gifts of jewelry that she said she was saving for her daughter, when they would be reunited one day, which she still hoped would happen when her "darling angel" was older, and the truth about her birth would be less traumatic for her. And without being able to see her daughter, Marguerite never returned to the States after her fruitless visit in 1960.

She sold their home in Naples in 1974, nine years after Umberto's death, when she could simply no longer afford to keep the castello, and could no longer bear being there without him. The money she got from the sale allowed her to move to Rome, to an apartment, where she had apparently lived carefully for twenty years, until she became alarmed by her dwindling funds. She had lived frugally in Rome for all those years, having sold the horses, cars, and property. Umberto had had some other properties, which she had sold too. He had left her everything when he died.

She talked about trips Umberto had taken her on, to Paris, where he had given her magnificent gifts. And throughout her letters, whenever she mentioned one of her husband's gifts to her, she declared her intention to give them to her daughter one day. But she had still been so young at the time that it probably hadn't seemed necessary to do anything serious and legal about it yet.

Her letters became sadder when she got older. She wrote them less often, and seemed to have given up hope of ever meeting her only child. She mentioned that Fiona had written to her when her "darling angel" got married, and again, many years later, when her son was born. Marguerite was nearly sixty by then, and still living in Rome. She had no desire to visit the States, or have any contact with her family. The only person she wanted to see was her daughter, which she considered impossible by then. The letters made that clear. She was still convinced that her sudden appearance in her daughter's life, after so long, would be nearly impossible to explain, and would only disrupt her life and make her unhappy. In Marguerite's view, the moment had come and gone, and would only cause her daughter to suffer, which was the last thing she wanted, so she never contacted her, even as an adult. She believed it was too late.

She wrote sadly of leaving Rome in the letters, which by now she no longer had any intention of sending to her daughter. They were a kind of diary she had kept over the years, of major events and landmarks in her life. She wrote to her daughter as though she was still a child. And when she left Rome to move back to New York, she felt as though she was leaving the only country that had been home to her. But at seventy, she expressed a need to go back to her roots, and believed she could live less expensively in a small apartment in New York. She spoke of that intention, and then of the apartment she had gotten, and of selling two pieces of jewelry, which she would be able to live off of for some time. She appeared to live a small, frugal life, careful of every penny she spent. There were no frills. Her fire seemed to have gone out by then, along with all hope of ever seeing or meeting her daughter. Her life was in the past. She spoke of Umberto often, nostalgic about the glorious years they had shared. And in one of her last letters, she said that she was going to write a will, leaving all her jewelry to her only child. She said that with the exception of the two rings she had sold, she had kept all of it, as souvenirs of Umberto's love for her, and the only gifts she had to leave her daughter.

Her last letters became rambling, writing about the past, her bitter regrets about being forced to give up her child, the happy life she had shared with Umberto, and the deep love they had for each other. But throughout, Jane had the sense that there had always been a dark shadow over her, the absence of her child.

She wrote of going to Paris with Umberto in her last two letters, as though they were recent trips, and Jane realized that dementia had set in by then. They were dated four years earlier, and her handwriting appeared to be shaky. She referred to her daughter as though she were a little girl, and wondered where she went to school. It was sad watching her decline in the letters, and sensing how lonely and alone she was. She seemed to live surrounded by her memories of people who were no longer with her. She appeared to be slowly losing her grip on life. But the one thing that was clear throughout was how much she had loved her daughter, and although she had never gotten around to writing the will she talked about for many years, it was equally clear that she had intended to leave the jewelry to her daughter, as the only objects of value she had. She herself was well aware that it was no substitute for the years that had been stolen from them. She never actually

mentioned her daughter by name, but it was obvious that she viewed her daughter as her only heir.
And in the last letter, she wrote again, for the first
time in many years, about going to see her daughter, meeting her at last, and trying to explain to her
what had happened, and why she had never come
back or contacted her. It tormented her till the very
end.

There were tears rolling down Jane's cheeks when
she finished the last letter. Marguerite had painted
a portrait of lost love, and a mother who had been
robbed of her child, and had never stopped loving
her for an instant. The only open question now
was who that daughter was. There was no name,
nothing to go on, no clue as to who or where she
was. And given the age of her daughter, it was possible that her only heir might no longer even be
alive.

Jane went back to Harriet's office at the end of
the day with a heavy heart.

"Find anything?" Harriet asked her expectantly.
She was hoping for a handwritten will, slipped between the pages of the letters, that had previously
gone unnoticed.

"Lots," Jane said sadly. "I think she had a daughter she gave up at eighteen, before she left for Europe. She never saw her again. She tried to regain
custody of her seven years later, and her parents
stopped her. There was something about a falsified birth certificate that named Marguerite's par-

ents as the child's parents. She was going to contact her at eighteen, and went to New York to see her, and changed her mind, afraid to disrupt the daughter's life. She never saw her again, or tried to contact her. She makes it clear that she saved the jewelry for her, and intended to write a will to that effect, but she never did. The dementia had already set in, at the end of the letters—she was in her late eighties by then. I have no idea who the daughter is—she is never named in the letters, and I don't know where she is. She may not even live in New York anymore, or she could be dead. She would be in her seventies now herself. The story is just so sad. There's a whole life in those letters, but nothing we can use to find her only heir."

"Let's just hope she saw one of our notices and contacts us." But it seemed unlikely to both of them. The trail was cold, and the child Marguerite Pearson had given up and referred to for more than seventy years as her "darling angel" was impossible to find without a name.

It was all Jane could think of as she took the subway to Alex's apartment that night after work. Alex had a date, and Jane was going to work on her final paper that she still needed to finish for graduation. But the words "darling angel" kept dancing in front of her eyes as she sat at her computer screen. Jane couldn't imagine anything more painful than Marguerite giving up her child. No matter how much she and Umberto had loved each other, it was the absence of her daughter that had colored Marguerite's life, and explained the tragic look in her eyes in some of the photographs. And all the jewelry she had saved for her, for so many years, was going to auction now, into the hands of strangers, instead of to Marguerite's child. It was one of those terrible injustices and ironies of life.

# Chapter 13

Phillip took the Air France flight to Paris that left New York just before midnight, and was scheduled to arrive at Charles de Gaulle by noon, local time. It would give him a late start to his day by the time he arrived in the city probably around two, after he got his luggage, went through immigration, and caught a cab for the hour's drive into town. But he would still have time for several appointments before the end of the working day. He preferred the night flight, where he could sleep on the plane for five or six hours, and arrive in good shape. It was the one he always took when Christie's sent him to Paris once or twice a year, or more, for important sales there.

The plane took off on time, and he ate a quick snack of cheese and fruit, and skipped the rest of the meal, although the food was always good. Other passengers preferred getting all the perks they were offered, but a serious meal after midnight was less appealing to him than sleep. And he settled down under a blanket with a pillow an hour after they took off. The pilot had said the flight would take six and a half hours, half an hour longer than usual, due to heavy winds. Phillip was asleep before the plane set out over the Atlantic north of Boston.

He slept soundly until the announcement that they were beginning their descent toward Charles de Gaulle Airport in Roissy, and would land in thirty minutes. He had just enough time for a cup of coffee and a croissant, and to brush his teeth, comb his hair, and shave before they arrived, and was back in his seat looking presentable and rested in time to land. It was gray and rainy, and he didn't mind. He loved coming to Paris, whether for jewelry or art, and he was planning to visit some of his old pals from the art department when he went to London after the Paris sale. But he had work to do in Paris in the meantime.

He caught a cab easily after he cleared immigration, and told the driver in halting French to take him to the Four Seasons on the Avenue George V. Christie's always paid for comfortable accommodations, and after walking past the spectacular flowers in the lobby, the room he was given was pleasant and pretty. He showered, and was at the

Christie's office on the Avenue Matignon just after three o'clock. The Magnificent Jewel sale, including Marie-Antoinette's historic jewelry, was scheduled for the following night, and his Paris counterpart, Gilles de Marigny, roughly the same age as Phillip, said that interest in the sale was high, and they had a lot of telephone bids on their books already, and every important museum in Europe had come to see the royal jewels, and would be bidding on them.

They talked business for a little while, and about politics at the Mother House in New York, and then Phillip went to the exhibition rooms to see the lots on display. It was a very impressive sale, and made him think of Marguerite's jewels again. He didn't have time to call the archives department at Cartier until six o'clock. They were happy to report to him that they had made good progress on his inquiry, and had found the records of the eight pieces he had asked about, and working drawings for many of them, except those that had been purchased at the store and not been made to order for her. They said they would be happy to show him the files and working drawings the next day, which was the day of the Christie's sale, when he knew he couldn't get away, so he made an appointment for the day after. He was looking very pleased when he got off the phone. He then placed a call to Van Cleef and Arpels, but the person he hoped to see, who was in charge of their archives, was out of the country and not expected to return for two weeks. But they promised to send him copies of everything they found in their records about the pieces Umberto had bought from them.

Details of the provenance and even working drawings that Christie's could include in the catalog would be very beneficial to the sale, especially for serious jewelry collectors who wanted to know everything possible in an item's history, both about the person who owned them, and about the creation of the piece.

"Good news?" Gilles asked him as he walked into the office Phillip was using for his brief stay.

"I think so. We just got a very interesting estate sale from the court in New York. An abandoned safe deposit box in a bank, which contained a fortune in magnificent jewelry given to its owner while she was married to an Italian count. Some beautiful pieces. Cartier has most of the drawings in their archives—eight of the items were purchased from them in the forties and fifties. There are twenty-two lots in all. We're putting them in the May sale."

"Sounds like a good one," Gilles said pleasantly. He had a pretty young wife and three children whom Phillip had met on earlier trips to Paris, but they had no time to socialize on this trip right before such an important sale.

"I hope it will be," Phillip said about the Pignelli sale, and then they looked over the bids for the next day that clients had placed as absentee buyers, and there would be many more on the phone and in the room. The sale was expected to bring in millions of euros and important buyers from all over the world.

Phillip left the Christie's office at eight, and walked back toward the hotel, then decided to keep on walking for a while. The Eiffel Tower was lit up, and there was a hint of spring in the air. He sat down at a small, busy bistro and ordered a glass of wine and a light meal, and got back to the hotel at ten o'clock, after watching the people and enjoying the atmosphere of Paris. He always loved it here. It was the most beautiful city in the world.

He watched the news on CNN in his hotel room, read the faxes that had been sent to him by his office after Paris office hours, and checked his messages in New York. It was only four-thirty there, not too late to return calls or do business if he needed to, but he had nothing important to tend to, and by eleven o'clock he was sound asleep, and woke up at seven the next morning, not sure where he was for a minute. And then he remembered that he was in Paris, and it was the day of the sale. He ordered room service for breakfast, read **The International Herald Tribune** and **The New York Times,** and walked to the Christie's office, and arrived just before ten o'clock.

It was a busy day after that. He and Gilles ate sandwiches at his desk, going over final details just

before the sale, and were in the auction room before seven, when the sale was scheduled to begin.
A well-known auctioneer would be presiding, with
several jewelry experts associated with the sale to
verify the pieces. And there was a bank of a dozen
telephones on one side of the room, at a long table.
The men and women at the phones were already
calling some of the more important bidders to verify that the lines were good, and that the phone
numbers they had for them were the right ones.

Gilles and Phillip took their places at the back
of the room to watch the bidding, and after an
announcement of one correction in the catalog
and two lots that had been withdrawn, the auction
began on time. Marie-Antoinette's historical items
were scheduled for later in the sale, to create anticipation, but the opening bids were strong. The
first three items went for three times the estimate,
which wasn't uncommon on an important sale
with a high degree of interest. And half an hour
later, an antique diamond necklace went for ten
times the high estimate, and caused a ripple in the
room, after two clients on the phone waged a bidding war against each other, with excellent results
both for the seller and for Christie's. The hammer
price was just under a million dollars. Gilles and
Phillip exchanged a glance of satisfaction. It was
going to be a great sale.

And when Marie-Antoinette's pieces finally
came up, well into the sale, they went for roughly

what the house had expected. Two were purchased by private collectors, as Gilles whispered to Phillip, five others were purchased by museums, and the best piece had been saved for last, an elegant diamond tiara she was said to have worn at court as a young girl when she was first queen. It sold for two and a half million euros, just over three million dollars, and was sold to the Tate Gallery in London. And the bidding ended with a surprise, which Gilles was familiar with, and Phillip had heard about but had never actually seen happen.

The instant the hammer fell, a small bearded man in a brown suit stood up in the third row and declared in a firm voice that carried throughout the room, "I claim this item for the museums of France, by the power vested in me by the government." There was dead silence in the room, as the uninitiated tried to figure out what had just happened. But Phillip already knew the procedure. When an item was historically important, a government representative was sent to the sale, waited for the bidding to end and the hammer to fall, to establish its current market value, and then claimed it for the government of France, and the successful bidder would lose the item, in this case to the Louvre. It was always a source of great disappointment to a successful bidder to lose the desired lot at the last minute, but it was a risk, and Christie's had warned their important clients of the possibility before the sale. The government representative had let the other items go to public sale, but not the tiara. A portrait of the young queen wearing it was already in the Louvre, of which Christie's had been aware. The auction continued after that, and it added even more excitement and drama in the room. Each of the lots sold, some at staggering prices, and when it was all over at ten o'clock, people claimed their items, or made arrangements to have them sent. Many of the lots had been purchased by well-known jewelers in London and New York. And one of the highest bids had been made by a private buyer in Hong Kong. It was one of those nights when Phillip had no regrets about not being in the art department. It had been a terrific sale, and a thrill to be part of it, particularly when the tiara was claimed by the museums of France, although neither he nor Gilles was surprised.

"Good one," he said to Gilles when they left the auction room after it cleared. It had been one of the most successful sales they'd had in years, although the lots had been consigned by many people, not just one famous person, whose whole collection was sold, such as the Elizabeth Taylor sale. Their single-owner sales, particularly of famous people, were usually the more important ones. But sometimes those from a variety of provenances did equally well, as this one had.

Phillip was still revved up about it when he got back to the hotel, and for lack of someone else to tell, he called his mother about it, but she was out. She was so busy with the many things she did and was interested in, the art classes she still took, boards she served on, and friends she went out with, that she was hard to get hold of at times. He thought of trying to reach Jane after he left his mother a message on her voicemail, but he felt a little foolish calling Jane about it. He didn't know her that well, and she would either be at work, or on her way home by then, so he let it go.

The next day was exciting for him. After helping Gilles with some of the paperwork and arrangements resulting from the auction the night before, which were considerable, he went to his appointment at Cartier at eleven, on the rue de la Paix, and met with the head of the archives department. He was waiting for Phillip with a folder on his desk. He had the inventory of items Phillip had sent him, and went down the list chronologically, rather than in the order Phillip had listed them, having no idea when the pieces were created. He was an older man, who was intensely knowledgeable about the pieces Cartier had made for important clients, what period of their work they represented, how they differed from other pieces they had designed, and whatever was unusual about them, and he loved sharing the information, and showing their working drawings to those who were interested. He was deeply proud of their work. He had worked for Cartier for thirty years.

He explained to Phillip that the thirty-carat emerald-cut—meaning rectangular (the style of cut referred to any color stone, not just an emerald, which Phillip knew of course after two years in the jewelry department at Christie's, although he hadn't known it before)—emerald ring with triangular emerald trillions of four carats each on either side, was the first piece the Conte di San Pignelli had commissioned from them. And the notes on the exquisite and immaculately neat working drawings indicated that it was a wedding present for his bride. He ordered it in late 1942, and the ring took six months to complete. It was a magnificent piece, Phillip knew from having seen it in New York. Umberto had bought the pearl and diamond choker for her a year later, for her birthday, and the measurements of Marguerite's neck were duly noted on the worksheets.

"She had a very long, thin, aristocratic neck, like a swan," the archivist from Cartier said with a smile. They had a photograph in the file of her wearing the choker sometime later, which Phillip wanted to reproduce for the catalog with their permission, with a credit to Cartier's archives listed beneath it. Marguerite was smiling in the photograph, wearing a white satin evening gown, and looked exquisite on her husband's arm. "We also sold him the very important pearl necklace on your list, which was an item we apparently had in the store, and we did not make it for her. They were natural pearls, which are even rarer now." Phillip remembered it perfectly from the inventory. The pearls in the long strand were of an unusual size, and a smooth creamy color, unblemished and flawless. "We sold that to the count a year after the choker, at almost the same time, so it must have been a birthday gift as well."

There was a very handsome diamond brooch that was noted as an anniversary gift after the war. And one of their famous tiger bracelets in white diamonds and onyx that was also for an anniversary. The twenty-five-carat oval "pigeon's blood" Burmese ruby ring was for their fifth anniversary and had taken a year to make, according to the notes in the file. "Probably to find the stone, which was unusually large for a Burmese ruby of that color." The forty-carat white diamond emerald-cut ring had been his tenth anniversary gift to her, and he had purchased the large yellow diamond ring for her to mark their twentieth anniversary, in 1962, three years before he died.

"She had some of our best, most memorable pieces. We wonder where they are sometimes, and then they surface and we become aware of them when heirs put them up for auction, or in situations like this one. I imagine it will make a very handsome sale," the Cartier archivist said. "Would you like me to send you a copy of our files: the

drawings and the occasions?" It was precisely what
Phillip wanted, and he had struck gold at Cartier.
The information they provided would give even
greater meaning and value to the pieces, and be
valuable to the people who bought them, whether
jewelers for resale, or privates who would want to
know everything about their origins, and who had
owned them.

"The count was a very generous man," Phillip
commented before he left.

"He must have loved her very much," the man
from Cartier said discreetly. He himself was en-
amored with the history of their pieces and had
dedicated most of his career to their archives, and
adding information about the new creations. It
was his life's work.

Phillip thanked him for his time and the excellent research, told him where to email the drawings for the catalog, and then they shook hands
and said good-bye and he left. Phillip stopped for
lunch at a sidewalk café, thinking about what he'd
learned at Cartier, and then went to Van Cleef and
Arpels, even though the head of the archives department was away. His visit there was briefer but
also instructive. The number-two person in the
department was able to tell him that the invisibly
set sapphire necklace and earrings, in a typical style
from the 1940s, had been a birthday gift, a simple
diamond pin had been a Christmas gift, and a sapphire ring and bracelet had been a Christmas gift

as well. The stones in the Van Cleef pieces weren't as large, but the settings were remarkable, the quality exceptional, and the pieces really lovely.

He hadn't contacted Boucheron about some of Marguerite's less important pieces. Umberto seemed to have a strong preference for Van Cleef and Cartier. And she had jewelry from a few other Paris jewelers that no longer existed.

Christie's own in-house jewelry experts had determined that Marguerite's small diamond tiara was an antique, and thus impossible to trace. They were certain it was French, but said it might have been purchased in London. The remainder of her jewelry had been made in Italy, notably two pieces by Bulgari, whom Phillip hadn't had time to contact yet. But his trip to Paris had been fruitful. He had a wealth of information about Marguerite's jewelry now, even their original prices, which bore little relation to their value now. The prices had been astronomical when they were purchased, but more than seventy years later, the price of jewelry and gemstones had multiplied exponentially. And stones of the caliber of her jewelry were almost impossible to find in the modern world.

Phillip went back to the Christie's office after his appointment at Van Cleef, and he had nothing more to do. He had been sent to the Paris sale as an observer and to lend a hand, but his work was over, and the Paris office could manage the rest. He was taking the Eurostar to London that night, mostly to show his face and check in at their London office, as long as he was in Paris anyway. And he always liked going to London, and seeing his friends in the art department. He said good-bye to Gilles, who wished him luck with the May sale.

He stayed at Claridge's in London, and took a walk down New Bond Street, where he admired the wares of Graff and the other important jewelers. They sold a lot of Graff pieces at auction, with flawless stones and beautiful designs, which were known to go for high prices, and Laurence Graff purchased stones from them as well to incorporate in his designs. He was known to buy incredibly valuable stones in rare colors, like pink and blue diamonds, in the largest sizes he could find. He had become the modern-day Harry Winston, with remarkable pieces at extraordinary prices. Phillip enjoyed looking in Graff's windows on his walk. Despite Phillip's preference for art over jewelry, Graff's pieces were best in show, and he admired him for that.

And on the way back to the hotel, he looked into several art galleries as well. And the next morning, he went to the Christie's office, and met with his British counterparts there, and discussed their upcoming sales. It was nice to see them and have a serious conversation, and not just exchange impersonal emails with them, and he advised them in greater detail about the May sale in New York. They were interested in hearing about the di San

Pignelli estate, how it had come to them through the surrogate's court, and his recent discoveries about the pieces at Cartier and Van Cleef. And when he went to pack late that afternoon, he decided on the spur of the moment to go to Rome after all, to complete his research, and had the concierge book him a flight at nine P.M. It was an easy hop from London, and they reserved a room for him at the Hassler. He wasn't planning to stay long, he only wanted to see the jewelers there. There were only one or two he planned to visit the next day.

After a brief delay at Heathrow, he arrived at the hotel in Rome just after midnight. His room was not large, but comfortable with a small balcony and decorated in lush yellow satin and antiques and had a beautiful view of Rome. The city was alive and bustling at that hour, with all the chaos and electricity he loved about it, and people in the streets. He poured himself a short brandy, and stood drinking it on the terrace, admiring the view under a full moon. As beautiful as Paris was, he always thought that Rome was the most romantic city in the world. And it depressed him a little to be standing there alone. It made him think that his mother was right, and he should be making more of an effort to meet someone, and do more than spend every weekend working on his boat. It would have been nice to have company in Rome with him, although he had come for business.

He slept soundly after the brandy, on a canopied

bed, and woke up at eight the next morning. He had a strong Italian espresso, and was at Bulgari on Via Condotti when they opened at ten o'clock. Both the emerald and diamond bracelet and the lacy diamond bracelet in Marguerite's safe deposit box were from there, but with regret they told him that they no longer had records that went back that far. Many of their older records were destroyed in the war. It had been a long shot coming to see them, and a good excuse to go to Rome as long as he was in Europe for the Paris sale. He wandered along the Via Condotti after that, and stopped in at Prada to buy a shirt, and by one o'clock, when many of the stores closed for lunch, he had finished his business there.

He went to a trattoria for a plate of pasta and a glass of wine, and as he watched the lively scene around him, another thought came to mind. He really didn't need it as research for the catalog, but he suddenly felt an irresistible pull to go to Naples, to see the château the Pignellis had lived in there. There was a Roman address on some of her papers too, and he had the cab driver pass it on the way back to the hotel. It was a handsome but innocuous building, where they must have had a Roman pied-à-terre. But her main address for thirty-two years had been in Naples, which he assumed had been the count's principal residence and family seat. He was aching to see it now. He didn't have a heavy schedule when he went back to New York, and was tempted to add one more day to his trip for the detour to Naples, and inquired about flights when he got back to the hotel at two-thirty. The concierge told him there was one from Fiumicino Airport to Naples at six o'clock, which he could easily catch, and they offered to book a room for him at the Grand Hotel Vesuvio, which they assured him was very agreeable. And feeling as though he were taking a leap into space, he asked them to make the reservations for him for both hotel and flight.

His mission to discover more about Marguerite Pearson di San Pignelli was beginning to take over his life, and he was faintly embarrassed by his obsession with her, but it was irresistible. An hour later, he was in a cab on the way to the airport, headed for Naples, with no concrete idea of what he hoped to discover there. All he knew was that he felt compelled to go. Something was beckoning to him and he wasn't sure what it was. He wished he could talk to Jane, and wondered if she'd understand, or think he was insane. Neither of them had a tie to this woman, and yet she had snagged their hearts.

The flight landed at Naples International Airport in Capodichino and Phillip took a cab to the hotel and checked in. His room had a balcony and a spectacular view of the Bay of Naples. It was a city he felt less comfortable walking around in, and it had a dicey reputation for street crimes, mostly by pickpockets, so he had dinner at the excellent Caruso Restaurant on the ninth floor. And he arranged to rent a car for the next day, which was delivered to the hotel. It was a serviceable no-frills Fiat sedan, and he had gotten careful directions from the concierge about how to reach Marguerite's address, which he assumed was the château. The concierge had told him it was at the very edge of the city in a beautiful location, although a bit out of the way. And as he drove there, Phillip could see Mount Vesuvius in the distance, and he thought about Pompeii. He had gone there with his parents as a boy and had been fascinated by it, not only the relics and artifacts, but the people who had been covered with lava and killed instantly, and mummified just as they had been that day, engaged in their ordinary activities. He remembered it vividly still, and it had made a deep impression on him as a child. He had wanted to know if there were volcanoes in New York, and was relieved to hear there weren't. The memory made him smile.

It took him a good half hour to reach the edge of the city in Neapolitan traffic, where people drove even more erratically than they did in Rome. And he was glancing at the directions, when he turned a corner and suddenly saw it, a beautiful small château. It was an elegant structure with a tall wall around it, and enormous old trees inside the walls. There was a large double gate, and he could see a cobbled courtyard inside. He checked the address he had written down, and saw that he'd arrived. He parked the car and got out to look around. He hesitated at the open gate, and saw two gardeners and a man in casual clothes directing them, and pointing at the gardens as they nodded. He was a tall man who looked to be in his sixties with a thick head of white hair, and he turned to glance at Phillip with a quizzical expression and then walked toward him when he finished with the gardeners. Phillip didn't know what to say, and his Italian wasn't adequate to explain why he was there.

**"Posso aiutarla?"** the man asked clearly in a deep sonorous voice. His face was lined, but his eyes were lively, and he looked nothing like the count in the photographs, who had long, lean aristocratic features, and was very thin and tall. This man appeared as though he enjoyed a good meal and a good laugh. His eyes were friendly but questioning as he gazed at Phillip, having asked what he could do to help him.

"Do you speak English?" Phillip asked him cautiously, not sure what he'd do if he didn't. His motive in being there was too complicated to explain in sign language, and was sketchy at best. He really didn't need to be there—he had just wanted to come, out of curiosity about Marguerite.

"Small," the man answered, holding up two fingers to indicate very little, as he smiled.

"I wanted to see the château," Phillip explained slowly, feeling slightly foolish. "I know someone who lived here a long time ago." That was a stretch too, since he really hadn't known her, but only about her.

The man nodded that he understood. "A parent? Grandmother?" he asked. Phillip didn't know that the word for **parent** and **relative** in Italian was the same, but he got the idea and shook his head. And he could hardly say "No, a woman whose jewelry we'll be selling at Christie's, whom I never met but am fascinated by," which was the case. And then he suddenly remembered the copies of the photographs of her he had in his computer case in the car, and went to get them, indicating to the man to wait, which he did patiently.

Phillip returned with them a moment later, and showed him the photographs of Umberto and Marguerite in front of the château, with the gardens and some of the stables, which Phillip guessed must have been behind the château, or maybe didn't exist anymore. And when he saw the photographs, the older man's face lit up immediately, and he nodded enthusiastically.

"Umberto and Marguerite di San Pignelli," Phillip said, pointing at them, and the man nodded again.

**"Il conte e la contessa."** He said their titles, and Phillip nodded and smiled.

"Are you of the same family?" Phillip asked him, and the man shook his head.

"No, I buy ten years ago," he said clearly. "He die a long time ago. No family, no children. He die, she sold house, go to Rome. Other people buy, make house very broken, then sell to me. They have no money, so they sell me." His English was broken, but he had no problem conveying to Phillip what had happened. Marguerite had sold the house after her husband's death, moved to Rome, and the people she sold it to had run it into the ground for lack of money, and then sold it to him. And he seemed to be taking good care of the place. And the Ferrari and Lamborghini that Phillip could see in the courtyard indicated that he had the money to do it.

**"Il conte era molto elegante, e lei bellissima,"** he said, talking about how elegant Umberto was, and how beautiful Marguerite had been, as he looked through the photographs. "Very sad, no children for house," he said. He would have liked to know more about Phillip's interest in the place but didn't have a sufficient grasp of English to ask him about it. Nonetheless, he beckoned Phillip to come inside and look around. And feeling grateful for the warm reception, he followed the new owner into the house. And once within the walls of the château, Phillip found himself walking through beautiful rooms with handsome antiques, and wonderful modern art that married well in the decor. The walls were painted soft, subtle pastel colors, and from the upper floors, where he took Phillip on a tour, he had a spectacular view of the sea.

"I love very much this house," the man explained, touching his heart as Phillip nodded. "Good feeling, very warm. It belong to **il conte**'s family four hundred years. I am from Firenze, but now Napoli too. Sometimes Roma. Galleria d'arte," he said, pointing at the paintings and then at himself, and Phillip assumed he meant that he was an art dealer, and the paintings on the walls were impressive, by well-known artists whom Phillip easily recognized. He took out his business card then, showing him as a vice president of Christie's, which the owner of the château recognized immediately, and was visibly impressed.

**"Gioielli?"** he said, pointing to the word **jewelry** on Phillip's card, and he nodded.

"Before, **prima**,"—Phillip used one of the few Italian words he knew—"art, paintings." He pointed at the art on the walls. "Now, **adesso, gioielli,** but I prefer art."

The man laughed as he understood, and seemed to agree, and then referred to Umberto and Marguerite again.

**"La contessa aveva gioielli fantastici,"** he said,

pointing to the photographs of Marguerite in some of her jewels. "I hear this. Very famous jewels, but then no money when **il conte** died. Many cars, horses, **gioielli,** so she sell house. And maybe very sad here after he die, especially with no children." Phillip nodded agreement. The owner of the château was creating a vision, even with few words, of a couple who had spent a great deal of money, and perhaps begun to run out of it at the time of Umberto's death, so she had sold the château, and moved to an apartment in the building he'd driven past in Rome. She had probably lived on the proceeds from the château for quite some time, and then gone back to the States. From all Phillip had gleaned so far, from the small apartment where she had lived in Murray Hill, and the nursing home in Queens, she had lived simply in New York. Her days of glory had been here, while Umberto was still alive. After he died, all that was left was the value of the jewels, which was considerable. But she had never sold the jewelry for money to live on, perhaps out of love for him, with the exception of two rings. It had obviously been a powerful love story, the memory of which had endured for the rest of her life, and long after his.

Thinking the same thing, the Italian pointed to the pictures of them and touched his heart with a tender look, and Phillip nodded. That was precisely what had brought him here, and the man he was conversing with, however awkwardly, seemed to understand. He took his own business card out to give Phillip then, and he had guessed right. His name was Saverio Salvatore, and he owned an art gallery of the same name, with addresses in both Florence and Rome. It had been a fortuitous meeting, and Phillip enjoyed talking to him. As they walked back to the courtyard and Phillip thanked him in both Italian and English, Saverio looked at Phillip warmly and pointed to a particularly endearing photograph of Marguerite and Umberto.

"You send to me? I like for this house. It was their home for many years." Phillip agreed to immediately, and said he would send him several. It touched him that the new owner wanted to have their photographs. Their love story endeared them to everyone.

The two men shook hands before Phillip walked out of the gate, and Saverio waved and wandered back into the house. They hadn't toured the grounds, which were extensive, but Phillip had seen enough. He had gotten a strong sense of what their home had been like, and how and where they'd lived. It was a very grand life. And it gave him a warm feeling that the man who was living there cared about and respected them. Their memories were not forgotten. And Phillip felt a feeling of peace wash over him as he started the car and drove back to the hotel.

The trip to Naples had served no useful function for Christie's, or the sale of Marguerite's things, and yet he knew that in coming here, he had done the right thing. He was certain of it. And he was going to keep Saverio's card, and hoped they'd meet again. He had every intention of fulfilling his promise, and sending him the photographs of Umberto and Marguerite.

# Chapter 14

Phillip called his mother that weekend, when he was back in New York. He wanted to have dinner with her on Sunday night, and tell her all he had learned about Marguerite, her jewelry, and that he had even seen the house where they'd lived. He knew that she'd be interested, and it gave more substance to the story now. Marguerite was no longer a complete mystery to them, she had been a woman with a home, a man who had loved her, and a favored life. She was not just a name on a safe deposit box at the bank, who had owned a collection of extremely valuable jewels. Knowing now that she was running out of money, was down to two thousand dollars when she died, lived in a tiny apartment for many years, had ended her days in a seedy nursing home in Queens, and hadn't sold the jewels to live more comfortably, was even more touching and intriguing. The jewelry from Umberto had obviously meant a great deal to her.

He wanted to say all that to his mother, and tell her all about the auction in Paris, and the rest of his trip, including the dramatic moment when Marie-Antoinette's tiara had been claimed by the government for the French museums. He knew she would love hearing about that. And he was surprised to hear her sounding somewhat somber when he called, or serious. And she said she wanted to see him too. She seemed as though she had something to say.

"Are you okay, Mom? Is something wrong?"

"No, I just want to talk. I have some decisions to make."

"Is it your health?" he said, with a feeling of panic.

"No, darling, I'm fine. Just some other stuff. I want your excellent advice." He knew that she sold some of his father's stock certificates from time to time. She was invested in a solid fund, where she didn't have to worry about the insurance money she had inherited when his father died. And she liked asking Phillip's advice.

"Sunday night?"

"That's fine, have a nice weekend." But he was concerned about her after they talked. She gave him the impression that she had a serious matter on her mind, and he hoped she wasn't lying to

him, and that her health really was all right. As an
only child, he felt responsible for her, and worried
about her, no matter how youthful and independent she was. She was still seventy-four years old,
even if she didn't look it or act it.

He thought about Jane Willoughby again that
weekend too. He wanted to call her and tell her
about the results of his trip, and his research about
Marguerite, and he decided to invite her to lunch
again, boyfriend or not. He had learned a lot about
Marguerite in Europe, and wanted to share it with
her.

While he worked on his boat, Jane was moving into her new apartment. It was a small one
bedroom in the meat-packing district near Alex,
and she was delighted with it. Her parents were
going to help her pay the rent, until she got a job.
Jane hadn't heard a word from John since she had
moved out. The waters had closed over her without
a trace. It was as though he had forgotten she'd existed, which was hurtful at best. And she assumed
he was with Cara and didn't care. It was a tough
lesson for Jane, and she was sorry she hadn't moved
when things started to go sour months before. The
last six months had been a total waste of time, and
his blithe ignoring her, with the excuse of school
and projects, had been insulting.

Jane had taken a day off from work that week
and gone to IKEA to buy the basics she needed
since she had no furniture, and Alex helped her put

it together. She was good with a screwdriver and a hammer. And by Sunday night, Jane was moved in, and the place looked great. It gave her a new lease on life. She and Alex ate popcorn and watched a movie that night to initiate her new home.

Phillip left Long Island on Sunday afternoon a little earlier than usual. It was raining, he knew there would be traffic, and he was anxious to see his mother. He stopped and bought a bottle of rosé wine he knew she liked, and at five o'clock, he rang her doorbell, and she looked surprised to see him.

"You're early!" she said with pleasure as he handed her the wine, which pleased her too.

"It sounds like we have a lot to talk about, so I thought I'd give us some more time," he said easily as he walked into the apartment. He could tell she'd been working—he could smell the fresh oil paints, a familiar scent he loved and always associated with his mother, and had all his life.

She poured them each a glass of wine a few minutes later, and they sat down in the cozy living room. She was in her favorite old leather armchair, and he on the couch, as he looked at her quizzically. "So what's up? You first." He'd been worried about her for two days.

"It's kind of a long story," she said with a sigh, and took a sip of the wine. "I knew about it the last time I saw you, but I needed some time to think about it. It came as kind of a shock." He was more sure than ever, as he listened to her, that she had a health problem, and he nearly held his breath as he listened, but in spite of what she was saying, she looked healthy to him, and no different than before.

"I told you that I went to see Fiona, my old nanny. I wanted her to help me make sense of something. When I looked at the photographs you gave me of Marguerite, nothing earth-shattering struck me about her. I guess I could see some vague family resemblance, but all she had were American Anglo-Saxon good looks, and let's face it, all WASPs look the same," she said dismissively, and he laughed at his mother's typical irreverence.

"Well, not always," he responded, and she smiled.

"I didn't see anything remarkable about her, in terms of looks. But what rocked me to the core were the photographs of the little girl. There aren't a lot of photographs of me as a child, as I didn't have doting parents, to say the least, but when I looked at those pictures, I was certain that they were me. There is no name written on any of them, but I was the same age as that child on those dates, and in a couple of them, I was absolutely sure. What I couldn't understand was why my photos were in the safe deposit box, what were they doing there?

"I went to see Winnie about it, and I had a strange idea. I was suddenly suspicious of the fact that there were no photographs of my older sister Marguerite. Supposedly, my mother was so devastated by her death that she destroyed them all, and any physical evidence of her, which always seemed odd to me. Wouldn't she have carefully preserved every shred of memories of her lost daughter? Your grandparents were unbearably uptight, cold, judgmental people, and I suddenly began wondering what if Marguerite didn't die? What if she had fallen in love with an Italian count, of which they would have strongly disapproved I'm sure, and what if they only said she died, and she had been alive and living with an Italian husband for all those years? What if it was not a coincidence of name, and Marguerite di San Pignelli was in fact my oldest sister? They are the same age, and I don't know why but I suddenly became overwhelmingly convinced that might be the case. Winnie was only four when she left, and I was a baby, but I wondered if she'd ever suspected Marguerite was alive, or heard something that made her question what we'd been told." Valerie looked at her son intently.

"And what did she say?" He was intrigued by what she said.

"That I was senile. That I'm insane, that our parents would never do a thing like that. She liked them a lot better than I did, and they were nicer to her. More important, she was just like them, I never was, so they always tried to pound me into thinking and behaving like them, and I couldn't.

She told me what I thought was preposterous, that our parents would never lie to us, and the photographs weren't me of course, and all children looked and dressed like that at the time, which is partially true. But that child's face was so like me, and my eyes. I got nowhere with Winnie, and we had a huge fight.

"And that night it occurred to me to go and see Fiona, and ask her what she knew. I figured she might know more about the circumstances in which my sister left. Years later, we were told that she had gone to study in Europe, in Switzerland, since there was a war on. But why would you let your daughter go there during a war, and if she went to England, why did she die in Italy? We were never allowed to ask questions about her, or even mention her name, and I was always curious about her. So I thought maybe Fiona could tell me something, and she'd recognize the photographs of Marguerite, if it was she, since she came to work for us two years before my sister left. So I drove to New Hampshire to see her. She's ninety-four, but clear as a bell." Valerie seemed breathless as she went on with the story, and Phillip listened, with no idea what would come next.

"I showed her the photographs and asked her if Marguerite di San Pignelli was my sister. And I was heartbroken when she said no. But I was in no way prepared for what she said next. She told

me that Marguerite was my mother. She got pregnant by a boy she loved at seventeen. He was just
shy of eighteen at the time. Both sets of parents
were outraged, and wouldn't let them get married
and separated them. Marguerite was sent away to
a home for wayward girls in Maine, to have the
baby in hiding and give it up for adoption. A few
weeks after she left the city, the Japanese hit Pearl
Harbor, the boy was drafted and sent to boot
camp, and then to California for training, and was
killed in an accident almost immediately, and apparently Marguerite refused to give up the baby,
so her parents, my grandparents, disappeared with
her, and returned to New York a few months after
the baby was born, pretending the baby was theirs,
but obviously hating every minute of it. They put
Marguerite on a neutral Swedish ship to Lisbon,
from where she went to London. She was never
going to Switzerland. And a year later they said
she died of influenza, and got rid of her forever, as
far as they were concerned. In actual fact, she met
the count in London when she got there. She was
alone at eighteen in a foreign country, with a war
on. He was kind to her, they married very quickly,
and he took her back to Italy with him, to live at
his family home in Naples. But her parents had
banished their own child, Phillip. Their firstborn
daughter, just to avoid a scandal," she said with a
look of outrage, and tears in her eyes. "They just

cut her out of their lives forever, and kept her baby, even if they didn't want it, and never loved it. Fiona says that Marguerite and the count tried to get her baby back several years later, and her parents did everything to defeat her and scare her off and threaten her, to keep the story quiet, and she eventually gave up. And all Fiona could do was send her photographs of her daughter periodically, until she left us ten years later.

"But Phillip," Valerie said, her eyes welling up with tears, which overflowed now, "that baby was me. Marguerite was my mother, not my sister, and my grandparents stole me from her, and pretended to be my parents and hated me forever because of the disgrace my birth would have meant to them. I lived a lie all my life, and was robbed of my mother, because of them. Marguerite Pearson di San Pignelli was my mother. I have no idea what to do about it, or who one tells something like that to, or even if it matters at this point. She's dead." She felt like an orphan again as she said it, just as she had the day she found out. "But there's no question. She was my mother. It is the weirdest of coincidences, even more so than we ever thought it could be, or than I thought when I started to wonder if she was my sister. It was like I was meant to find her, when you got called to do that appraisal from Christie's. She was your grandmother, Phillip. And the mother I never knew, and should have." The tears spilled down her cheeks and Phillip put his arms around her and held her. He had never seen his mother as bereft except when his father died. Valerie cried softly as he held her.

"Did you tell Winnie?" he asked her, and she nodded.

"This time she believed me. She still made excuses for them and said she's sure they thought they were doing the right thing. But keeping my mother from me all my life, treating me like an unwelcome intruder, banishing their daughter and pretending she was dead, could hardly have felt like the right thing, even to them. Winnie begged me not to make a fuss about it, or even say anything. Originally, she accused me of being after the jewelry, but in a way this is all much more shocking than wanting to be the heir to a fortune in jewelry. It's a hideous lie propagated by my grandparents, and they must have ruined Marguerite's life, having stolen her only child from her. And the poor woman died alone." Valerie dried her tears and looked deeply moved by it, as Phillip thought about what she had just said.

"I wasn't thinking about the jewelry, just about what all this meant to your mother, and to you. I agree, it's an awful story." But now there was the jewelry to consider too. "The truth is, Mom, you are the heir to the jewelry. You're her only child. And if that's true, you should have it."

"It belongs to Winnie too—she was her sister. But I really don't care about the jewelry. It won't bring my mother back now."

"No, but she would want you to have it. I think there's a reason why she hung on to it for all these years, even when she had so little money left. Either she kept it out of love for Umberto, or she hoped to find you one day and give it to you."

"If that were true, she'd have written a will, and she didn't," his mother reminded him.

"You don't know what she was thinking or what condition she was in, in the end. The simple fact is that these things belonged to her, and you're her only daughter. I'm not sure what we do now. But there's a lot more to the story than meets the eye here, other than your grandparents' terrible behavior. Your mother left a fortune in jewels, and they belong to you." It was an outcome he had never in his wildest dreams expected, even when he had asked her about the coincidence of maiden names. He had thought Marguerite might be some very distant cousin, but not his maternal grandmother. It was an astounding revelation, for all of them. And they couldn't let the story lie where it had fallen. Now they had to do the right thing. Phillip didn't know what that was yet, but he wanted to think about it and make the appropriate decision.

When he calmed down from the shock of the

information his mother had shared with him, he told her about his visits to Cartier and Van Cleef, and what he knew about the jewelry now, and its origins and the meaningful occasions on which it had been given. And he told her about visiting their home, the château, and meeting Saverio Salvatore in Naples, the current owner of the château, what a charming man he had been, and the little he had known about Marguerite and Umberto. It all fit together now, a perfect puzzle, with few pieces missing.

"I'd like to see it one day," Valerie said wistfully, about the home where her mother had lived for thirty-two years with the stepfather she had never known. Valerie was slowly acquiring a family she never knew she had, who even posthumously seemed more real to her than the parents she'd grown up with.

They talked long into the night, eating in the kitchen, and putting all the pieces together as they looked at the photographs again. Valerie admitted to him as they finished the wine that she wanted to do a portrait of her mother from the photographs he'd given her. She seemed to want to cling to her now, like the motherless child she had once been, and heal the tragic losses of the past.

Phillip was deeply moved by all of it when he left and went home that night. There was so much to think about, about the past, present, and future, and some decision had to be made about the jewelry. And all Phillip could think of was that he had to call Jane in the morning. She probably wouldn't know any more than he did about what his mother had to do now, but clearly they had to do something. What, remained to be seen.

# Chapter 15

Phillip called Jane the next morning before she had time to take her coat off in her office. He was still at home.

"How was your trip?" she asked him, obviously happy to hear from him. She had been thinking about him that morning.

"Very interesting," he said, feeling distracted and sounding serious. He had been awake most of the night, thinking of what his mother had told him, and what he had to do now to help her. He cut to the chase. "I was wondering if we could have lunch today. I have something I'd like to discuss with you." Given the tone of his voice, it sounded like business, not romance, and she couldn't imagine what it was.

"Sure. Of course. Where would you like me to

meet you?" He suggested another restaurant near his office, that wasn't too noisy, and had good sandwiches, burgers, and salads. He didn't want to be distracted by fancy food, intrusive waiters, or noisy customers. They agreed to meet at twelve-thirty, and he was already at the table when she got there. He was wearing a blazer and a sweater and gray slacks, and she had dressed casually as well, not expecting to have a lunch date. And she could see from the look in his eyes that he was worried about something.

They both ordered club sandwiches, and agreed to share a salad, and as soon as the waiter had taken their order, Phillip turned to her, and told her about his trip to Europe, the visits to Van Cleef and Cartier, and the château in Naples. She was touched to hear everything he told her, and then he took a breath and decided to plunge into the deep end and tell her the rest. It was very personal and very moving, but having shared the adventure this far, he thought she ought to know.

"Jane, my mother has been doing some sleuthing herself, and some amazing information has turned up. As it turns out, there was more than a coincidence of names here. A lot more." He told her then what Valerie had learned from Fiona and what she had told him the night before, that he hadn't yet fully absorbed. "It seems incredible and stranger yet that you would just happen to call Christie's for this appraisal, and it led to my mother discovering

the truth about her birth, her mother, and a whole
mystery has unraveled right before our eyes. Fact
is definitely stranger than fiction. And weirdest of
all, my mother turns out to be Marguerite di San
Pignelli's direct heir, and Marguerite is my grandmother. Talk about strange." He looked bowled
over as he said it, and Jane was amazed. As she listened to him tell his mother's story, the similarity
of what she had gleaned from the letters had struck
her, and she was stunned. "I'm not sure what we
do now, or how we prove to the court that my
mother is Marguerite's rightful heir. She can't just
walk into surrogate's court and say 'Hi, she was my
mom.' And since her grandparents faked the birth
certificate in some way, claiming her as their own,
I don't suppose that will be easy to prove either.
Not to mention the fact that the auction is in two
months. I'm sure it will all fall into place in the
end, but I'm not sure what the next step is, and I
wanted your advice. What do you think?"

She could hardly find words to answer him for a
minute, and then instinctively switched into legal
gear. There was no doubt in her mind what he had
to do. "You need to call a lawyer, and fast. You
can't sort this out on your own. You need to advise
the surrogate's court that an heir has been located,
your mother needs to come forward officially, and
then you'll need to provide proof. How long that
will take, what the steps are in the process, or what
proof they will require, I don't know. But a lawyer

will. This isn't my area of expertise. How is your mother taking this, by the way? It must be a terrible shock to discover that the people she thought of as her parents cheated her out of her real mother, and kept them separated from each other all her life. It's really heartbreaking to hear stories like that. I know it happens, but it must be an awful feeling for her," Jane said with compassion in her eyes. Marguerite's poignant story, and his mother's, had reality for her now and touched her deeply.

"She's very upset, and I can't blame her. She really isn't thinking about the jewelry at this point, just about the mother she lost, and I gather that her grandmother was never nice to her. She was a very cold woman, and I guess she always held against my mother the circumstances of her birth, unfair as that is. But in spite of all that, we have to deal with the jewelry too. It can't be sold now that there is a rightful heir, without that heir's permission, and my mother will have to be legally acknowledged as the heir first. And I have no idea if that will take days or months." He looked worried about it, and so did Jane.

"I don't know either," she admitted. "The timing of that could be anything, and courts never move quickly, particularly when they're handling the estates of deceased people who can't complain about how long it's taking." They both smiled at that.

"I also don't know if my aunt Edwina is going

to make a claim on the estate. Marguerite was her sister, and she may want a part of it too."

"You need to call an attorney immediately," Jane reiterated. "I can get a recommendation if you like," she offered helpfully.

"I have someone in mind," he said quietly.

"Call them today," she urged him, as he nodded and paid the check, and then thanked her for listening, and for her good advice. It helped being able to talk to her, and he appreciated it. She was still awestruck that destiny had led her to call Phillip, and that his mother was the child whom Marguerite wrote about in her letters, and had grieved for most of her life. The force of it was overwhelming. "When Harriet had me read the letters in the safe deposit box, I was still hoping to find a will. I didn't, they were only letters, but the whole story is there. Everything you just told me, from her mother's side. Leaving the baby she called her 'darling angel' in New York, being forced to disappear, arriving in London during the war, meeting the count, marrying and living with him, and attempting to get her child back when she was seven. They did what they could, and were stymied by her parents at every turn. She went back to see her when the child was eighteen, to tell her the whole story, and once she saw her from a distance, she was afraid to disrupt her life and ruin it, and trade her daughter's respectable life for a scandalous one, and she went back to Italy without seeing her, and eventually just gave up.

"She wrote letters to her lost daughter for more than seventy years. They were love letters to her child. She never named her, and she always said that she was going to leave the jewelry to her. She was going to write a will, but she obviously never got around to it. And you can tell from her letters that her mind was no longer clear in the end. She was lost in the past. There is nothing in the letters that would provide adequate legal proof, except if your mother can prove that Marguerite is her mother. But it's all there, the whole sad story from beginning to end, and some sweet times too. She was happy with the count, but the most powerful force in her life was her missing child. I still have the copies of the letters in the file. I'll scan them for you. It's a sad story, but it will tell your mother how much her mother loved her during all those years they lost and never had as mother and child." She could only guess at how much the letters would mean to Phillip's mother. They were her mother's voice speaking to her.

Phillip looked overwhelmed by what she had just said. And it would be an important testimony to give his mother, to know how her mother had felt.

"I'd be very grateful to you if you sent me the copies of the letters. They might be tough for my mother to read, but maybe healing in a way too.

All she knows now is from other people. Hearing it in her mother's letters would be an incredible gift."

"I'm so happy I read them," Jane said quietly, even if they hadn't yielded a will, which would have been more useful to him.

They went out to the street then, both of them a little dazed by what they'd shared. And to distract them both from the heavy emotions of their discovery, he decided to inquire how things were going with her boyfriend, not expecting anything to have changed.

"Actually," she said, smiling up at him once they were on the sidewalk outside, "some things happened that changed the situation for me. I moved out. I just moved into my own place in the meat-packing district, and I love it."

"Are you still seeing him?" Phillip asked, hoping she wasn't.

"No, I'm not," she said quietly. "He was cheating on me, and I just found out. I should have given up six months ago, when the relationship went sour, but I thought it would work out. It didn't. And he's moving back to L.A. with her." It had been a total bust, as Phillip could deduce, and he hoped it hadn't been too painful for her. She seemed calm and philosophical about it, and even relieved.

"Could I invite you for dinner sometime?" he asked her, just as he had before, and this time she nodded and looked pleased.

"I'd like that a lot," she said with a warm smile, and he promised to keep her informed about his mother's situation, and what they would be doing to confirm her as Marguerite's heir. He had a feeling it would be complicated, and maybe a lengthy process. And she promised to send him the copies of Marguerite's letters that afternoon. He wanted to copy them, and read them himself. He felt enormous compassion for his mother over what she'd just learned.

"I'll call you," he promised, and after kissing her on the cheek, she wished him luck. He hurried back to his office then to contact his cousin Penny. She was the attorney he had in mind. She worked for a great firm, was a partner herself, and always gave him good advice. He called her as soon as he sat down at his desk, and she walked out of a meeting to talk to him. As cousins and only children, they had always been extremely close. Penny was forty-five years old, and had three teenage children, a thirteen-year-old son, a fifteen-year-old daughter who drove her crazy, and an eighteen-year-old son who was in his last year of high school. They were the grandchildren Winnie complained about constantly to her sister.

"What's up? Did you get arrested?" she asked hopefully, and he laughed.

"Not yet. I'm still working on it. Listen, something has happened, this is a biggie. Can I come down to your office and see you?" She worked on

Wall Street, and her specialty was tax and estate law, so this was right up her alley.

"When were you thinking?"

"Now? Later? In ten minutes?"

"Shit, I'm in meetings till six o'clock. If it's important, I'll ask my housekeeper to stay late and feed the monsters."

"It would be great if you could do that," he said honestly.

"See you at six then. You're not in trouble are you? Tax fraud? Embezzlement?"

"Thank you for your faith in me," he said, smiling ruefully.

"You never know. Crazier things have happened."

"Not crazier than what did happen. See you later. And Penny, thank you."

"No problem. See you at six."

He had three hours to wait until he saw her, and half an hour later Jane scanned Marguerite's letters to him, and he sat at his desk all afternoon, reading them, as tears streamed down his cheeks. Knowing all he did now, it seemed a tragedy to him that Marguerite had been robbed of her child. Even more so for her than for his mother, who had no idea what she'd missed. Marguerite knew exactly what she'd lost and mourned it all her life.

The firm Penny worked at had an impressive name and a big reputation, and she had a handsome office. She had been a full partner for several years, and when Phillip walked into her office, she got up to hug him. She was a good-looking redhead, with a great figure, and a husband who was crazy about her.

She sat back at her desk after hugging him, and he took a seat across from her and told her the whole story. His mother's secret illegitimate birth, her grandparents claiming her as their own, with a birth certificate that had been doctored and paid for, and falsified at birth that her grandmother was her mother, their "disappearing" their oldest daughter and keeping Valerie from her, and then the coincidence of his doing the appraisal on Marguerite's intestate estate, his mother's guesswork, and the information the old nanny had provided her, which appeared to be accurate but was unofficial. He told her about Marguerite's letters too, which confirmed it all in depth and her own words.

"So what do we do now, to establish my mother as her mother's rightful heir?" Penny thought about it for a moment, and jotted some notes on a pad, as she had done during his whole astonishing recital. But as an attorney, nothing surprised her anymore. She had heard far stranger stories, although Phillip's was remarkable.

"First, we send someone to get a statement from the nanny. At ninety-four, we don't want to dilly-dally. If she dies in her sleep tonight, the story, and the corroboration, dies with her. I'll try to get someone up there tomorrow. Do you think she'd be willing?"

"As I remember her, she's pretty chatty. Also, she wanted my mother to know the story. I don't know why she didn't tell her sooner. But at least she did now. If I hadn't done that appraisal, my mother would never have seen those photographs, and would probably never have found out who her mother was, or that our grandmother wasn't really her mother." The story was so amazing, it shocked them both.

"Fate moves in strange ways," Penny said, and firmly believed it. "My next suggestion may not be something your mother wants to do, but it will simplify the whole story. I want her to get a DNA test. We'll need an order to exhume her mother's body, my aunt and your grandmother, I guess," she said, considering it. "We have to get the court's approval for that. And I don't see why they would balk at it, as long as we're willing to pay costs, which I assume we are." He nodded confirmation. "And if it's a match, it's pretty straightforward. The court would then confirm your mother as the rightful heir, and what she does with the property after that is up to her. It takes six weeks to get the results of the DNA, and if it's a positive match, it's a done deal."

"What about your mother? Would she be a direct heir too, as Marguerite's sister?" Penny thought about it for a moment, and knew how unpredictable people were when estates were involved, but she thought she knew her mother better than that, and her financial circumstances. Penny's father had left her a very substantial fortune, and his parents had established a sizable trust for Penny. There was no need for the two women to fight over the money.

"She could certainly make a claim on the estate," Penny admitted, "but I think we should leave that up to the sisters. Let them work it out and come to an agreement. My guess is my mom won't want it, and will be happy for your mother, and figure she deserves it, particularly after they cheated her out of her rightful mother. Let's see what our moms work out between them over that. Is the jewelry worth a great deal?"

"According to our estimate, twenty to thirty million, before estate taxes of course, which will cut that amount in half." But it was still an impressive amount. Penny whistled.

"That's a nice chunk of change." It could leave Valerie with ten to fifteen million dollars after taxes. She'd be set for life, even more so than with her late husband's insurance. "This really is an amazing story. It feels like the hand of destiny is on this one. One forgets that good things do happen to good people, not just bad ones. This would be nice for your mom."

"Yes, it would," Phillip agreed, and for him one day, but he wasn't thinking about that.

"Well, let's get started. I'll send someone up to see the old nanny tomorrow. Shoot me an email with her details. You ask your mom about the DNA test, and have her call me, and I'll prepare an order to exhume Marguerite's body. It's all less complicated than it sounds. And if there's no opposition to her being the rightful heir, there's no problem." At least the end of the story would be simpler and happier than the beginning, and hopefully with a good result for his mother, which was some consolation, although the jewelry, and proceeds from it, were no substitute for a mother.

It was seven-thirty when Phillip left his cousin's office, and he called his mother as soon as he got home. She was painting. He told her what Penny had said, and she rapidly agreed to the DNA test, and gave him Fiona's address at the nursing home in New Hampshire, and said she'd call and warn her that someone would be coming to take a statement from her. When Valerie called Fiona, she said she would be happy to tell the story to the investigator when he arrived.

Valerie was excited now to get the result of the DNA test. She was planning to call her doctor about it the next day. She seemed to have a deep visceral need now to prove that Marguerite had been her mother, which no one was denying. At least not now, not anymore. But she wanted to confirm it officially, as though to prove to herself that she'd had a mother who loved her after all.

Finally, Valerie called Winnie. She just wanted to let her know what she was doing. Winnie listened carefully to what Valerie told her, and sounded somewhat jangled when she responded.

"It's all so messy," she said, sounding unhappy. "Exhuming bodies, DNA tests. I wish we could just let it lie." But then Marguerite's estate would go to the state, which seemed wrong to her too. But she hated all the mess, and facing the reality that her parents had been liars. She wasn't angry at Valerie anymore, she just wished that none of it had ever happened, or they hadn't found out. She was a little annoyed at Fiona for telling Valerie the story. Winnie had preferred to be an ostrich all her life. And so had her parents. And it was painful for Winnie to admit they were liars.

"I know you think I'm doing this for the money," Valerie said sadly, "but as hard as it is to believe, I'm not. I just want to prove she was my mother. I never felt as though I had one. Now I do." It was too late for it to change anything, and it seemed childish of her to Winnie, and she had had parents after all, even if they weren't her real ones, but she could hear how much it meant to Valerie, and there was no stopping the process now. Pandora's box had been opened. "And you have a right to a share of the jewelry too," Valerie told her. "She was your sister."

"I don't want anything from her estate," Edwina said firmly. "Henry left me more than enough. I wouldn't know what to do with it. And his parents took care of Penny. She has all she'll ever need, and so will her children. I've set up generation-skipping trusts for them. Just worry about you and Phillip. If she really was your mother, that's only right." Winnie was not an easy person, or a particularly happy one, but she was honest and fair and had no intention of fighting with Valerie over the estate, or even expecting part of it. "If I turn out to be your aunt and not your sister, you can take me to dinner," Winnie said with a wintry smile.

"If you want, I'll take you to Europe," Valerie promised. "I want to see where she lived. Phillip just went to visit the château in Naples." Valerie sounded wistful as she said it.

"I always get sick in Italy," Winnie complained. "The food is too rich. The last time it gave me diverticulitis," she said, and Valerie laughed.

"Well, think about it."

"You can take pictures for me," Winnie said firmly, as Valerie admitted to herself silently that it would be easier traveling without her, but she was grateful too that Winnie planned to make no opposition to the estate, and wanted nothing from it. It would make the process simpler.

The next day, Valerie went to get the DNA test, Penny filed a request with the state to exhume the body, and get a DNA test of Marguerite, and she sent a licensed investigator to interview Fiona in New Hampshire. They were on their way. And Jane was in Harriet's office that morning, as soon as she arrived. "We have an heir to the Pignelli estate," she said, looking excited, as Harriet's eyes widened.

"Someone answered the ad?" Harriet seemed startled but pleased.

"It's a lot more complicated than that," Jane shared with her, and told her the whole story in detail, as Harriet listened in amazement.

The form came across her desk two days later, requesting to exhume Marguerite's body for a DNA match, and she submitted it to the court immediately to facilitate the process. And as Jane left her office, she couldn't help thinking that if she had gotten the clerkship she wanted in family law, and not at the surrogate's court, she would never have met Phillip, and his mother might never have discovered the truth about her own history.

He had invited Jane to dinner that weekend, and to visit his boat when the weather got warmer. It gave her something to look forward to. Her life was looking up these days. And all thanks to Marguerite Pearson di San Pignelli and the jewelry she had left in her abandoned safe deposit box. It was beginning to feel like a miracle to all of them.

When Phillip got the letters from Jane, he brought his mother a set the same night. She would get the originals eventually but he knew she would want to read them right away, and not on a screen.

He explained to her quietly what they were, and she started to cry even before she took them out of the manila envelope he had put them in. And she told him she wanted to read them alone, after she thanked him for bringing them to her. She suspected they would be painful, but she had no idea how excruciatingly poignant it would be to read of her mother's decades of suffering and never-ending sense of loss, having given up her baby daughter, only to grieve for her, for her entire life. Valerie sobbed for hours as she went through them intently, and went over them again, but when she had finished, she knew exactly how loved she had been. She wished that her mother had dared to approach her when she was eighteen, instead of fearing it would ruin her life. It wouldn't have—it would have improved it immeasurably to meet the mother who loved her instead of the one she had. And she wished that Marguerite had contacted her over the years, or when she moved back to New York twenty-two years before. At any point in her life, Valerie would have welcomed her with open arms, and now she would never have that chance. But now at least she knew who she had lost, the woman she had been, and the love her mother had had for her. Knowing that put balm on some very old wounds, of never having had a mother's love, except from her nanny Fiona until she was ten. She had never had maternal love from the woman who had pretended to be her mother, her own grandmother, who had taken her just to avoid the scandal and not from any deep feelings for her, of which she had none. If anything, she had resented Valerie all her life for how she'd been conceived. And she had thrown away her own daughter, while stealing hers from her. Two daughters had been lost, not just one.

It remained inconceivable to Valerie, and yet it had all happened, and all she wished, as she finished reading the letters, was that she could have held her mother once so they could tell each other how much they loved each other. Valerie would have given anything for that. But the letters would have to be enough, and they were an amazing gift, from the mother she had never known. She realized now in every fiber of her being that Marguerite had always loved her with all her heart and soul.

# Chapter 16

The night after Valerie had her blood drawn for the DNA test, she was painting in her studio, and the figure she'd been working on of the unknown woman had begun to look more and more like the photographs of Marguerite. There was an eerie, wistful quality to it, like a mystery emerging from the mists. There was something sad about the painting, and Fiona's words about her natural mother and father kept echoing in Valerie's head, that they had been like Romeo and Juliet. Fiona had said that Tommy's parents had been as upset as Marguerite's about the pregnancy, so they couldn't have harbored warm feelings for her either, as the tangible result of their son's foolishness. And even when he died, they must have not wanted his child, or they would have reached out in some way, and they never did, not that she knew, although maybe her grandparents had concealed that too. And by now, she was sure that her paternal grandparents would be dead, they would have been over a hundred years old, like her own. But she couldn't help wondering if some other member of the family had survived. Given how soon he died after Valerie was conceived, Tommy would have had no other children, but perhaps he had siblings or cousins. She had a thirst for her relatives now that nothing could quench. She wanted to know it all. She had half of the equation—now she wanted the rest.

She set down her brushes and left her studio, to sit at her computer at her desk, and she put Tommy and his parents' names into a search engine. She Googled them in different ways, using Tommy's birth date and a guess at when he was killed. Thomas, Muriel, and Fred Babcock—eventually the information came up that they were deceased. Then she tried Thomas Babcock, thinking that a relative might have named a child after her father, since he died during the war. She found one in New York, who was ten years younger than she was, which might have been about right, if Tommy had a brother who had named a child after him.

Feeling her heart pound in her chest, with a shaking hand, Valerie called the phone number on her cell phone, and held her breath while it rang. It would be just too incredible if she got it right on the first try, but the possibility of it was exciting.

She'd heard stories like this before, of people seeking long-lost parents, often who had put them up
for adoption, and as the result of a random call,
they were united via the Internet. She had become
one of them, children born out of wedlock, looking for their roots, compelled to find their parents
or relatives, trying to gather up the fragments of a
lost life before it was too late. Or was it already too
late? Were all of Tommy's relatives dead? Had he
been an only child?

A man answered on the third ring. He had a
pleasant voice, and Valerie launched nervously into
her story about Tommy Babcock and her mother,
seventy-five years before. Separated young lovers,
an unwanted pregnancy, and his untimely death
in the early weeks of the war. It sounded like a
strange story even to her, as she described it. The
man at the other end of the phone was silent as
he listened. "Did you have an uncle or a relative
named Thomas Babcock?" she asked hopefully,
and waited anxiously for his answer.

"Yes, I did," he said, "but I don't think he's the
one you're looking for. I had an uncle Tom, and my
grandfather was named Thomas too. I don't think
my uncle's your man, though," he said, chuckling.

"Why not?" Valerie asked, curious, and wondering if he actually was the right one. So many coincidences that had seemed wrong at first had proved
to be true.

"My uncle was gay. He was an early activist in

gay rights, and moved to San Francisco in the sixties. He was a great guy, and he died of AIDS in
1982. I don't think he fathered any babies. He was
a very talented set designer on Broadway, and became a well-known interior designer in San Francisco." His nephew sounded proud of him, but
this clearly wasn't who she was looking for. "I hope
you find some relative of your father's. It sounds
like a sad story. Why did you wait so long to look
for his family?"

"I only discovered the true story recently myself.
In those days, babies born out of wedlock were
pretty shocking, and no one talked about it."

"I guess that's true," he said kindly. "Well, good
luck." They hung up a moment later, while Valerie
wondered how many wrong Babcocks she'd have
to call, and if she'd ever find the right one, who'd
been somehow related to her father.

She tried the same name again, and dozens came
up, some as young as four years old, from a variety of states. And finally one of them struck her
as possible again. He was seventy years old, born
the year after the war ended, and he lived in Santa
Barbara, California, with his wife, Angela, and a
Walter Babcock, who was ninety-four years old.
The possible fantasy struck her immediately. What
if Tommy had had an older brother, who married
and had a son after the war, and named him after
his deceased brother? She believed that anything
was possible now. She would have liked to call

Fiona to ask her, but it was too late, she would be sound asleep.

Valerie sat staring at the names and number, desperate to call. She no longer cared if people thought she was crazy. She picked up the phone and called. It was only seven o'clock at night in California, and the worst they could say was that she had the wrong number and hang up. She had already decided to ask for Thomas Babcock, and not his father. Thomas would have been the nephew of her natural father, if she guessed right. A woman answered in a slight southern accent, when Valerie asked to speak to Thomas Babcock and closed her eyes as she waited. She had nothing to lose, except time and face, and she didn't mind losing either one.

A moment later a man with a deep, vibrant voice came on the line. He didn't seem upset to be called by a stranger, and she explained rapidly, and as clearly as possible, the reason for her call.

"I know this must sound crazy, but I was born in June 1942, out of wedlock, to a young woman named Marguerite Wallace Pearson, and a boy named Tommy Babcock. His parents were Muriel and Fred. My mother and father were seventeen years old when I was conceived, in New York. My mother was sent to Maine to have me in secret. My father went into the army right after Pearl Harbor and was killed in an accident in January 1942 in California, before I was born. My grandparents brought me up and claimed me as their own. They sent my mother away to Europe after I was born, and I never saw her again. I learned all this very recently, and never knew anything about either of my parents till now. I just located my mother, unfortunately six months after she died.

"And now that I know something about him, I was wondering if some members of my father's family were still alive. Maybe they knew the story of my parents and remember it. I was wondering if your father, Walter, had a brother who matches this description and died in the war." She fell silent then. Thomas Babcock had kindly and politely listened to her entire recital, even if he was the wrong one. Something about the way she told the story, and the impact of it, touched his heart. She sounded like a rational woman, and it moved him that she was searching for her parents at seventy-four. His assumption, though not correct, was that she must have an empty life. And he would like to help, if he could.

"Actually," he said, sounding very kind, "I was named after an uncle, who did in fact die during the war, at just that time. He was only eighteen, but he didn't have any children. He was my father's younger brother, and they were very close growing up, almost like twins, from what he says. He still cries when he talks about him, and he's ninety-four. I'd let you talk to him, but he's very frail now, he goes to bed early, and he's asleep."

"Is it possible that he wouldn't have known about an unwanted pregnancy, or wouldn't have told you about it, not to sully the memory of a beloved younger brother?" The man on the other end laughed in answer.

"It's possible, but not likely. My dad is a pretty straight-shooting guy, and can be bawdy at times. I think he would have told me, if he knew, or if something like that had happened. But I can certainly ask. Why don't you leave me your name and number, and I'll talk to him tomorrow, and get back to you if I turn up anything?"

"Thank you," she said, grateful and relieved. "I know this must sound stupid, and I don't know why this matters to me at my age, but it does. I think without knowing it, I've been looking for them all my life."

"We all need to know our roots," Tom Babcock said sympathetically. She gave him her name and number, and he said he'd call her either way, and then they hung up.

"Who was that?" his wife, Angie, asked him, as she finished cleaning up the dishes from their dinner. They lived in Montecito in Santa Barbara, and Tom's father was living with them. He was in a wheelchair now, but they didn't want to put him in a nursing home. They had agreed that he would stay with them till the end. They had four grown children and six grandchildren, and they wanted to set the example that elderly parents weren't to be discarded like old shoes, but were to be cherished and respected, even when it was inconvenient and sometimes hard. And he was a sweet old man, though he had been failing rapidly for the last year.

"It was some woman in New York who is older than I am, and says she's the illegitimate daughter of a man named Tommy Babcock, who died during the war at eighteen, and a young teenage girl he was in love with. She's only just learned about them. Her mother is already dead, and she's trying to find relatives of his. I don't think we're it. I promised her I'd ask Dad, but he'd have told me something like that. He's never been one to keep secrets," Tom said, as he put an arm around her, and she agreed.

Angie was from South Carolina, and they had been married for forty-three years, happily so. His father had settled in California, in La Jolla, after being stationed in San Diego after the war, and Tom had been born there, and lived in California all his life, although his parents were originally from New York. He and Angie had met at UC San Diego, married right after graduation, moved to Santa Barbara, and had been there ever since. And their adult children lived in Santa Barbara and L.A., and they saw a lot of them.

Tom was an architect, and still active in his field. He always said retirement wasn't for him. And his father had run a successful business, and retired at eighty-three. Angie was an interior designer and frequently worked with Tom. They were happy, busy, and fulfilled, and still involved in their careers, and the kids were doing well. They had many friends, and they were friendly, loving people. Tom's warmth and kindness had come across on the phone, which had given Valerie the courage to tell the story, although he didn't appear to be the right one. And it had taken so much energy to call him that she didn't call any of the other Thomas Babcocks after that, and went to bed.

The next morning after he helped his father shower and shave, and got him dressed and into his wheelchair, Tom told him about the call the night before.

"Some woman from New York called here last night, looking for you, Dad." His son teased him a little—he hadn't lost his sense of humor yet. "She said she heard you were a handsome guy." Walter Babcock guffawed and didn't believe a word of it, and then his son explained the reason for her call. "She said that her parents were a couple of seventeen-year-olds in New York in 1941. Her mom got pregnant with her, and was sent away to have the baby, and I think her grandparents brought her up, and they never let her see her mother. She never even knew about her till now. She said her dad was killed in an accident right after he was drafted in January 1942, before she was born, when he was just eighteen. She only just learned about all of it. She found her mother, but she'd already died, and now she's looking for her father's relatives, to touch base with her roots, and meet them. She sounded like a nice person, and she's seventy-four years old, so she's no kid. The story sounded like Uncle Tommy, except you never told me about a baby. She said her mother's name was Margaret Pearson, something like that." It was close enough. "Maybe you didn't know?" Tom asked his father casually, and his father looked agitated and sounded angry.

"I would have known if he got some girl pregnant. Tommy would never have done a thing like that. Of course it's not him. What's wrong with that woman, at her age, throwing dirt at the reputation of people who've been dead for seventy-four years? She should be ashamed of herself. I hope you don't talk to her again." He was frowning in his wheelchair and looked fierce, and his son had started his day off on the wrong foot. He still considered his brother's memory sacred, and was furious at what she'd said and tried to do.

"I told her I'd call her either way," Tom said easily. "She sounded serious about it. It must be sad not to know who your parents are until you're seventy-four years old, and never have met either one."

"At her age, she shouldn't care. Doesn't she have kids?"

"I didn't ask," Tom said honestly. "Maybe not.

But even if she does, you read stories like this all the time, or see them on TV, of eighty-year-old people looking for their hundred-year-old mothers who put them up for adoption. I think those things haunt people forever. I'm glad it wasn't Uncle Tommy. It must be terrible for that poor woman to have never known her parents." He hadn't known his uncle either, but his father had talked about him all his life. He had never fully gotten over his younger brother's death.

Tom rolled his father into the kitchen for his breakfast then, and their housekeeper and a male attendant arrived to take care of him. They never left him alone. And then he and Angie left for work together. Tom called Valerie from his architectural office, and told her about the conversation with his father.

"I'm really sorry, Mrs. Lawton. I would have loved to come up with some relatives for you. It's a touching story, and I hope you find the right people. I'm afraid I came up dry out here." He didn't tell her that his father had been outraged by the story, which he himself had found heart-wrenching.

"Thank you so much for trying," Valerie said pleasantly, grateful that he had spoken to his father and even called her back, and didn't dismiss her as a lunatic. But stranger things had happened, it might have worked, and been the right Babcock. "I knew it was a long shot. It was really a stab in the dark. I don't know where to go from here." Although there were many more Thomas Babcocks she hadn't tried.

"Maybe a detective agency, if it's worth it to you?" he suggested.

"I'd never thought of that," she admitted, "but this is all very new to me, the search for lost parents. I always thought I knew who mine were. It turns out I didn't."

"Well, good luck," Tom said, and they hung up, and he forgot about it.

And for the next three days, the housekeeper and male nurse said Walter had been impossible. Cantankerous, difficult, in a bad mood, restless, and he had hardly eaten. And when Tom walked into his father's room when he came home from work at the end of the three days, he found his father crying, which frightened Tom. He had never seen him that way, and his father turned to him with tears rolling down his cheeks.

"What's up, Dad? Are you feeling sick? Do you want me to call the doctor? Joe and Carmen said you're not eating." And he had rejected Angie's dinner too the night before.

"It's that woman," he said in a choked voice.

"What woman? Carmen?" The housekeeper had been with them since their kids were young, and she had always been kind to him. "Has she been giving you a hard time?"

"No," he shook his head miserably, and looked like he had shrunk in the past few days. "The one who called you and told those lies about Tommy. Why would she do a thing like that? He was such a good boy." He was genuinely frantic about it, and Tom was worried it might be an early sign of dementia, although he'd had none before. But he was desperately upset and agitated.

"Of course he was, Dad," Tom tried to soothe him, but his father was inconsolable over what he considered the insult to his late baby brother, whom he revered as a saint. "She's just looking for her father's family. You can't blame her for that. She didn't mean any harm by it."

"He never got anyone knocked up," Walter insisted, and continued crying.

"She just got us off the Internet, Dad. She never knew Uncle Tommy."

"She's as bad as her mother was," he suddenly said fiercely, in a tone his son had never heard him use before. "I never liked her. She just wanted to trap Tommy, and she got what she deserved. They sent her off to some prison camp for bad girls in New England somewhere. My parents never let Tommy see her again. He thought he was in love with her, he even wanted to marry her, but Dad wouldn't let him. And then he was killed. I don't know what happened to her. It didn't matter after that." He was crying harder, as Tom stared at him.

"You knew her?" His father wouldn't answer him and looked out the window with tears streaming down his cheeks.

"He hardly talked to me once he fell in love with her. She put a spell on him. He said he was going to marry her." It was obvious to Tom that his father had been jealous of her, and the love the two young people had shared. And it sounded like they'd paid a high price for it, separated from each other, punished by their parents, the baby taken from the young girl, by her own parents, never to be seen again, and the boy she loved killed while she was pregnant with his baby. He could only feel sorry for her, while his father was still angry and jealous of her, and had lied to his son about it, to protect his brother's memory.

"Dad, why didn't you tell me? These things happen, especially in those days. It must have been a terrible scandal back then," Tom said sympathetically.

"It would have been. Our parents never let that happen. They covered it up immediately, and so did her parents. No one wanted that baby. I don't know what happened to it, but it got what it deserved and so did its mother. Marguerite. I hated her."

"I think that was 'the baby' I was talking to on the phone the other night. And I don't agree with you about her getting what she deserved. What did she do to deserve that? Seventy-five years later, she's still looking for her parents, and trying to figure out who they are. That doesn't seem fair to me. Because two teenage kids fell in love with each other? Come on, Dad. You're her uncle. And what if she's a nice person? Is this what Tommy would want you to do to the girl he loved, or their baby? What if it were your child and you'd been killed—would he pretend he knew nothing about her, and ignore her? I'm ashamed of you, Dad. You're bigger than that. At least we can tell her she found her father's family. I'm sure she's not going to ask you for money." Tom smiled at him, trying to lighten the moment.

"How do you know? The Pearsons were pretty fancy, although they lost most of their money in the Depression. They thought they were better than everyone, and then look what happened. Their precious daughter got knocked up. Our mother was ready to kill her. She forbade Tommy to ever see her again. He cried all night over it, and then her parents sent her away the next day. I think he went to see her once, at the home, and then he got sent to California, and died right after that." Tom had never heard his father so harsh, and the whole story sounded like a nightmare, especially for both young people, who had been treated like criminals by their parents. Tom felt sorry for both of them. But clearly Valerie had touched a nerve with the story. His father hadn't recovered from it yet. "I don't want anything to do with her," Walter barked at him, and Tom quietly left the room a few minutes later, to let him calm down. And he went to tell Angie what had happened. She was stunned too. Walter had lied to protect the memory of his brother, and had no regrets about it.

"What are you going to do?" Angie asked him as they shared a quiet dinner in the kitchen that night, after his father went to sleep. He had finally calmed down a little after he'd vented about it. And Tom didn't bring it up again.

"I'm going to find her number and call her tomorrow when I get to the office. I hope I didn't throw it away. And I'm going to tell her Dad lied to me. He's never done that before."

"You know how sensitive he is about his brother," Angie said gently, but Tom looked shocked, and disappointed.

"Can you imagine what a nightmare that must have been for those two kids, especially in those days? And look at it, she never saw her mother or even knew who she was, or her father. And who knows, maybe if he'd lived, Uncle Tommy might have married her and she'd be our aunt Marguerite," remembering his father had corrected him about the name. "Instead she was an outcast, and their child was a lost soul. It's a terrible story," he said, profoundly upset by it. And as he said he would, he called Valerie first thing the next morning, when he found the paper still on his desk with her number on it.

She was painting when he called, squinting at

the portrait of Marguerite. It was noon in New
York on a blustery March day. And she didn't recognize the voice when she answered.

"Mrs. Lawton?" he asked cautiously.

"Yes."

"Tom Babcock. We spoke the other night, about
my uncle, and my father." She knew who he was
the moment he said the name.

"Of course. I didn't recognize your voice at
first." She smiled as she said it. "You're so nice to
call me back. I'm really sorry I troubled you, I was
just hoping you were the right one." She sounded
faintly embarrassed in the clear light of day, since
his father hadn't known anything about it and
hadn't known her mother.

"I owe you an apology," Tom said bluntly, with
sincere regret in his voice. "My father lied to me.
He's never done that before. I don't know what to
say, except how sorry I am. I didn't mean to mis-
lead you. My father did know your mother, and
he knew the story. He just didn't know what happened to the baby, and I guess no one ever talked
about it in those days. It must have been a terrible
time for your mother and my uncle."

"Oh my God." She sounded like she had just
won the lottery. "Your father is Tommy Babcock's
brother? He's my uncle?" There were tears in her
eyes and in Tom Babcock's. She was clearly so
moved that it touched him too.

"And I'm your cousin. I don't know if it's a blessing for you or not, or something to celebrate, but you found the family you were looking for. And I'm so sorry my father misled me," he said again. "He revered his brother, and I don't think he ever got over losing him. The idea of besmirching his memory, over an unwanted pregnancy, was just too much for him."

"I understand. It was a big deal then. The poor kids must have been desperate. It's hard to imagine, and then your uncle died, and my mom must have been even more lost. Her parents banished her forever after I was born, and pretended she was dead. They sent her to Europe during the war, at eighteen, and never saw her again. And my grandparents pretended I was their child. That's pretty heavy stuff."

"It certainly is. I'm sorry you never knew her."

"So am I," Valerie said sadly. "I have some photographs of her now. I just got them recently, and know more about her life. She never had other children. Just me."

"Do you have children?" Tom asked, curious about her, now that they were related.

"One, a son named Phillip. He's wonderful. He's thirty-four and works at the auction house Christie's, in the jewelry department. He has a master's in art history. His father was an art history professor, and I'm an artist, a painter."

"I'm an architect, and my wife is an interior designer. And we have four grown kids, six grandchildren."

They were suddenly a family, and they were both excited. And Valerie sounded shy when she asked the next question.

"Do you suppose we could ever meet?"

"Of course," he said kindly. "We're first cousins."

"Your father wouldn't have to see me, if it would upset him." He was very old, and she didn't want to give him a heart attack or kill him.

"I would expect nothing less of him," Tom said firmly. "I'm sure his sainted brother would have seen his daughter if the situation were reversed, if everything Dad says about him is true, about what a great guy he was, although he was just a kid. It's sad to think of my uncle dying at eighteen." Valerie agreed.

"If it's not inconvenient, maybe I could come out in the next couple of weeks." He didn't know what her circumstances were and if she'd expect to stay with them, which would be hard with a total stranger, even if they were long-lost cousins. "I could stay at the Biltmore," she said quickly. "I've stayed there before."

"I'll talk to my wife and we'll arrange it," he promised. "And Valerie," he said in a gentle tone, "I'm glad you found us."

"So am I," she said as tears rolled down her cheeks. It wasn't exactly like finding her father, but it was close enough. She could hardly wait to meet them, and was excited when she hung up. She was waiting for the results of the DNA test, to make it official, but she knew in her heart what the results would be. And it was important to her to find her father's family too, if she could.

She heard from Angie two days later, and they agreed on a weekend that worked for both of them. It was ten days away. Valerie could hardly wait to meet the family she had never known, and they could only be a thousand times better than the one she had growing up.

# Chapter 17

The following week when Phillip called her, Valerie casually mentioned that she was going to California for the weekend, and he was surprised.

"What are you doing out there? Some kind of art show?"

"No, I'm going to visit my cousins," she said, with mischief in her voice. She had been in great spirits ever since she'd found them.

"What cousins? We don't have cousins in California." The only cousin he had was Penny.

"We do now. I got busy on the Internet one night. I was trying to find relatives of my father's. I tried some different combinations, and I got lucky on the second shot. I found his older brother and my father's nephew. His father denied it at first, because of the disgrace at the time, and he was trying to protect his brother. And then his son called me back when he realized that Tommy's brother had lied about it. And now I'm going out there to meet them." She sounded like a kid at Christmas.

"Are they good people?" Phillip was worried— he didn't want anyone being unkind to her. He thought she was being a little naïve, particularly if her father's brother had initially been dishonest and hostile.

"They seem like it. Tom, my cousin, is an architect married to a very nice woman. I talked to her—she's an interior designer. They have four grown kids. They live in Santa Barbara, and they have grandchildren. Tom's sixty-five, and she's a few years younger. Walter, my father's brother, is ninety-four, and apparently very frail." She knew all about them, and until now he had heard nothing about it.

"Well, you've certainly been busy. Do you need me to come with you?" He had plans that weekend, but would have gone with her if she'd asked. He didn't love the idea of her facing these people alone, but she had no qualms about it.

"Of course not. I'll be fine, but thanks for asking. I'm just staying the weekend. I have a busy week next week with a board meeting at the Met."

"Well, call me from out there. Where are you staying?"

"At the Biltmore." She made it sound like an adventure, and Phillip was smiling to himself when he hung up.

He told Jane about it at dinner that night. It was their second date. He had taken her to dinner and a movie the week before, and it had gone well. And they were planning to spend the day together on his boat that weekend. Jane was looking forward to it.

She was touched when she heard about Valerie's plans to fly to California to meet her father's relatives. It seemed very brave of her, and she said as much to Phillip.

"This seems to mean a lot to her. I think she felt like such an outsider growing up, and so disapproved of, that she's hungry now to meet the relatives she never knew she had, if that makes sense."

"It does. But knowing what we do now, about her background, it must have been so hard for her as a kid."

"I don't think it was easy. She's very different from her sister, and the grandparents who pretended to be her parents. She's a much warmer person. Her mother must have been more like her. It's a shame she never knew her," he said sympathetically.

And then he added, "I'd like you to meet my mother sometime." Jane looked pleased by the suggestion.

"I have to meet **Sweet Sallie** first," she said, referring to his boat, and Phillip grinned.

"You have to be aware that she will always be my first love. She's been the woman in my life till now."

"Believe me, I get it. My father would give up our whole family to keep his boat. You don't try to come between a man and his sailboat."

"Then everything should be just fine," he said, pleased.

They'd had a nice time so far going out to dinner, and he'd gotten a glimpse of her small, cheerful apartment when he picked her up for their second date. She had made magic with the things she'd bought at IKEA, and had turned it into a cozy home, and she'd only been there a short time. It was the kind of thing his mother would have done.

They talked a little over dinner about the DNA results they were waiting for. The order to exhume Marguerite's body and perform the DNA test had been approved and signed by the judge the week before, and they had another five weeks to wait for the results, but there seemed to be no doubt in anyone's mind now what they would be. It was clear from everything Fiona had told her that Marguerite was her mother. And Jane commented that she would have left the surrogate's court by the time the results came in. She had to attend two more months of classes, and then she was due to graduate from law school in June.

"And what are you going to do after you graduate?" he asked her over dinner.

"Pass the bar, and get a job at a law firm." She had résumés out at several top firms, but hadn't heard anything conclusive yet. And she would have to focus on review for the bar exam soon. "And I want to go home to Michigan for a couple of weeks to see my parents before I start work." It sounded reasonable to him.

The time he spent with her sped by, as they talked about a variety of subjects, and got to know each other better. He had never met a woman as easy to be with. Everything felt simple and natural when he was with her. And he had a feeling that his mother was going to like her too.

The real test came when he drove her to Long Island that weekend. He picked her up at her apartment at nine in the morning, and was relieved to see that she was wearing jeans, a warm jacket, and sneakers. The last girl he had invited to the boat had showed up wearing a miniskirt and high heels. And he was even more impressed when she helped him with the sails, and slipping the moorings. Her father had taught her well, and she knew exactly what to do. He had brought a picnic lunch for them, and he threw the anchor in a small cove where there was shelter, bright sun, and a gentle breeze.

"This is perfect," she said, smiling at him, obviously enjoying the day as much as he was. There was something about being on a sailboat that allowed you to forget all your worries, and just enjoy the wind and the sea.

They stretched out on the deck in the sun afterward. It was still too cold to go swimming, and
as she lay there with her eyes closed, enjoying the
warmth of the sun, he leaned over and kissed her,
and she slipped her arms around his neck and
smiled at him. Neither of them said a word but
just enjoyed the moment, and then he rolled over
on his side next to her and propped himself up on
one elbow.

"How did I get so lucky?" he said happily. "I
thought I was just going to do some boring appraisal, and instead I found you." Phillip felt like
it was meant to be. She felt the same way about
him. And she was well aware that she could have
still been miserable with John if she hadn't had the
guts to leave him. She was glad now that she had,
and hadn't let it drag on till June.

"You just like me because I'm a halfway decent
sailor," she teased him, and he grinned.

"Yeah, that too. I like you because you're smart
and kind and a good person, not to mention beautiful." He kissed her again then, and he lay holding her for a long time, but they went no further.
They both knew it was too soon, and didn't want
to rush things. They wanted to savor the beginning,
and see where it went. There was no hurry. And a
little while later, they set sail again, and enjoyed
the afternoon on **Sweet Sallie.** They were tired and
relaxed when they finally sailed back toward the

dock, and she helped him tie the boat up, and they walked to his car hand in hand.

"Thank you for such a nice day," she said, and he could see that she meant it. It had been a perfect day for both of them.

They cooked dinner together at her apartment that night, and watched a movie. They sat close to each other, and he kissed her. It was after midnight when he left, promising to call her the next day. She had already agreed to go back to the boat with him the next weekend. She was beginning to look like the perfect woman to him.

# Chapter 18

Before Valerie left for California for the weekend, she called Winnie to tell her she was
going out of town. She always tried to check in
with her, in case Winnie needed anything. Valerie
liked to let her know her plans, and then she could
call Penny, or someone else, like her housekeeper,
if she needed help with anything.

"Where are you going?" Winnie asked her,
sounding suspicious.

"To California," Valerie said vaguely. She wasn't
sure if she wanted to tell her who she was visiting,
or why.

"What are you doing there?"

"I'm going to Santa Barbara, to see friends."

"That's an awfully long way to go for the weekend." Winnie hated going anywhere, and said she

liked sleeping in her own bed. She had never been very adventuresome, even when she was young. "What friends do you have in Santa Barbara?" She couldn't recall Valerie ever mentioning them, and of course she was right. She looked years older than Valerie, and acted it, but her memory was still acute.

Valerie decided then that there was no escaping it, and told her who she was going to see.

"You found them on the Internet? Are you crazy? What if they're ax murderers or awful people?"

"Then I won't see them again. I'm staying at a hotel, the Biltmore, if you want to reach me. And they might have the same concerns about me. They don't know me from Adam. I called them out of the blue with my story. They were extremely nice about it. I just want to meet them, and see how it feels." She was acquiring new relatives and a whole new life.

"Why do you need them now, at your age? What difference will it make?" She was finding the whole thing unsettling, first Valerie's horrifying discoveries about Marguerite, and then her insistence on the DNA test. It had been her own daughter's idea, and Winnie wasn't pleased about that either. And now she was going to meet her alleged father's family, who might turn out to be dreadful people. Why couldn't she just let the dead rest? It was all so upsetting.

"I'm not sure," Valerie answered her honestly.

"I just feel it's something I have to do. That boy was my father, and this is his family. I want to meet them, and see if I feel any kind of connection to them. I never felt any with the people I thought were my parents, and were my grandparents."

"And you think you'll feel connected to an uncle and a cousin you've never met? What could you possibly have in common with them?"

"I don't know. That's what I want to find out." She was on a mission, and the trip was a pilgrimage of sorts, to honor the past. She hadn't told Winnie about her mother's letters. She felt tender and protective of them, and Winnie always had something negative to say about everything. But the Babcock connection seemed less private to her, and she was willing to share that.

"You might not have felt any connection to your biological father either. They were just kids." But the Babcocks were her family, whatever Winnie thought. "Be careful, Valerie. Take care of yourself."

"I will. Don't worry. I'll be fine." Winnie grumbled a grudging good-bye. And Valerie left for the airport a few minutes later. She felt carefree and young, about to discover another part of her life, her history, and herself. And nothing about it felt wrong, despite Winnie's misgivings. She never trusted anyone or anything, which was part of her negative view of life, just like her mother's. They were so much alike, and more and more with time.

Winnie had turned into her mother as she aged. Valerie couldn't imagine anything worse.

The plane landed in Los Angeles on time, and she rented a car at the airport, for the two-hour drive to Santa Barbara. She was going to check in to the hotel first and call them. Angie and Tom had invited her to dinner. She was slightly nervous about meeting them as she drove north, but mostly excited about the discoveries they would make.

It was late afternoon by the time Valerie got to the Biltmore and checked in. She took a walk for a few minutes, through the Coral Casino, the swim club that was across the street from the hotel and owned by them. And then she went back to her room and called Tom to tell him she had arrived. He asked how the trip was, and she said it was fine, and she thought he sounded nervous too. This was emotional for all of them, especially his father, who had said he wouldn't meet her and would stay in his room when she came to the house. Tom wasn't going to force him to see Valerie, but he told his father he thought he was wrong.

"I'm not going to meet that girl's illegitimate baby. Why should I?"

"Because she's your brother's daughter, and your niece," Tom said again, but his father just turned stone-faced and looked away.

Tom had offered to pick her up at the hotel,

but Valerie insisted she could drive herself to their home, and she headed toward Montecito at six o'clock, and followed the directions he had given her to their house. When she got there, she saw that it was a big sprawling Spanish-style home with a wide circular driveway perched high on a hill, with a beautiful view. The house was substantial, and the grounds extensive, perfectly manicured and well designed, and there was a large swimming pool and tennis courts off to the side. She walked up the front steps and rang the doorbell, and a moment later the door opened and Angie appeared. She was an attractive blonde with a wide smile, and right behind her a tall man appeared, who looked like a teddy bear, and the only trait they seemed to have in common was the same snow-white hair. Without hesitating, Tom gave her a warm hug, and Angie kissed her hello. Valerie had worn a pale blue cashmere sweater and gray slacks and was carrying a blazer in the cool air, and wondered if she was too informal. Angie was wearing a dress and high heels, and Tom was wearing a shirt and tie and a suit in her honor. But the atmosphere in the house was informal, and they walked her through the beautifully decorated home to a patio with heaters outside, where they could enjoy the view.

Angie told her they had bought and remodeled the house when the children were young, and it was a little too big for them now, but they loved it. And they had good living quarters for Tom's father, who was with them now. He had been living with them since Tom's mother died ten years before. But Valerie saw no sign of Walter, as they drank white wine and got to know each other. They seemed like warm, kind people and made her feel at home. And she was surprised by how at ease she was with them, as though they had known each other all their lives. They were that sort of people, with an easy California style, but Valerie felt something more.

The conversation turned toward her being an artist, and Tom surprised her by saying her father had been a talented artist too, and that Walter had many of his drawings, and some of his paintings. It explained where her own talent had come from, since no one else in her family had had any interest in art. It was one of the things that had drawn her to her husband when they met.

They chatted for an hour before dinner, and then went inside. Angie had organized a beautiful table and meal, and the housekeeper had stayed to serve it. Valerie noticed that the dining room table had been set for three, and remembered that Tom had said his father went to bed early since he was so old. And Tom excused himself before dinner to go and check on him.

He found his father in his bedroom in his wheelchair, looking out the window and scowling.

"Are you going to come and meet her, Dad? She's a lovely woman."

"No, I'm not."

"She's older than I am. She's not some kid, or some hippie. You at least owe her that."

"I don't owe her a damn thing," he growled, and spun around to turn his back on his son, who quietly left the room. It was like dealing with a child. He had never seen his father behave like this and didn't like it. And he knew that Valerie would be disappointed not to meet him, after coming this far.

Instead, as he walked back to the dining room, Tom picked up some framed photographs on the way, then showed them to Valerie. They were photographs of her father, as a boy and in his teens. There was one of him at the age he must have been when he was in love with her mother, and another of him in uniform right before he left New York for the West Coast. And she was struck immediately by the resemblance, not only to her but to her son. Valerie looked far more like him than any of the Pearsons. And he was a very handsome young man. Tom was watching her intently as she looked at the photographs and then back at him.

"You look a lot like your father," he said softly as they sat down to dinner. Valerie nodded, thinking how remarkable it was that she had found them. She could have called all the wrong Thomas Babcocks, but she hadn't. She had honed in on the right one, on the second try. And now she was here.

"Does your father look like him too?" she asked, curious about him.

"Not really. He looks more like me, although he's smaller now than he was. He's lost a lot of weight." She nodded, wondering when she would meet Walter and how that would feel.

They talked about a variety of subjects during dinner—music, art, theater. Angie said they went to L.A. often for cultural events, but they liked living in Montecito, and having more space and better weather, and Tom's architectural practice had always been there. Tom said the children had loved growing up in Santa Barbara, and only one had moved to L.A. They talked about their children, and Valerie showed them a photograph of Phillip. Tom commented on how much he looked like his grandfather too. The Babcock genes had been strong in both Valerie and her son. And Angie proudly showed her photographs of their grandchildren, whom she adored.

Valerie asked if they ever came to New York, and they said not often enough, but they were busy with work and their kids. And they didn't like leaving Tom's father for long periods of time. They were obviously dedicated to their family, and responsible people. And Tom smiled at her at the end of dinner.

"I never had a sister, and I have no cousins. I like having a cousin now. I wish you'd found us sooner," he said warmly.

"So do I," she said, and meant it. "I didn't even know you existed, or about any of this until very recently. It all came as a surprise, not to say a shock." She laughed. "But in a funny way, it's a relief. I never fit in to the family I grew up in, and I always felt they resented me and disapproved of me, and I didn't know why. Now I know. It wasn't really about me, it was their disapproval of the circumstances of my birth, not something I'd done wrong, which was how I felt. I don't think my mother ever got over it. It takes a lot to banish your own child and declare her dead. It broke my mother's heart, never seeing me again. Our nanny used to send her photographs of me, which was how I made the connection when I saw them."

She told them about Marguerite's safe deposit box then, and the jewelry, Phillip doing the appraisal, by sheer coincidence, and Fiona's admission to her of what had really happened so long ago. "I would never have known about your uncle, my father, if I hadn't gone to see her, and she hadn't told me. She was surprised I never figured it out, but my grandparents hid it well. Even my birth certificate was falsified and showed them as my parents. They went to great lengths to conceal the truth from me. I wonder if they had any contact with your grandparents after I was born, or if they never spoke again. Apparently none of them wanted my parents to get married, and they were certainly very young. And it would have been a terrible scandal among the people they knew in those days."

"I never heard a word of it," Tom admitted over coffee and dessert. "My father even denied it when I asked him about you. It must have really shocked him to have it surface after so many years. Nobody ever mentioned Tommy having a child."

"You'd think someone would have been curious about me, but I guess it was just too upsetting to face it, so no one did. I would have liked to meet your grandparents." But meeting Walter would be enough. She hoped he would be well enough to see her during her brief stay. Tom had said during dinner that he was having a rough spell—he didn't tell her that his father was refusing to see her and behaving like an angry child. He didn't want to hurt her feelings after the effort she'd made to come out and meet them. He was glad she had. They shared many common interests, and were as open-minded as she was, despite their conservative appearance. They were bright and fun and interested in the world, in sharp contrast to Winnie, whom she'd grown up with and was so shut down, and negative about so many things. Angie and Tom really seemed to enjoy life, just as Valerie did.

She stayed at their house later than she'd planned, and got back to the hotel after midnight, after promising to come back and see them again the next day. Angie had offered to take her to the local antique shops the next morning, and Tom wanted to show her his architectural office, which he was very proud of, and they took her out to lunch afterward. He obviously had a very successful practice and had built many of the houses in Montecito that they drove by. And during lunch, Tom asked her what was going to happen to her mother's jewels. She had told them about the Christie's auction in May, and explained that she was currently waiting for results of the DNA test, which would confirm her as Marguerite's heir.

"It's more of a formality."

"I'd love to see the jewelry," Angie commented, and Valerie promised to send her the catalog of the sale.

They had organized a dinner with their children that evening, and even their son from Los Angeles came. They had gone all out, and Valerie was touched by the warm reception she got from everyone. It was remarkable considering that she was the long-lost illegitimate cousin and niece that no one had even known about. And now they all acted as though they had been waiting for a lifetime to meet her. Except for her uncle Walter, who was continuing to refuse to leave his room. All his grandchildren asked where he was when they arrived.

"Grampa's not feeling well. He's resting in his room," Tom said simply. Two of them went to see him, and Tom's oldest son came out and commented to his father.

"Wow, Gramp is in one hell of a foul mood. What happened?" He had never seen him that way before.

"It's a long story." He didn't want to explain now, in case Valerie overheard him and was hurt by her uncle's refusal to meet her. He had lost hope of his father becoming reasonable by then.

Valerie thought Angie and Tom's children were wonderful. The conversation was lively and fun at dinner, and she was sorry Phillip hadn't come. But she hoped to come back again, and promised to bring him next time. She wanted them to meet him too.

They were talking and laughing after dinner, as Tom served champagne to everyone, and he was just toasting his new-found cousin when they were suddenly aware of another presence, and all heads turned to see Walter wheel himself into the room with a stern expression.

"What's all the noise out here? You people could wake the dead." He was a dignified-looking, very old man, and he wore a proper suit, with a white shirt and tie, and had put on his shoes, and Tom knew it had cost enormous effort to do so by himself, and he was proud of him, as he handed him a glass of champagne.

"You look terrific, Dad," he said gently, as Valerie smiled at him from across the room, and then walked toward him respectfully, and extended her hand. His disapproval of her was plain on his face, but it didn't deter her. She had been waiting to meet him.

"It's a great honor to meet you, sir," she said softly, and he hesitated for a long moment. Then he shook her hand as his eyes bored into hers. He wanted to dislike her as much as he had hoped to, but he found he couldn't, and tears filled his eyes as he looked at her, and then he finally spoke.

"You look so much like your dad, even at your age." And then he smiled. She took out the photograph of Phillip to show him then, and he stared at it hungrily. "I guess that's how Tommy would have looked at his age." She sat down next to him, and they talked for a long time, as he slowly mellowed in the face of her gentleness and grace. "Your mother was a very pretty girl," he admitted. "And I know she loved him. He loved her too. I always worried about what would happen between them, it was a flame that was just too bright, and I was afraid they'd get burned. I was at Princeton when it all happened, and when I came home, all hell had broken loose, and she was already gone. And then Pearl Harbor, and we were both drafted. I shipped out before he did. He was desperate about you. He didn't want Marguerite to give you up. He wanted to marry her when he came back, but he never did. And I never knew what happened to you after that. They told my parents that you'd been given up, and that was the end of it. My mother didn't believe them and thought there was something suspicious about it, but I think they didn't want to know. I think because Tommy died, they wanted to find you after you were born, but it was all too difficult then, it was easier to just let it go. We never spoke of it again. And then we heard that your mother died, and the whole story died with her. It was a chapter that was closed." He stared at her in amazement. "And now here you are." He looked at her sternly for a long moment. "You took a long time to show up."

"I'm sorry about that. I didn't know any of it either. They never told me anything. I just found out a few weeks ago. Too late to meet my mother, sadly. She died last year, before I knew. We never saw each other again after she left, I was only a few months old."

"She was a beautiful girl," he said again. Valerie didn't tell him that she had married Umberto. He didn't need to know. And it was a lot for him to absorb. It brought up all his sadness at losing his brother, although he seemed very interested in her son, and wanted to know more about him. And she told him she was an artist, and he had Valerie wheel him into his room so he could show her some of her father's paintings, and they were very good.

Walter was tired then, and said he was going to rest for a while. The young people were making too much noise, and it had been a big evening for him.

"Will I see you tomorrow?" he asked her, with anxious eyes.

"If you'd like to. I'm not going back to New York till tomorrow night. And I'll be back again."

"Bring your son next time. I want to meet him. He looks like a fine boy."

"He is. I think you'd like him." He nodded, as he gazed at her.

"I'm sorry they made such a botch of it for you," he said gruffly. "You're a good woman. She probably was too. It sounds like she had a hard life if she never saw you again, and they said she was dead. I hope she was all right in the end."

"I hope so too," Valerie said softly, and he nodded and patted her hand. And before she left his room, she leaned down and gently kissed his cheek, and she saw that there were tears in his eyes, but he was smiling when she left.

She went back to the others, and they talked for a while. Angie and Tom's youngest daughter played the piano, and they all sang. And it was late again when she left.

Valerie invited them all to brunch at the Biltmore the next day, and afterward she went to visit with Walter. He showed her all of Tommy's drawings and paintings, and photographs of them as children and young boys. He told her stories about her father that made her laugh, and by the end of the day she felt as though she had met her father as well as her uncle and cousins. He gave her a photograph of Tommy to take with her. And when she kissed Walter goodbye, she promised to come back soon. She wanted to see him again and didn't want to wait too long at his age.

"He loved meeting you," her cousin Tom told her before she left. He didn't tell her how resistant Walter had been before she had arrived, and how she had totally captivated him. He was her biggest fan by the end of her stay. He had come alive again talking to her. "I'm sorry you didn't know him when he was younger. He was a terrific guy."

"He still is," she assured him, and they all hugged each other and promised to stay in touch. She thanked them for everything, and as she drove back to the airport in L.A., she was so happy she'd come to meet them. It had been one of the most important weekends of her life. She had a real family now, one where she was welcome and belonged. She could hardly wait to see them all again.

## Chapter 19

The results of the DNA test came at the end of April, and were no surprise. Marguerite Wallace Pearson di San Pignelli was Valerie's mother. Valerie hadn't doubted it, but hearing it was like an affirmation of who she was, and gave her back the identity that had been stolen from her at birth.

She called Winnie after they told her, just to let her know, and Winnie sounded shaken and tearful.

"I know it's stupid," she said, sniffing, "but I feel like I just lost the only sister I had."

"I can be as big a pain in the ass as your niece, as I was as your sister. And I don't care what you call me. Nothing's changed." But a lot had changed, and they both knew it. Valerie had gained an important piece of her history, a part she had never even known was lost. In spite of her mother's coldness to her, she had been a happy person and had made peace with not being loved as a child and had overcome it, in great part thanks to Lawrence. But the lack of love she'd endured as a child was unnatural, and now she knew she had been deeply loved by her real mother. It completed her, and added a part of her that she hadn't known was missing. It filled her with a profound and satisfying sense of peace. It was like coming home after a long journey. She wasn't an outcast anymore, or a misfit. She had had a real mother and father, and knew who they were, even if they were no longer alive. For some strange reason, it gave her more confidence in herself. And it made Winnie feel more vulnerable somehow, and more alone. She was the only one left of her generation, even if she and Valerie were only four years apart. And all their parents' lies had been exposed, in spite of Winnie's futile attempts to protect them.

Penny called Valerie after the results came in, and said that there would be a hearing in surrogate's court, to confirm that Marguerite was her mother, and Valerie was her heir. She said that she would have to pay inheritance taxes on the value of the jewelry, and had nine months to pay it. She was going to use the proceeds from the Christie's auction to pay the taxes, and keep the rest. Penny asked her if she still wanted to sell the jewelry now that she knew for certain that Marguerite was her mother, and Valerie discussed it with Phillip. She said that she couldn't imagine wearing any of it, although it was spectacularly beautiful, but it was all much too showy for her. She preferred to sell it and invest the money wisely, and let someone else enjoy the jewelry, which wasn't suited to her life. All she wanted to keep was the box with her mother's crest ring, the locket with her baby picture in it, and the wedding ring from Umberto. She wanted to sell the rest.

Penny had her mother sign a release that she wished to make no claim on the estate, and that would be filed with the surrogate's court as well. And Phillip notified Christie's that the Pignelli jewels were no longer being sold to benefit the state, but a rightful heir had been located, and the sale would proceed as planned. They were going to add an insert to the catalog, notifying buyers of the change. It made no difference to them, but it was a technicality they had to observe.

The hearing in surrogate's court was set for two weeks before the auction. Penny would be there, and Phillip with Valerie. Harriet would be the clerk for the case, and Jane had promised to come, although she would be leaving her position as clerk at the court two weeks before the hearing to finish her classes at Columbia. And she was already busily preparing for graduation. Her parents were flying to New York for it, and she wanted Phillip to meet them.

And after the results of the DNA test came in,

Phillip invited Jane to dinner to meet his mother. They had been dating for six weeks by then, and were seeing a lot of each other, almost every night. It wasn't by any particular plan or agreement, it just seemed to work out that way, and they went sailing every weekend. And **Sweet Sallie** was not a wedge between them, but a bond, and something they enjoyed doing together.

Phillip invited both women to dinner at La Grenouille. He wanted it to be special and festive, and to make it a celebratory evening when his mother met Jane. He didn't admit it to either woman, but he was nervous about it. What if they hated each other, or considered each other rivals for his attention? Anything was possible, and he thought women were unpredictable that way, and just when you wanted them to like each other, they didn't. Even Valerie, who was normally sensible. She had always preferred the women he liked least, and disliked the ones he was crazy about, although there hadn't been many of those, and Valerie usually had valid reasons for her opinions, and proved to be right in the end. So the evening was important to him.

He picked Valerie up at her home, and Jane met them at the restaurant, feeling slightly daunted by the elegant surroundings, and the fact that she was meeting his mother, which scared her. She wasn't sure what to expect from his description, and she knew how close they were, and how much he respected what she thought.

Jane felt shy at first, but Valerie made an effort to put her at ease, and by the end of the first course, the two women were getting along famously, and Valerie told them about her visit to the Babcocks in Santa Barbara, and how much fun it had been. And they talked about Jane's plans after graduation, and when she passed the bar exam. The evening sped by, and afterward they dropped Valerie off at home. Phillip walked her into the building, and she gave him an emphatic thumbs-up. By the time they got back to Jane's apartment, Phillip was exhausted, and realized that he had been tense all night, wanting it to go well.

"I love her!" Jane said enthusiastically, as Phillip collapsed on her IKEA couch. He had enjoyed the dinner, but there had been a knot in his stomach all night, hoping for the best, and fearing the worst. "She's like talking to someone our age, only better," Jane said, and he laughed. It was an apt description of his mother.

"She's very lively and youthful. I forget how old she is sometimes." And she certainly didn't look anything close to her age.

"If I'd met her without you, I'd still want to be friends with her," Jane explained. "She's such a real person."

"I feel that way too," he confessed. "I'd like her even if she weren't my mother." It was a high compliment from a man his age.

"She doesn't seem possessive. I thought she'd hate me."

"She loved you," he reassured her. It had been a perfect evening for all three of them, and a superb dinner. And the sommelier had chosen excellent wines for them. "At least that's behind us. You've met her. Now that's done," he said, looking relieved, and Jane laughed at him.

"You look like you went over Niagara Falls in a barrel tonight."

"I think I did. I never know how women are going to react to each other, especially my mother." But she had been easy and fun, and great company, and she and Jane had enjoyed several good laughs at his expense, particularly about his passion for his boat.

They talked for a while longer, and then went to bed. He'd been staying at her apartment a lot lately. She had mentioned it to Alex, who had been impressed, and had referred to him as "a keeper." Jane was beginning to think so too, although it was early days yet. They were still in the honeymoon phase, but it was showing no sign of abating. Things just kept getting better and better.

He wrapped his arms around her when they went to bed, and he'd been so stressed all night that instead of making love to her, as he usually did, he mumbled a few words, hugged her closer, and fell asleep, as Jane lay smiling next to him. Even without making love, it had been a very good night. And if she had passed muster with his mother, as he said, it had been a great one.

The day of the confirmation hearing of Valerie as Marguerite's daughter and sole heir, it was pouring rain. She and Phillip arrived in a cab. Penny got there a few minutes later looking drenched, and Jane shortly after. Winnie came, as a gesture of respect for her newly discovered niece, although she had no part in the proceedings. And Harriet Fine was there with all the records and files and evidence to present to the court. She was pleased to see Jane, and realized for the first time that something was going on between Phillip and Jane.

"So that's the way it is," she said with a wry smile, and Jane blushed. But she was no longer clerking there, and she had left Harriet on good terms. And Harriet was in a much better mood than she had been in for a while. Her mother was doing better, and was staying with her again. She knew it wouldn't last forever, but for now things had improved, and she was happy to have her home.

The confirmation hearing was brief and perfunctory. Harriet presented the file to the court. Penny represented Valerie, who solemnly swore that all the evidence and her statements were true and correct and she was in fact Marguerite di San Pignelli's heir. Winnie cried when the judge confirmed it, and Valerie was beaming afterward.

"Now you get to pay taxes on the estate," Winnie said to her smugly.

"I know." Valerie smiled at her. "The auction will take care of that." Valerie was sorry to see all the beautiful pieces go, but it made no sense for her to keep them. Phillip had already brought her the small box with the gold pieces, and Valerie was wearing the crest ring and the locket. She had put her mother's gold wedding band away.

And as they left the court, Winnie commented to her that she should use some of the money to buy a decent apartment, and finally move out of the one she'd lived in for years.

"I love my apartment," Valerie said, shocked. "Why would I move?"

"You could have more space, a bigger studio, better furniture, in a nicer neighborhood." Winnie had never liked SoHo and thought they were all crazy to live downtown: Valerie in SoHo, Phillip in Chelsea, her daughter in the West Village. It suited them, but Winnie couldn't understand it. None of them would have wanted to live on Park Avenue, uptown, as she did. It was too far from the places they liked to go to, and the things they wanted to do. But Winnie was from another era. And Valerie was one of them, and had lived downtown far longer than any of the others. "I guess you'll always be a bohemian," Winnie said ruefully, and Valerie laughed.

"I hope so."

They were in good spirits as they left the building. They all had to go back to work, and school in Jane's case, and Valerie went to make some arrangements she'd been planning for weeks.

And that night she called Fiona and told her the results of the DNA test, and about the hearing that day. Fiona was happy for her. Things were working out as they should have. She was just sorry it had taken so many years.

"If you hadn't told me the truth when I came to see you, none of this would have happened," she said gratefully.

"I should have done it years ago," Fiona said seriously, "instead of waiting for you to come and ask me." She sounded tired on the phone but relieved. She said her daughter had been to see her that day. Her children were good to her, and Valerie was pleased to hear it. And then Valerie told her what she was planning. She hadn't told anyone else yet, and Fiona approved. They both agreed it was the right thing to do.

"You have your mother back now," Fiona said gently. "And no one can take her away from you again. I'm sure she's watching over you, and she'd be very proud of you. She always was," Fiona said softly.

"I love you, Fiona," Valerie said when they hung up. And Fiona loved her too. In the end, Fiona had returned her mother to her. It was her final gift to both Valerie and Marguerite.

# Chapter 20

On the weekend before the Christie's sale, Phillip and Jane went sailing on Saturday. It was a beautiful May day, and the following day was Mother's Day. He was planning to spend the day with Valerie, and she had finally shared her plans with them. She had bought a good-size plot at a beautiful, peaceful cemetery on Long Island, had it landscaped, and had made arrangements to move Marguerite and bury her there. She had visited Marguerite in the crowded dreary cemetery where she was buried, after Fiona had told Valerie her story. And she wanted to honor her mother with a better final resting place. It was a small thing she could do for her, a final gesture of love and respect. She had told Phillip he could bring Jane along to the brief graveside service. Winnie was coming, with Penny, and afterward they were going to lunch, although Penny was going back to her husband and kids for Mother's Day, and not joining them for lunch.

Phillip and Jane were sailing in gentle winds on Saturday, when he told her he had to go to Hong Kong in September, to participate in a sale of important jades, and he asked her if she wanted to come along. His trips to Hong Kong were always interesting and fun.

"If I'm not working yet," she said practically. "If I am, I probably can't get away." He loved going to Hong Kong for the jade sales, and would have liked to go with her. "I'll keep it in mind," she promised. She had two interviews scheduled in the coming week, and one the week after. And then it would be graduation. She was already deep in her review for the bar exam, and hoped she passed it on the first try, which wasn't always the case, but it would be embarrassing not to. Phillip had been impressed by how much she studied, and how hard she worked, although it was cutting into their time together, but he knew it wouldn't be forever. She was taking the bar exam in July. And after that he hoped to take her on vacation. They'd been talking about going sailing in Maine, which sounded wonderful to both of them. She was the first woman he'd ever known who thought so.

\*   \*   \*

The service that Valerie had organized on Mother's Day, for her mother, was short, poignant, and respectful.

It paid homage to the mother she would have been, if she'd had the chance. Valerie had bought a large plot, with two big trees on it, and the white marble headstone said "Beloved Mother," and then Marguerite's name, and the dates just beneath it. She'd asked a minister to say a brief service, and Valerie stood for a long moment at her mother's gravesite, wishing her peace, and then they all left the cemetery together.

Penny drove back to her family in the city, and the others went to lunch at a nearby restaurant with a cheerful garden. And afterward they went back to the city too. Valerie felt as though they had closed another chapter as they drove home. And the four of them talked about the upcoming sale. Phillip had said there was enormous interest in it, and he was expecting some very high bids on the phones. Some of their most important jewelry clients had already placed absentee bids. Marguerite's collection of beautiful pieces had already created quite a stir, and the section of the catalog dedicated to her was impressive, discreet, and elegant. The caption above it said "Property of a Noblewoman," as Phillip had suggested and she'd agreed.

Phillip had very properly advised Christie's of his relationship to Marguerite, once he discovered he was her grandson. And they had decided to allow him to work at the sale anyway, although he wouldn't be the auctioneer. He would be taking phone bids. Valerie had invited Jane to go to the auction with her. The anticipation was mounting, and with her mother respectfully acknowledged and buried now, Valerie was ready to move on.

The night of the auction, Valerie arrived a few minutes early at the main auction room with enormously high ceilings and neat rows of chairs. Phillip had reserved a seat for her in the second row, on the aisle, and she could observe the auctioneer at the podium, and the long bank of phones easily from where she sat. She had worn a plain black dress and her mother's small locket and gold ring. The men who worked for Christie's were all wearing dark suits and ties, the female employees were wearing black suits or proper dresses, and the women in the audience in the bidders' seats were expensively dressed and wearing jewels. It was a very elite group. There were also several well-known jewelers in the audience. The cream of New York was there, with an equal mix of European buyers, jewelers, and celebrities.

Marguerite's pieces were the most important in the sale. And people were perusing the catalog, with the photographs of Marguerite and Umberto looking glamorous, interspersed with the photographs of the jewels. Christie's had done it just right, to enhance public interest and keep the aura of mystique about her, without cheapening it with sensationalism or anything vulgar. It was top notch. And no one had suspected an event like this when Jane called Phillip for an appraisal and he appeared at the bank to view the contents of the safe deposit box.

Jane got there seconds before the sale began, and took her seat next to Valerie, with an apology for being late. She was afraid it might have already started, but it hadn't. She was wearing a pale blue silk suit the color of her eyes and looked very pretty as Valerie, with her white hair in a French twist, smiled at her, quiet and distinguished. She felt as though they were paying homage to her mother that night, and in a way they were. She felt a flutter in her stomach, wondering if the sale would do well. It was hard to imagine that it wouldn't, after the care Christie's had taken. And she was partly sad too to be parting with items that had obviously been important to her mother, and that she had held on to for so long, but it made no sense to keep them. They weren't appropriate for Valerie's life, even if they had been to her mother's, more than half a century before, in another world. She wondered who would buy them, and cherish them as Marguerite had. Each one had been a gift of love from the man she had married.

Valerie patted Jane's hand with a smile, as the

auctioneer stood at the podium but hadn't started yet. Valerie glanced at Phillip then, who smiled at his mother, wishing he could sit with her too, to lend his support. Valerie had invited Winnie, but she said that the excitement of the bidding would make her nervous and give her palpitations. She preferred to hear about it the next day, and learn the final results. It was so like Winnie not to be there, and Valerie wondered if it saddened her too to see her sister's possessions disappear. She had never known the sister who had supposedly died. Her story had turned out to be completely different from the one they were told. But Marguerite was her sister, and Winnie had lost her too.

Tom and Angie Babcock had called Valerie the night before the sale to wish her luck. She had sent them a catalog, and Tom had shown it to Walter. Angie said he had nodded and looked at each photograph carefully, and he had said that she had grown up to be even more beautiful than she was as a young girl. He realized then that she had married, but Tom said he wasn't upset by it. He had expected her to, she was a very pretty young woman. He was sorry life hadn't worked out better for her and she'd lost her little girl. It was odd how things happened sometimes, and for his brother Tommy too. Valerie couldn't help wondering what their life would have been like, or hers, if their parents had let them marry. Marguerite would have been widowed almost immediately, but at least their secret would have been out in the open, and she would have stayed in New York with her daughter. Valerie's life would have been completely different with her real mother, and her childhood, happier. But tonight was not about Marguerite and Tommy. It was about her and the count who had showered her with jewels and a golden life for more than two decades.

The auctioneer was a tall, serious man with a deep, booming voice, who was well known to their important clients, and Christie's knew he would handle the auction well. The bidding began at exactly seven-fifteen. The first lot in Marguerite's collection was number 156, which Phillip had said would take about two hours to get to, so they had time. They had one hundred and fifty-five lots to sell before hers, which went through lot 177. And there were only a dozen lots being sold after hers, mostly loose stones, and two very important diamond rings, which were expected to go for over a million dollars each. Marguerite's jewelry was in good company that night.

Valerie followed the bidding closely, whispering to Jane from time to time about some particularly impressive or beautiful item. Jane had noticed and commented to her in a whisper that the better pieces were going for about four times the estimate, and one or two went for six times the estimate, which was good for both the sellers and the house. The estimates on Marguerite's pieces had been set high, with strong reserves, which meant that they could not be sold for less than a certain amount, to preclude their being sold for below their value. The estimates had been the subject of considerable discussion, determined by the makers and the size and value of the stones, all of which were of top quality and sizes that were almost impossible to find nowadays. The pieces in her collection were extremely rare now, more so than Marguerite ever knew or could have hoped when she kept them. If she had sold even one or two, she could have been more comfortable at the end of her life, which tugged at her daughter's heart, knowing that she had been preserving them for her.

The earlier items in the auction sold one by one, and the auctioneer's voice droned on. There were a couple of bidding wars, one notably between a well-known jeweler and a private buyer who simply refused to lose the piece. The jeweler dropped out after driving the price up, and the private buyer paid ten times the estimate for it, but seemed thrilled.

And then finally they were at lot 155 at nine thirty-five, and Valerie took a deep breath as the hammer fell for a sapphire cocktail ring by Harry Winston that went for three hundred thousand dollars, just over the estimate, but within range. It was purchased by a jeweler who would sell it for twice that on Madison Avenue. And they were up next. Jane squeezed her hand as the simple Van Cleef diamond pin came up first. Two women held up their paddles with their bidding numbers immediately. As Jane had already noticed, the major jewelers who were known to Christie's held up no paddle, but made subtle, nearly invisible gestures to signify their bids, and the auctioneer knew their bidding numbers by heart. But the privates used the paddles, with rare exceptions. A few of the celebrities in the audience didn't use the paddles either. Everyone knew who they were. You had to look closely to see who was in the race. And the jewelers tended to let the privates get in a frenzy first, and then stepped in.

Three other bidders joined them for the diamond pin, as Valerie and Jane watched, fascinated. Some of the bidders were clearly jewelers, but one of the women refused to let go, and at the very end the man sitting next to her, presumably her spouse, discreetly put up a hand, the auctioneer saw it and nodded. The man's bid was prevailing, and then just before the hammer went down, one of the jewelers jumped in again and the woman who had wanted the piece looked crestfallen, and her husband bid again with a determined expression. And this time the hammer fell and it was hers. She kissed the man who had bought it for her, and was smiling broadly, as the diamond brooch from Cartier came up next. And all the underbidders from the previous piece leaped in heatedly right from the beginning. Christie's had set the stage well, trying to capitalize on moments such as this.

The bidding on the Cartier brooch went faster and higher and was more furious, and it sold for twice the price of the Van Cleef piece. Valerie realized then that she was holding her breath, and slowly exhaled as they brought up the next piece. An image of it appeared on a large video screen at the same time. Valerie glanced at Phillip, but he was busy on the phones, and had a bank of three of them in front of him, so he could keep people on hold at the last minute as they waited for their lots to come up. There was tangible excitement in the room, and the first two pieces were the least exciting of Marguerite's jewels and had sold extremely well, better even than Phillip had expected, and when he glanced over at his mother and their eyes met, he nodded and looked pleased.

The Cartier tiger bracelet was sold next. Phillip had explained to her that the bracelets like that one were collectors' pieces, and that that particular one hadn't been made by Cartier in forty years, so it was an important piece for connoisseurs. It was a classic example of Cartier's work. The bidding on it was hot and fast, mostly among jewelers, with some privates, and the hammer fell at just under a million dollars, to a well-known collector of fine jewelry who lived in Hong Kong. He had bought it for his wife, who already owned many examples of Cartier's tigers. They had been favorites of the

Duchess of Windsor too, and appeared in many books.

They moved on to the pearl and diamond choker then, which wasn't one of Valerie's favorites but was pretty. Her mother had had such a thin, elegant neck that it had been too small for Valerie when she tried it on. It was very much of a bygone era, but had an antique elegance to it, and it became the object of a bidding duel between two well-known jewelers who sold antique jewelry at enormous prices and could ask anything they wanted. It went for the high estimate, which was a respectable amount for the piece.

Marguerite's Boucheron pieces sold after that, and went for good, solid prices to individuals who liked them more for the design than for the value of the stones, which were handsome nonetheless, and they brought a good price as well.

They went back to Van Cleef then, with the invisibly set sapphire necklace and earrings. Phillip had predicted it would go high. It was an exceptionally fine example of their famous invisible setting technique, and the necklace was large and flattering on the neck. It went for close to a million dollars, as Valerie watched in fascination. Jane never took her eyes off the podium and the auctioneer, mesmerized by the action. You had to look around the room carefully to see who was bidding. Some of the bids were very subtle with a nod, a facial expression, a single finger, or a barely raised hand.

The long strand of natural pearls came up next and was again hotly battled over by connoisseurs who knew the value of pearls of that size and quality, of a kind that was no longer available in the modern world. Valerie nearly fell out of her seat when they went for two and a half million dollars, which Phillip had told her they might. He was smiling broadly—they had gone to one of his clients on the phone, who was thrilled. She was calling from London. She had stayed up till after three in the morning to bid on them over the phone. But she was successful and delighted, which made it all worthwhile.

The remaining Van Cleef items came up after that, a sapphire ring and bracelet, which sold for top prices to jewelers who knew they had a market for them, one in Los Angeles and the other one from Palm Beach. They were well known to Christie's, and the auctioneer recognized them immediately.

They moved on to Marguerite's Italian pieces then, two from Bulgari that sold at very high prices, and some others from unknown jewelers who no longer existed, but the pieces were pretty and did well. The emerald and diamond bracelet from that group was the most impressive and sold for five hundred thousand dollars to an unknown buyer no one recognized, and the diamond bracelet that looked like lace doubled the high estimate and sold to an Italian buyer on the phone, who was not a client of Phillip's, but whom Christie's knew well. Most of their buyers in this rarified category preferred pieces by big-name jewelers, which were also a good investment, but sometimes the lesser-known pieces surprised everyone if someone fell in love with them.

The bidding was taking more time than usual because there was so much competition in the room, so much interest, and so many buyers on the phones. By ten forty-five, there were five pieces left, the antique French diamond tiara and the four important rings from Cartier, which were the big events in the sale. The auctioneer began with the tiara, which sold to an antique dealer in Paris. The thirty-carat emerald ring was the first of the final group, and you could feel the electricity in the room. Without thinking about it, Valerie took Jane's hand in her own and held tight. She was about to watch the last of her mother's only possessions dispersed, but for a vast fortune she would one day leave to her son, as a final blessing from her mother.

The bidding started slow and high. The auctioneer opened at five hundred thousand dollars, and it was double that within minutes, and then double again, and then it moved up in hundred-thousand-dollar increments. The hammer came down at three million dollars, and there was a gasp in the room. It was the highest price obtained at Christie's recently for an emerald of that size, but it was clearly worth it. It was purchased by a private buyer from Dubai, a handsome Arab man with three beautiful wives, and he was generous with them. One of them had fallen in love with the emerald ring.

The twenty-five-carat ruby ring was next, with its astounding deep color, and it sold very quickly to another private buyer for five million dollars. Phillip wasn't surprised. The successful bidder was also well known to them though not one of his clients. The jewelers had stopped bidding on the final lots, because the privates were willing to go too high to make it worthwhile for them to resell. They were letting the important rings go, which were the cream of the sale.

The forty-carat emerald-cut white diamond ring looked spectacular on the video screen when the image came up. It was D color, the best and purest color there was, and internally flawless, which would drive the price up even further. The bidding was strong and moved in hundred-thousand-dollar increments rapidly to the price of nine million dollars, sat there for a minute as the auctioneer scoured the room and checked with the Christie's representatives on the phones. Just as he was about to drop the hammer, it went to ten, with an eleven-million-dollar bid on the phone instantaneously, and a final bid brought it to twelve million dollars, and it stayed there. The hammer dropped, and there was a sigh in the room, as though relieved that it, was over. It had been Valerie's favorite piece, along with the ruby ring, but it was out of the question that she would keep it, she had nowhere to wear it in the life she led. She preferred to invest the money for her son to inherit one day. And purchasers had to pay an additional twenty percent to the house for their commission for items under a million dollars and twelve percent if over a million, which added another one million four hundred forty-four thousand dollars to the final price, which actually brought the large white diamond to thirteen and a half million dollars, which was almost unthinkable.

The fifty-six-carat yellow diamond ring was the last piece. Valerie had a death grip on Jane's hand by then, and didn't even know it. The color was categorized as "fancy intense," the designation for yellow diamonds, and it was internally flawless as well. It became a battle between two privates, and at the last second Laurence Graff, the legendary London jeweler, stepped in, and swept it up for fourteen million with a stony, deadpan expression that gave nothing away as to whether he thought he got it for a good price or not. But he was brilliant at purchasing the best stones in the world, and he clearly knew he could get more for it set in his own design and with his name attached. With the buyer's commission added, he had paid well over fifteen million dollars, almost sixteen.

With the sale of the yellow diamond, the disposal of Marguerite's jewels was over. They had brought a total of forty-one million dollars. Phillip had predicted they would bring between twenty and thirty, but Christie's had handled the sale so elegantly that they had done even better than anticipated, particularly with the buyers' commissions added. The house had done well, and so had Valerie, as the owner of her mother's estate. They would have to pay the auction house the ten percent seller's commission, which was four million, one hundred thousand dollars of the hammer prices, which meant they had gotten almost thirty-seven million dollars from the sale. She had to pay inheritance taxes on the estate now, which would be eighteen and a half million, which left her with eighteen million dollars to invest, which would benefit Phillip one day. But there was far more involved in this sale than money, although that was certainly a factor. The sale had been deeply emotional for her, and she was grateful to her mother for keeping what she had to the very end, even in hard times. She had given her daughter the security and comfort for her later years that Marguerite had never had herself, and had unknowingly included her grandson in the blessing.

The lots after Marguerite's in the auction sold very quickly. The loose stones, all colored diamonds, went to Laurence Graff again. Two pink diamonds were noteworthy, and a pale blue one. And the two "important" diamond rings at the end of the sale went to private buyers for far less than Marguerite's white and yellow diamonds, which had been the star items in the sale.

The sale ended twenty minutes after the last of Marguerite's pieces sold. It was eleven-thirty, and the auction had gone on for four and a half very intense hours. Valerie stood up, looking as though she'd been dragged by a rope, and was exhausted. It had been incredibly stressful, but well worth it. She didn't look unhappy about what they'd given up, but relieved over what they'd gained. It was an enormous windfall for her, and ultimately Phillip. She hugged him as soon as he left the bank of phones and joined them. Valerie had been talking to Jane, who was bowled over by what she'd seen, the beautiful pieces, the fascinating buyers, the excitement and tension in the room. It had been like an action-packed thriller all night.

"I felt like I was in a movie," Valerie said in a shaken voice. It had been particularly hard for her, wondering what would happen. At one point she had fantasized that nothing would sell, which Phillip told her could never happen with items like these. But she had never fully understood their enormous value. It was almost impossible to conceive of for the average person. And it was all new to Jane too, who stood close to Valerie, feeling just as stunned, as Phillip hugged them both. Only the heads of Christie's, the head of the jewelry department, and the court had known that he was indirectly one of the beneficiaries of the estate.

"We did great!" he said to his mother. "Better than the high estimates." And the reserves they had put on them had never come into play. They had sailed right past them in each case. "Let's go celebrate!" Phillip said to both women, although he was tired too. It had been a long night, and working on the phones with high bidders, he had to pay close attention that he didn't miss their bids, misplace them, misinterpret what they'd said, or misunderstand them, despite sometimes heavy accents or poor English. The calls were recorded for review later, in case of a dispute, which sometimes happened. There were large amounts of money involved, and people didn't take it lightly if they missed out on a piece they wanted due to the incompetence of the person bidding for them. Phillip had had his senses, especially his hearing, finely tuned all night. And he was pleased for his clients who had been successful, and above all for his mother. In a way this would be a form of closure for her, and she could move on, with all she knew of her mother now and how loved she had been. It changed everything for Valerie, even more than the sale.

Phillip suggested that they go to the Sherry Netherland for a drink, and he shepherded them out of the building, after he told his colleagues he was leaving. And as they followed him, Valerie looked like she was in shock, and Jane was dazed.

"I don't know how you can say auctioning off jewelry is boring," his mother said in the car. "I had my heart in my mouth all night. I think Winnie would have had a stroke and dropped dead." They laughed at what she said.

"I have to admit, tonight was anything but boring, but this was a very special sale. The items were incredible, thanks to your mother. And it was meaningful for me because of you. But most auctions aren't like this," he said, smiling at her. "Tonight was incredibly exciting, but this kind of sale happens once in a blue moon, or once in a lifetime. Some of the big art sales are like this too. But I have to admit"—he smiled at her and then at Jane—"I really enjoyed this one. Who wouldn't?" And the results had been better than even he had dreamed, especially for his mother, who was set till the end of her days, as was he now, if they invested the money well. She had wanted to call Winnie and tell her about it, but it had been too late by the time they were through. By then, Valerie knew, she was asleep.

They stayed at the bar at the Sherry Netherland until two o'clock in the morning, trying to wind down, and talking about every aspect of the auction. Valerie was still exhilarated when they dropped her off at her apartment, and Phillip and Jane went back to his. Valerie had the feeling they were together all the time now, and on his boat every weekend, although she didn't ask.

Jane had another month of classes, and then graduation. She had invited Valerie to attend and said she wanted her to meet her parents. Valerie had promised to come, and was beginning to suspect it was serious between them, although they'd only been dating for two months. But she was exactly what Phillip needed, and his mother hoped he was smart enough to know it. Jane was good for him, and he seemed happy. But he was a grown man and had to do what he wanted, and suited him. And now Valerie was going to do the same. She had promised herself she would go to Europe for at least a month, or even two. She wanted to see where her mother had lived in Rome after Umberto died, before she came back to the States, and also visit the château in Naples where they had lived together. It was going to be a kind of pilgrimage for her, and she wanted to float around Florence, maybe Venice, or wherever the spirit moved her to go. She could do anything she wanted now. For the rest of her life. Thanks to Marguerite.

Valerie fell asleep that night, thinking about the auction. What a dazzling night it had been!

# Chapter 21

Valerie spent the next few weeks planning her trip, and just trying to adjust to everything that had happened. Sometimes it was hard to believe it was real.

She went back to visit Fiona once, to thank her, and the old nanny seemed sleepy, and more tired than she'd been before, although she was just as clearheaded. Everything Fiona had told her in their previous visit had changed Valerie's life forever. It was strange at her age, but Valerie felt more confident now, and no longer apologetic for how different she had been all her life from the people she was related to.

Angie and Tom had sent her an email, congratulating her on the successful sale. They had read about it, and thought the results were wonderful. They were happy for her, and were begging her to visit them again, and they were thinking of coming to New York for a long weekend in the fall. They said Walter was doing well, although little by little he was slowing down, and had had some minor health problems lately that he'd never had before. At ninety-four, it was to be expected, but at least he was happy, well cared for, and comfortable.

Jane finished her final paper, after giving up two weekends on the boat to do so. And as she'd promised her she would, in June Valerie attended Jane's law school graduation and met her parents. They all had a lot to talk about. Jane's parents were nice people and more sophisticated than Valerie had expected. They went to Chicago frequently to see every play, opera, symphony, and ballet that came through there, and went to Europe once or twice a year. Jane's mother had been a psychologist before she married, and was still an avid skier, who skied the French Alps every year, and went helicopter skiing in Canada, which was arduous. She was a very attractive, still young woman with a lot of energy and many interests. Jane's father was the CEO of a major insurance company and an intelligent, interesting, handsome man. They were crazy about Phillip when they met him, and enjoyed meeting Valerie. Jane's mother confided to her how worried she was about Jane not wanting to settle down and, according to her mother, being too dedicated to her career. As an only child, they were more focused on her, which Valerie understood.

"It's tough sitting on the sidelines once they grow up," Vivian Willoughby said to Valerie. She was an attractive blonde, with a terrific figure, and looked a lot like her daughter. She was in her early fifties but seemed ten years younger than she was, and so did her husband, Hank. He was fit and athletic, and had the chiseled tanned face of a sailor from being on his boat every weekend in all weather. He was a very attractive man. And they all had a good time. Valerie had enjoyed meeting them.

Jane had graduated cum laude. She had three interviews with law firms that week. One of them, by sheer coincidence, was Penny's firm. Phillip was very proud of Jane too, and had put a good word in for her with Penny, just in case it helped. She still had to take the bar exam in July, although Phillip was certain she would pass it. Jane wasn't as sure.

"We wanted her to come back to Detroit," Vivian confided to Valerie as they stood around after the graduation ceremony. Jane looked very official in her cap and gown. "Or at least Chicago, but she loves it here. And I guess if she gets a good job in New York, or if she and Phillip get serious, she'll never come back." She looked wistful but resigned about it. "It's not easy having an only child. You put all your eggs in one basket."

"I know. Phillip is an only child too." Valerie smiled. "So is my niece. Her mother still worries about her too, and my niece is forty-five, happily married, has three kids, and is a partner in a law firm. They're our kids forever, no matter how old they are." Valerie was far more relaxed than Vivian, and very open-minded about whatever her son did. Jane's mother was more intense, although Jane seemed normal and sane in spite of it.

The Willoughbys had invited everyone to lunch at The Carlyle, Phillip and his mother, and Alex, who had attended the graduation too. And they spent a pleasant afternoon celebrating Jane's successful completion of law school. Looking back, it seemed easy to her now, but it had been brutal along the way. She knew John had graduated from business school the day before. She hadn't heard from him since the day she moved out. She wondered if he was going to L.A. with Cara now. She didn't miss him, and she was having fun with Phillip, but it felt strange to her that she no longer had any contact with a man she'd lived with for almost three years. It had worked out for the best, and her mother told her how much she liked Phillip and his mother, after lunch, when they had both left.

"He's a lovely man," Jane's mother commented,

"and his mother is a fireball. She said she's leaving for Europe and planning to tour around Italy on her own, and having an art show of her work when she gets back. She's going to visit friends or relatives in California, she said something about possibly taking a class at the Louvre in November, and she's on the board of the Costume Institute at the Met. I couldn't keep up with what she was saying. She made me feel like a slug," Vivian said, sounding admiring and overwhelmed. They knew about the recent auction and were impressed by that too.

"Me too." Jane laughed about Valerie, and there had been all the excitement and stress of her finding out about Marguerite, dealing with the surrogate's court, DNA tests, and the auction. Valerie had never slowed down for a minute.

Jane and Phillip spent the weekend with her parents. They went to a Broadway play and had dinner at "21." The women shopped, while Phillip and Hank went to a boat show and compared newer sailboats to their classic ones, and talked sailing and boats for most of the weekend, and even managed to sneak in a brief visit to Phillip's boat, and Jane's father loved it.

It was all very enjoyable, but Jane was happy when they left. She said entertaining her parents was a lot of work—making sure they had fun, were doing what they'd planned, and were eating where and when they wanted to, liked the restaurants, and weren't too exhausted. She had loved seeing them, but was happy to kiss them good-bye, and go back to her own apartment with Phillip and collapse onto her bed for a quiet Sunday night.

They wound up making love almost as soon as they lay down, and then later foraged for dinner in the fridge. She was standing naked, eating some leftover chicken, when she asked him what he was doing that week, and he laughed.

"Making love to you, I hope, if you're going to stand around like that." She smiled and put the chicken down, and wrapped her arms around him.

"Best offer I've had," she said, and kissed him.

"I'm taking my mother to the airport on Tuesday," he said in a muffled voice as he kissed her neck, and held her round, firm bottom in his hands. "Other than that and work, I have no plans. Why?"

"I want to study for the bar this week. I thought maybe we could steal the day on Friday, and spend three days on the boat next weekend. I can bring my books." She was happy to have graduation behind her. She had the interviews for jobs that week, but otherwise her life was slowing down. She had reached a major goal.

"Music to my ears," he said, referring to three days on **Sweet Sallie,** and then he picked her up and carried her back to bed. It was a perfect Sunday night.

*     *     *

Winnie went to see Valerie on Monday afternoon to say good-bye while she was packing. She was almost finished, and they stopped to have iced tea. Winnie had hay fever, as she always did at that time of year, and she looked emotional to see Valerie leave.

"How long will you be gone?" she asked wistfully.

"I don't know. Three weeks, a month, more. Maybe six weeks. I just want to float around for a while. It's been a stressful few months." It was a major understatement. Winnie still felt shaken by everything that had happened, especially learning the truth about her parents, which was still painful for her. She hadn't recovered from that yet, although Valerie looked better than she ever had, and strengthened and validated from what she'd learned.

"I think I like you better as my aunt," she teased Winnie. "It makes me feel young." And she looked it. Winnie really did seem old enough to be her mother, although they were only four years apart.

"Don't say that. I'm still upset that we're not sisters anymore." There were tears in her eyes as she said it.

"You'll love me as your niece," Valerie said, leaned over to kiss her cheek, and put an arm around her shoulders. It was easier to make light of the serious situation that had surfaced. Winnie's anger and accusations were forgotten. The two women had made peace, mostly due to Valerie's forgiving nature and happy disposition. And things had turned out well. "Why don't you meet me in Europe? It would do you good."

"No, it wouldn't. I hate the way you travel. You dash around all over the place, you change plans every five minutes, you check in and out of hotels. It would put me over the edge. I want to go somewhere and sit and not move. And I don't want to be packing every five minutes either."

"Why don't you rent a house in the Hamptons?" Valerie suggested.

"It's too expensive," Winnie said sourly. "I can't afford it." Valerie gave her a pointed look that said she knew better. Winnie always cried poor.

"Yes, you can and you know it. You're just too cheap to spend the money," she accused her, and Winnie laughed sheepishly.

"That's true," she confessed. "Penny's renting a house in Martha's Vineyard for the summer. She said I could come up for a weekend if I don't nag the kids."

"Could you do that?" Valerie wasn't sure she could, and neither was Winnie. Her grandchildren drove her crazy, and her daughter, whom she criticized constantly.

"Probably not," Winnie said honestly. "They're just so rude and badly behaved, and so noisy, and Penny lets them."

"They're just kids, and they're actually pretty good. They don't do anything bad in my studio

when they visit," Valerie said easily. She liked
Penny's kids more than Winnie did.

"You're better with them than I am. I have fun
playing cards with them, but other than that,
they make me nervous. They move around all
the time. I'm always afraid they're going to spill
something or break something, and most of the
time they do." Valerie had seen her in action with
her grandchildren, and she agreed with Penny—it
was nerve-wracking for all involved.

"If they make a mess, you clean it up. You could
stay at a hotel at the Vineyard," she suggested, but
Winnie didn't want solutions. She was always married to the problems.

"Why spend the money?"

"Well, you can't sit in your apartment in New
York all summer," Valerie said firmly, but she could
see that Winnie wasn't convinced.

"Why not?"

"It's depressing. You have to think of somewhere
to go, or something to do."

"I'm not like you. I'm happy at home by myself."
Their mother had been that way too. It seemed
grim and mournful to Valerie. She wanted to be
out and around, meeting new people. She could
hardly wait to leave for Europe the next day. "I'm
going to miss you," Winnie said softly. "Call me."

"Of course. I'm starting in Rome, to see where
my mother lived before she moved back here. And
then I'm going to Naples to see the château. Phil-

lip says it's beautiful, and it's been restored by the current owner. He didn't know my mother, but Phillip sent him some photographs of her and the count, at the owner's request. He has a soft spot for them." Phillip had given her Saverio Salvatore's address and phone numbers, and told her to look him up, so she could see the château, and she spoke enough Italian to get by on the phone, more so than Phillip, who had struggled with the language when he met him, although they had managed with the gallery owner's fractured English. Phillip had noticed that Italians spoke more French than English, and his French wasn't all that great either. His mother's was better.

"Well, don't forget to call me while you're running all over Europe," Winnie reminded her.

"I won't." Penny had just finished settling the estate for her, and Valerie had paid the inheritance taxes from the proceeds of the sale. She felt free as a bird. "And I want to hear that you're doing more than just sitting home and playing bridge."

"I have a tournament this summer." Winnie brightened at the prospect.

"Good. Do something else too. It's good for your health." Winnie nodded, and was genuinely bereft as they hugged when she left. She felt as though she were losing her best friend now, after losing a sister in learning the truth about Marguerite. She had been mourning her illusions now for months. Everything seemed different. Valerie and

Penny had discussed it, and Winnie's daughter had insisted she'd adjust. Valerie wasn't as sure. Winnie had fought hard all her life to defend their parents, and never criticized them or questioned what they did. She had trusted them completely. Having the blinders torn off her eyes to face reality had been hard on her, and Valerie thought she was depressed. Winnie just wasn't a happy person, and now less so than ever. But at least they had made peace after their raging battles over Winnie's parents. Winnie was still inclined to make excuses for them, to her daughter, but she didn't dare say a word in their defense to Valerie anymore. She had been proven right in her feelings about them for years.

Valerie hoped Winnie would be all right over the summer, and went back to packing after she left. She could hardly wait to leave the next day.

# Chapter 22

Phillip picked Valerie up at her apartment at four o'clock on Tuesday, having left work early to do so. She had two good-size suitcases, and a tote bag to take with her on the plane, full of books, magazines, and her iPad. She had to be at the airport at five, for a seven P.M. flight to Rome. And she looked like an excited kid when he got to her house and put her bags in the trunk. She chatted animatedly all the way to the airport about her plans, to visit museums she'd never been to before in Rome, gallery exhibits in Florence, and the Uffizi, where she'd been countless times and always loved, and the château in Naples. And she would see after that. Maybe a driving tour in Tuscany, or a stop in Paris on the way home. She planned to be in Italy for most or all of the trip.

"Wait a minute. How long are you going to be gone? Two years?" Phillip teased her.

"Maybe." She laughed. She felt carefree and excited about the trip.

"It sounds like it. Don't forget to come back. I'll miss you," he said sincerely. He was happy to see her so lighthearted since her discoveries about her real mother. Knowing that she had missed an entire lifetime with her had been agonizing, but learning more about her, the life she had led, and the fact that she had hungered for news of her daughter and had been prevented from coming back to her, had helped Valerie bond with her, even after her death. Learning how much her mother had loved her made up for her loveless childhood. It had healed an old wound that Valerie never acknowledged but was always there. She had finally freed herself of the disturbing echoes of parents who had never approved of her, and had been unkind to her all her life. Now she was ready for new adventures, even at seventy-four.

When they got to the airport, he helped her check in her bags, and get her boarding pass for the flight, and she lingered on the sidewalk with him for a little while, before going into the terminal. "Have a good time with Jane while I'm gone," she told him, looking motherly for a moment, while still trying to respect his freedom of choice as a man. "It was nice meeting her parents. They seem like good people. I enjoyed them." Phillip did too, to a point.

"They get a little intense sometimes," he said quietly. Jane never pressured him, but he sensed that her parents might, especially her mother. She made it clear she would like to see Jane married, a goal Jane didn't care about for now.

"I hope you don't say things like that about me," Valerie said, and he smiled.

"Hardly. You're too busy doing your own thing." He knew all she wanted was for him to be happy, whatever that meant to him. She left how he achieved that, and with whom, up to him.

"I like seeing you with a good woman, and I wouldn't want you to wind up alone. But you can figure out all that for yourself," she said simply, and then added, "Jane is a nice girl." He smiled as she said it.

"Yes, she is, and she's a good sailor too. And she'll be a good lawyer. She's interviewing with Penny's firm. It would be pretty funny if she winds up working there." Penny and Jane got along well too. They'd had dinner together several times, and he and Jane were going to spend the weekend with Penny and her family at Martha's Vineyard over the Fourth of July.

He liked the fact that his mother never pushed him about his personal life. She was too busy with her own, and the way she lived, enjoying her life to the fullest, served as an example to him. It was one of the things he had admired about his parents' marriage—they loved and respected each other and gave each other space to be who they were. They had never been confining, stifling, or possessive, or tried to change anything about each other. They were tolerant of each other's quirks. It had been a partnership that truly worked. He had seen few other relationships that did, and none of his own. Until now, with Jane. And it meant a lot to him that Jane and his mother liked each other, and got along.

He could tell that Valerie was anxious to go inside then, and he hugged her and kissed her good-bye, feeling an instant of panic, like a parent sending a child off to camp.

"Take care of yourself, Mom . . . be careful . . . don't do anything stupid . . . . Naples is full of pickpockets—watch out when you're there . . . ." He suddenly had a thousand instructions he wanted to give her, and she laughed.

"I'll be fine. Take care of **yourself.** You can reach me on my cell, or send me an email." She hugged him again, waved as she left, and disappeared into the terminal, and he felt happy for his mother, after he left her and drove back to the city. He went to Jane's apartment, where she was studying for the bar, as she did constantly now.

"Did your mom get off okay?" Jane asked when she took a break, and he handed her a glass of white wine.

He grinned in answer to her question. "She was

so happy to leave, it was embarrassing. She loves to travel, and she practically ran into the airport. She can't wait to get to Naples and Rome. It'll be good for her." So much had happened to her recently, and the trip was going to be fun.

And at that moment, Valerie was chatting to the person sitting next to her on the plane, selecting a movie, and she had just ordered a meal and a glass of champagne. She was traveling Alitalia, and she had treated herself to business class, so she could sleep comfortably on the plane. When she'd mentioned it to Winnie, her now-aunt had chided her for the expense. And Valerie had responded that at their age they could indulge in some luxuries. There was no point saving it till they were a hundred. She was willing to spoil herself a little now, particularly after the jewelry sale. She had no intention of squandering it, but knew the trip would be easier and less arduous in business than coach, which seemed reasonable to her, though not to Winnie, who preferred to stay home and save the money entirely, and go nowhere.

She watched the movie and enjoyed her dinner of osso buco and pasta, with a glass of good Italian red wine, and then she settled down to sleep for what was left of the seven-hour flight. They were arriving at eight A.M. Roman time, and she hoped to be at the Hassler by ten, which would give her a full day in Rome. She had her mother's address on a slip of paper in her purse. She wanted to go there before doing anything else. It was why she had come to Rome. She was planning to visit museums and churches for two days, enjoy the city, and walk around. And then she was going to Naples to see the château, which was going to be a high point for her, knowing that Marguerite had lived there for more than thirty years. She had lived in the apartment in Rome for twenty. Italy had really become her home, although Valerie knew from her letters that her mother had been happier in Naples with Umberto, than alone in Rome after he died. Valerie could only guess that her best years had been at the Castello di San Pignelli while he was alive. Her life must have been very lonely after that, with no relatives in the world.

Valerie slept lightly on the plane, had a cup of strong coffee before they landed on time, and was among the first off the plane. She took a cab to the Hotel Hassler, and was given a small room similar to Phillip's when he was there in March, and she took a cab to her mother's old Roman address, as soon she had showered and changed into a long black cotton skirt, a T-shirt, sandals, and a Panama hat. She looked very casual and stylish with her long straight white hair streaming down her back, and she was wearing silver bangle bracelets on her arm. There was an arty, casual feeling to what she wore.

She stood outside her mother's apartment building, wondering which apartment she'd lived in. It was so long ago that she was sure no one who was there would remember or even know. She just liked being there, knowing that this had been her mother's neighborhood. It was a fashionable residential neighborhood called I Parioli, and people walked by her, or rode by on bicycles, as scooters wove through the cars in the heavy Roman traffic and horns sounded everywhere. She stayed there for a long time and then walked away, wandered into a little church nearby, and lit a candle for her mother, grateful that their paths had somehow crossed again. She touched the locket on her neck as she thought about it, and sat peacefully in the little church, thinking about her, as old ladies came and went to say rosaries or chat quietly with friends. Several nuns were cleaning the church, and it had a welcoming atmosphere. She wondered if her mother had ever gone there, and if she had still believed in any deity after the misfortunes that had happened to her. Valerie would have undestood if she didn't, and wouldn't have blamed her if not.

It was a pretty neighborhood, and she felt safe there as she walked the fairly long distance back to the Piazza di Spagna, where the hotel was, and the shops on the Via Condotti nearby. It was touching discovering her mother's world, and the life she had led during her half century in Italy, after she left the States. Valerie spent the rest of

the day visiting small churches, and had a delicious lunch of fish and pasta at a sidewalk café.
She practiced her Italian with the waiter, and
he understood her despite her mistakes. And it
amused her to notice that men looked at women
in Rome of all ages—she saw several male heads
turn as she walked by, and it made her smile. It
could never have happened in New York, but it did
here. Italian men made you feel female and desir-
able to the grave. And Valerie was still an attractive woman with her slim figure and still-beautiful
face.

She walked for hours that afternoon, and had
dinner at a small restaurant near the hotel. She
didn't like going to restaurants alone, but traveling without a companion, she had no other choice
and didn't want to eat in her room, so she just did
it, and enjoyed the food and a strong espresso afterward before going back to the hotel. She wrote
postcards that night to Phillip, Winnie, and the
Babcocks. Her family had grown. And the Babcocks were coming to New York for a visit in the
fall, to meet Phillip, and had invited her to dinner
and a Broadway play.

She did more of the same the next day, exploring churches and galleries, admiring fountains
and statues, soaking up the atmosphere of Rome
and watching the people around her. And the day
after, she flew to Naples. She had several texts from
Phillip asking how she was, and assured him she

was fine and enjoying Rome. She took a cab from the airport to the Hotel Excelsior, where she and Lawrence had stayed years before, and watched the sights along the way. She saw Vesuvius and the Bay of Naples, and remembered taking Phillip to Pompeii and his utter amazement and fascination with it, when she explained to him what had happened there.

And not wanting to drive around Naples alone and risk getting lost, she hired a car and driver at the hotel, who was available that afternoon.

She had lunch on the terrace of the hotel, and went outside to meet the driver afterward, armed with her mother's address, just as Phillip had done. She had Saverio Salvatore's phone numbers with her, but hadn't called him, and didn't want to disturb him if possible. She just wanted to see the château, and bask in a private moment, thinking of her mother as a young girl of eighteen with the man she loved, not long after Valerie was born.

The driver explained the sights to her as they drove past them. He spoke English very well, and pointed out churches and important buildings and homes, and told her some of the history of Naples. But the history that interested her most was her own. There was a lot of traffic in the city, and it took them a while to get to the far edge of the city where the castello was located, and when they got there, he stopped, and she got out of the car in silence, looking up with awe at what had been her mother's home. Marguerite had been a countess by then, loved by Umberto, and respected by all who knew her, according to what Saverio Salvatore had told Phillip when he was there.

Valerie stood at the gate for a long moment, cautiously, not wanting to intrude, but no one was there. The gates were standing wide open, and the courtyard was empty. There was a red Ferrari parked in an open garage that looked like an old stable, but the grounds were deserted. And feeling like a burglar, she walked in quietly in her sandals and jeans and the crisp white shirt she had worn on the trip with her Panama hat. It was a hot day, but the heat was dry, and her hat shielded her from the sun. No one stopped her, and she walked around for a little while, through orchards and past vine-yards and gardens and then walked back toward the château. She could easily imagine her mother walking there with Umberto, enjoying the view of the bay. It was a beautiful, peaceful place, and ap-parently very well kept. She saw two gardeners in the distance, but they never approached. She was halfway across the courtyard on her way back to her car when a silver Lamborghini roared into the courtyard, with the top down, driven by a man with white hair. He almost looked like Umberto for a moment, and Valerie was startled and embar-rassed when he looked at her and frowned. He got out of the car quickly and came toward her with a questioning look.

**"Sí Signora? Cosa sta cercando?"** She knew he was asking what she was looking for, and she would have felt stupid answering "My mother," and he would have thought she was crazy. He probably did anyway. She didn't feel properly dressed to be trespassing, in sandals and jeans and her battered old Borsalino straw hat.

**"Scusi,"** she said, feeling flustered as she apologized to him. **"Che casa bellissima,"** she said, pointing at the house and telling him how beautiful it was.

**"È una proprietà privata,"** he reminded her. It was private property. And she decided to shoot for the moon, at the risk of seeming even more foolish or intrusive.

**"Mia mamma era in questa casa molti anni fa,"** she said, feeling lame, telling him her mother had been in the house many years before, which was the best she could do in her rusty Italian. "La Contessa di San Pignelli," she said, groping for an excuse for her intrusion. **"Sono la sua figlia."** He frowned then as he looked at her. She had told him she was Marguerite's daughter.

**"Davvero?"** For real? "It is true?" he said, switching to English, which was easier for her, if not for him. He looked intrigued.

"My son came to see the house some months ago. I believe you met him, Phillip Lawton. He sent you some photographs of my mother and stepfather, the count and countess. He gave me your card.

Signore Salvatore," she said shyly, and he looked thunderstruck.

"He did not tell me they are his grandparents."

"It's a long story, but he didn't know then."

"And you are the beautiful countess's daughter. The photographs are in the house." He waved vaguely at the castello, fascinated by her now, as Valerie smiled back at him, grateful that he had remembered Phillip, and not told her to leave.

"I'm terribly sorry to intrude on you like this," she apologized, still feeling flustered and rude. "I came to Naples to see where my mother lived with the count. It's silly, I know. She's dead now, and I wanted to come to Italy to see her home." She didn't explain that she'd never known her in her entire life, and had only just discovered that Marguerite was her mother. It was too convoluted to explain in either language.

"Do you wish to see the house?" he asked politely, and she couldn't stop herself from nodding. She was desperate to. It was why she had come, and the main reason for her trip.

He took her on a more extensive tour than he had given Phillip. He showed her the count and countess's bedroom, where he slept now, their private suite with a beautiful library of antique books, and the little study where Umberto had worked at whatever he did, which Valerie didn't know or want to ask. There was a lovely boudoir and dressing room that had been her mother's that was empty now, with antique wallpaper that had been hand-painted, and looked like something from Venice in the seventeenth century and probably was. There were sitting rooms, and spare bedrooms that Saverio had turned into guest rooms, majestic chandeliers lit with candles, a noble dining room with a long table and tapestries and graceful chairs, the living room he used to entertain, and a big homey kitchen also with the view of the bay. The house was large and distinguished but not too large to be comfortable and inviting. She wished she could close her eyes and imagine her mother there, and she saw one of the photographs Phillip had sent him, on a grand piano, in a silver frame, in a place of honor. And as Phillip had, she noticed the impressive contemporary art the new owner had successfully mingled with the antiques, which had married well. He had either a good decorator, or great taste. The tour ended in the kitchen, where he offered her a glass of wine, and she hesitated. She didn't want to overstay or exploit his kindness unduly.

"I'm so sorry to disturb you," she said, looking uncomfortable, and he smiled.

"I know how it is with families. My mother die when I was a young boy . . . I always want to know about her. Like you perhaps?" he asked as he poured the chilled white wine into a glass and handed it to her, and then one for himself. He walked her out to a terrace where they sat down, and could view the perfectly manicured gardens, which he had restored. "A mother is very special," he said, and took a sip of the cool wine. "I like your son very much when I meet him. He is a good man." She smiled at the compliment for Phillip.

"Thank you. I think so too. Do you have children?" she asked him, and he smiled easily and held up two fingers.

"Two. **Un ragazzo a Roma,**" a boy in Rome, she understood. "**E la mia figlia a Firenze.** My daughter work with me in my gallery. My son is the director of my gallery in Rome. Art," he said pointing at the paintings inside the house. "Your son sells art for Christie's," he said, remembering, **"e gioielli."** Jewels.

"Yes. I only have one son." She held up one finger with a smile. "And I'm an artist." She pantomimed painting, and he looked impressed.

**"Brava!"** he complimented her, and they sat looking at the view for a moment, as she thought about her mother again. She could almost feel her here, where she had lived for a long time, and hopefully been happy. It was a warm, inviting place, and he explained to Valerie that he loved it, and touched his heart, as he had with Phillip. "You go to Capri now? Or Amalfi? Sorrento? Positano? On holiday?"

"No," she said, shaking her head. "Firenze." Florence. She hadn't wanted to go to a beach resort alone, and she knew that Capri was overrun with tourists at that time of year, and it hadn't appealed to her. The cities with their art treasures did. She'd been debating about going to Venice too. There was more to see there than in Positano or Capri, and museums and galleries she loved to visit.

"Me too," he said. "I go back to Firenze in a few days, to work. I am here to rest," he said, but wasn't convincing. He had driven in at full speed in the Lamborghini, which didn't seem restful to her. "I come here one time, two time in a month to relax." That made sense to her. "Otherwise, Firenze, Roma, Londra, Parigi. Business." She nodded her understanding of the cities where he worked, and they sat peacefully for a while, and then she stood up, having imposed on him for long enough. "Please call me when you come to Firenze, visit my gallery and meet my daughter," he said hospitably. "You have lunch with us."

"I'd like that very much," she said, as he walked her back to where her driver was waiting with the car. A man in a Mercedes drove into the courtyard then, and Saverio waved at him, as though he'd been expecting him. "I'm sorry I stayed so long. Thank you for the tour of the house." She looked moved and he smiled warmly at her.

"Not at all. It was a pleasure and an honor." He bent to kiss her hand, and she felt like someone very important when he did, even the pope. She wasn't used to the European traditions that were symbols of her gender and rank.

"**Mille grazie,**" she said, as the other man walked up to them and spoke rapidly to Saverio in Italian, and her host introduced them. "Valerie Lawton," she supplied.

"Signora Lawton, **a presto . . . a Firenze,**" he said, and left her then, and walked into the house with his guest talking animatedly. He couldn't have been nicer, just as Phillip had said. And yet again, with an uninvited guest. It had been a perfect visit for her, and she had seen enough. She had visited her mother's bedroom, her dressing room, where they ate, their living room and gardens. And it was Saverio's house now, not theirs. She was faintly embarrassed at what she'd done, barging in on him, but she was glad she had come to Naples nonetheless. But she knew she didn't need to come back again, she had seen it, and walked through her mother's home.

She spoke to the concierge at the hotel that night and made arrangements to go back to Rome the next day. She wanted to spend a few more days there, and then she would go to Florence, as she had planned. She didn't know if she'd have the courage to call the owner of the château when she was in Florence. She didn't want to bother him at work this time. Maybe she'd just wander into his gallery out of curiosity. But her pilgrimage was complete now. The rest of her trip would be just for pleasure. And Marguerite Pearson di San Pignelli could rest in peace.

## Chapter 23

Valerie's second stay in Rome, after returning from Naples, was even more interesting than the first. She looked up several galleries and museums she had wanted to visit, went to the Catacombs, which she'd always wanted to do, and discovered a myriad of small churches tucked away in narrow side streets, and she began to know her way around the city on foot. She loved being there, even alone, and she told Phillip all about it when he called her. They agreed on what a nice man Saverio was, and she told him about her visit to his home, and how welcoming he had been.

"He's a great guy. Our family seems to keep dropping in on him, and he's a good sport about it."

"I saw the photo you sent him of my mother. He had it framed on the piano, which was sweet."

"I think he has a crush on her," Phillip commented easily, and his mother laughed at the irreverence.

"So where are you going now?" he asked her.

"Florence. I'll figure the rest out after that." She had no set reservations after Florence and had wanted to play it by ear. And there was so much art she never tired of in Florence that she didn't want to rush to leave. She was thinking of renting a car to drive through Tuscany, which she didn't tell Phillip or he'd worry. "How's Jane?" Valerie asked him.

"Busy. She's taking the bar exam in three weeks. I probably won't get five words out of her till then. She's staying at her place for a few days, so I don't distract her." She had told him he was like a kid, trying to kiss and cuddle her all the time, and she had to work. So he was banished, but he had plenty to do to keep busy at work.

Valerie called Winnie that night too, as she had promised. She was fine, despite her allergies. She was in a bridge tournament, which kept her happy. Valerie told her she had been to Naples and seen the house, met its owner, and was back in Rome exploring the city.

"Better you than I. It's probably boiling hot there," Winnie said plaintively.

"It's hot, but I love it." Valerie sounded happy and relaxed. And the next day Valerie decided not to fly to Florence, but drive there instead. She rented a Mercedes, which would be solid on the road, and she would be safe. She had the doorman load her bags in the trunk, and she took the highway after she left Rome, and stayed on it until Perugia, where she left the highway and drove past Lago Trasimeno. Four hours after she left Rome, she reached Florence, and found her way to the Four Seasons Hotel Firenze, using the GPS. She felt supremely competent as she got there, and she'd had a great day on the road, and had stopped in Perugia for lunch.

She left the car at the hotel, checked into her room, and then walked through the Piazza della Signoria and bought a gelato. It was a gorgeous hot afternoon, and she couldn't wait to go to the Uffizi the next day. It was her favorite museum in Europe, and she and Lawrence had spent days there on their trips. It was Mecca to anyone who loved art as they did. It was Phillip's favorite too.

She walked around Florence for hours, and finally went back to the hotel and lay on her bed to rest. She laughed to herself in the room, thinking about how Winnie would have hated this trip and complained every minute of the way, about the walking and the heat, and Valerie's determination to see everything and leave no stone unturned in her travels. It would have been Winnie's worst nightmare and was Valerie's dream. She wondered if her mother had been more like her.

She fell asleep early that night and woke up as

the sun came up over Florence, which she could see from her room. She stood looking out the window at the city in the early morning light, which looked like a painting. She went for a walk, and came back for breakfast at the hotel, and arrived at the Uffizi just as it opened. She stayed there until it closed for lunch, walked some more, and then went back for the afternoon. And as she wandered through the streets afterward, she remembered Saverio's gallery, and looked at the address on his card, which she still had in her bag. She had no idea where it was, and stopped a policeman to ask. He told her in Italian, and indicated that it was very close, and she thought she understood and followed the direction that he had pointed, and when she turned a corner, it was there. It was a large handsome gallery, with a massive bronze sculpture in the window, and she was startled to see him through the glass, pointing emphatically at a painting and talking to a young woman.

Feeling hesitant but curious, Valerie walked in, and Saverio turned to look at her and smiled in surprise.

"Signora Lawton ... welcome in Firenze ... **brava**!" He seemed delighted to see her, as though they were old friends, and introduced her to his daughter, Graziella, whom he had been speaking to. The young woman spoke excellent English, and the two women conversed for a few minutes. She looked about Phillip's age or a little younger.

She went back to her office at the rear of the gallery a few minutes after they'd met, and Saverio continued to chat with Valerie in his easy, open way. "When did you arrive?" he asked her with a welcoming smile.

"I drove here yesterday," she said proudly, feeling accomplished, and he complimented her again with another **"Brava!"** "I've been at the Uffizi all day," she said, and he nodded.

"I grew up there." He smiled at her.

"Was your family involved in art?" she asked, wondering if he'd understand her. He did, but shook his head.

"No, my father was a doctor, and my mother a nurse. My father was very angry when I wanted to be an artist. But I have no talent, so I sell art by other people." He laughed. "He thought I was crazy. But I didn't want to be a doctor. He was very unhappy with me."

"Mine didn't want me to be an artist either." Her real father had been an artist, she knew now, but that was too complicated to explain.

"You must show me your work," he said with interest.

"Oh no," she said, feeling modest. She had recognized the important piece in his window, by a sculptor she admired. She wasn't in his league by any means, or didn't think so. And then Saverio turned to her.

"You will have dinner with us. Yes?" She hesitated and then nodded. She had nothing else to do, and he was friendly and interesting to talk to, and they shared a passion for art. "What is your hotel?" She told him, and he promised to pick her up at eight-thirty, and she left the gallery feeling brave and adventuresome again, as she walked back to her hotel. It was fun meeting new people. She had come to Europe for experiences just like this, after her trip to see her mother's home. Now she was free to play and relax, with the serious part of her travels over.

She had no idea where they were going for dinner, and didn't know what to wear, so she wore a simple black skirt, a lacy white blouse, and high-heeled sandals, with her white hair loose down her back and small diamond earrings Lawrence had given her for twenty years of marriage. And she carried a shawl in case it got chilly that night. She was waiting for him in the lobby when Saverio drove up in the red Ferrari. He looked very dashing in a well-cut blazer and white slacks with a blue shirt, his deep tan, and his mane of white hair. He came inside and found her and took her arm as they walked outside, and she got into the Ferrari with him and felt very racy, as he tore through traffic and wove among the other cars. She laughed as she glanced at him. It was slightly terrifying driving with him, but very Italian, and she liked it.

"You make me feel young again!" she said with a broad grin over the noise of the engine.

"You are young," he said, smiling at her. "At our age, we can do whatever we want, and we are as young as we wish to be." And then he added, "You look like your mother." He watched her when they stopped at a traffic light.

"I wish that were true," she said ruefully, "but I don't. I look like my father." She had just discovered that recently in Santa Barbara, from the photographs Walter had of Tommy. But there was a similarity of expression with Marguerite, that Saverio had noticed immediately.

"Then your father must have been a beautiful man." She smiled at the compliment as they roared off again when the light turned green. Saverio was very charming and exciting to be with, and probably a bit of a ladies' man. But it suited him, and he was so Italian. And he made her feel attractive.

They met his daughter at the restaurant, and her husband Arnaud, and they were delightful. She ran her father's gallery in Florence, and her husband was French and worked for a local TV station as a producer. They said they had a little girl, Isabella, who was two. And just talking about her, Saverio's eyes danced, and he showed Valerie a photo of her on his phone. She was wearing a tutu and had a halo of blond curls and a mischievous smile.

"You have grandchildren?" he asked her, and she shook her head.

"Phillip isn't married." She thought that explained it, but apparently not.

**"Allora?"** Saverio said with a purely Italian gesture. "My son Francesco is not married, and has two beautiful children with a very nice girl." Valerie smiled at what he said.

"My son hasn't done that yet," she said politely, and hoped he wouldn't. She was free-thinking and modern, but still had traditional values, although she knew she would have loved Phillip's children, whatever he did.

"Children always surprise you," Saverio said, and they both laughed. His English improved with the wine they drank at dinner, and his daughter and son-in-law spoke very good English. They had a very enjoyable dinner, and then the young people left them, and Saverio took her to a bar and restaurant with a spectacular view of Florence and the night sky. He was not ready for the evening to end, and Valerie wasn't either. She was having such a good time.

"So, Valerie," he said, curious about her. "You are married? Divorced? . . ." He was looking for another word but didn't know it.

"A widow," she supplied. "My husband died three and a half years ago." She didn't sound pathetic, just matter-of-fact. She had made her peace with Lawrence's death. They had had many wonderful years together. He had lived a good life and they had shared a great one.

"You are alone?" He looked shocked, and she laughed.

"Yes. At my age most women are, if their husbands die." She was sensible about it. She didn't expect to find a man or even want one. She was comfortable alone.

"Why? You are a beautiful woman, and very exciting. Why would you be alone?" It was difficult to explain to him, and she didn't want to, and say most men were not beating a path to your door. She hadn't been out with anyone since Lawrence died. She'd had invitations from widowed men she knew, but didn't want them. She accepted her solitary state and sometimes enjoyed it. And she and Lawrence had been good together. They had been so happy for so long. She didn't want to be greedy or foolish and expect to find that again, and then be disappointed.

"You must be alone only if you want to be," he insisted. "Do you want to be alone?"

"Not really. But I keep busy. I do many things I enjoy."

"But you do them alone?" She nodded. "That's terrible. I am seventy years old, Valerie. I do not consider my life over as a man." He was very definite and seemed as though he meant it. She was surprised to hear his age. She had guessed him to be in his early or mid-sixties. He was terrific-looking, and a very handsome man.

"It's different for men," she said simply. "Men have more choices. You can be with a twenty-five-year-old girl if you want to. I'd look pretty silly if I did that. Men start new families with young women at your age," she said. He shook a finger at her when she said it.

"No babies! I like women, not babies, or young girls." He was very clear about it, and Valerie realized with amazement that he was flirting with her. That hadn't happened to her in years, and she wasn't sure she wanted it to. But it was flattering, and it seemed to fit the scene. She was in Italy, and he was a charming, handsome, intelligent man. Maybe flirting with her wasn't such a bad thing. Winnie would have keeled over at the thought, but she couldn't imagine Saverio flirting with Winnie. The very thought of it made Valerie laugh. "I do not believe in age," he said with determination. "It is a very small idea. Like a small box. That box is too small for you. You have no limits, you are free." He wasn't entirely wrong about her, and she liked what he said. He was saying that accepting a belief in age was too limiting, and apparently for him too. It was certainly an appealing idea. They talked about it for a while longer, as best they could, and she was pleased to see that he had stopped drinking champagne since he was driving, but he encouraged her to have another glass and she did. There was nothing she had to do in Florence and could sleep in the next day. "I want to show you Florence," he said as he signed the check. She discovered as they left the bar that it was a club, and she wondered if he came here often, and if he dated a lot. He was everything people expected of Italian men, but he seemed sincere. And he confessed to her in the car about Marguerite.

"I am in love with your mother. I was . . . **la prima volta** . . . the first time I saw her photograph. She is a woman of magic and mystery. The count adored her." She wasn't sure how he knew that, but she believed him. Their photographs, her mother's letters, and the extravagant gifts he'd given her suggested that.

"I wish I'd known her," Valerie said softly.

"You didn't?" He looked shocked, and sad for her, as Valerie shook her head.

"I never met her. I didn't know she existed, as my mother, until recently. It's a long story." Too long to tell now, and he didn't pry.

"We will talk of it one day," he said, and sounded as though he meant that too. "We have much to talk about." And then she thought of something, and decided she wanted the answer to a question before their friendship went any further, if it did.

"Are you married, Saverio?"

"Why do you ask?" He turned to her with a curious expression.

"I just wondered."

"You think all Italian men run after all women." He shook his head and looked disapproving. "No, I do not run after every woman. Only the special women. Like you. And I am like you. My wife died when my children were small. She had cancer.

Graziella was five, and Francesco was ten." Like Valerie, he sounded matter-of-fact about it. It was a long time ago, longer for him. Thirty years. And he said he had never remarried. He had never met another woman he wanted to marry. Valerie was sure he had had a lot of women in his life in the past thirty years, but she liked him. He was lively and fun, and she enjoyed him. And she could sense that there was depth to him too.

He drove her back to the hotel and kissed her chastely on the cheek, not the hand this time. "May we have lunch tomorrow?" He amused her. She wasn't swept off her feet by him like a young girl, and there was no question he was a flirt and he loved women, but he was a delightful man.

"I'd love it," she said simply.

"Will you come to the gallery?"

"I will," she said.

"We will go to a restaurant with a very pretty garden," he promised her, and she thanked him and waved as she got out of the car. He watched her go inside, and then roared off in the Ferrari. It had been a wonderful evening, for both of them.

# Chapter 24

T he next day Valerie turned up at the gallery at twelve-thirty, and Saverio took her to the restaurant with the garden, which was as pretty as he said. They sat and talked for three hours, and she told him the story about her mother, and he was fascinated, particularly by how she had discovered her, through the safe deposit box and the photographs of her as a child and Fiona's confession of what she knew when Valerie went to see her.

"That is destiny, Valerie," he said with certainty. "Those are not accidents." And then he startled her with what he said next. "Perhaps our meeting is destiny too." It seemed too soon to her to say that, although it was an appealing idea, and always a possibility. She didn't comment.

He walked her back to the hotel then, and she spent a quiet evening, reading and making a list of what she wanted to see in Florence. And the next day they went to the Uffizi together. He had a thousand plans for what he wanted to do and show her. They drove through Tuscany on the weekend in the Ferrari with the top down. He took her to a dinner party given by his friends, many of whom spoke English. He introduced her to his son when he came to Florence. She met Isabella the Adorable. She was letting time drift by, and enjoying it thoroughly. For two weeks, she let life take its course, and then she wondered if she should move on, and travel some more. She mentioned it to him one night at dinner. He took her to a different restaurant every day.

"Why do you want to leave Florence?" he asked her in answer to her question, and she saw that he looked hurt. "Are you unhappy?"

"No, I'm having a wonderful time. But I can't stay here forever. And you have things to do, Saverio. You're a busy man, and you're spending a lot of time with me. Don't you want to go back to your own life?"

"No. I love to be with you." He spoke to her sometimes in Italian now, and she understood, if it didn't get too complicated. "There is space for you in my life." But she couldn't live in a hotel in Florence, to be with him. Still, she loved having a man in her life again, talking to him, sharing ideas, doing things with him. She had never known any man like him. He made her feel like a woman again, whatever her age. And the fact that he was four years younger than she made no difference to either of them. "Why don't we go to Rome for two days?" he suggested, and they drove to Rome two days later. He stayed at his apartment, near where her mother had lived in I Parioli, and she stayed at the Hassler again. He didn't press her to stay with him. He already knew her better than that. And if anything were to happen with them, she needed time to believe it was real, and he wasn't just playing. But he seemed to be very serious about her, and his children had been very nice to her too. His daughter Graziella had even said something about it to her at the gallery one afternoon when Saverio stepped out for a meeting and left her there for an hour to wait for him.

"You know, my father is more serious than he appears. He always seems like he's playing, and he loves women, particularly pretty ones." She smiled at Valerie. "He's a man. And he's Italian. But he has been serious about very few women in his whole life. And he has been alone now for a long time. He was in love with a woman ten years ago, and she died, like my mother. He has loved no woman since. I think he really likes you. And I promise you, he is not playing with you." Valerie was touched by what she said, and it was an insight into him that he hadn't given her himself. He had never mentioned the woman who died ten years before.

They had a wonderful time in Rome, and he showed her a side of the city she'd never seen before. The real Rome that Romans knew and loved. And when he walked her back to the hotel from a restaurant nearby on the second night, he kissed her on the Spanish Steps, and she was surprised to realize that there was more tenderness to it than passion. It felt like a real kiss from a real man who had real feelings for her, and she felt something stir in herself that she thought had died years before. He kissed her again when he walked her back to her room, but she didn't invite him in. She couldn't yet. And she was beginning to worry about what they were going to do. She couldn't just stay in Italy to be with him. Sooner or later she had to go back to New York. She tried explaining that to him, and he said the same thing he had said to her before. "Why?"

"What do you mean 'Why?' I have a life there, and a son."

"Your son is a man, Valerie, with a life of his own. One day he will marry, or love a woman. You don't have a job. You're a painter. You're a free woman. We could live in Rome, Paris, Florence, New York. At our age, would you give this up to be in one city, because you think you are too old to fall in love? That would be stupid and wrong.

Perhaps destiny or your mother wanted us to be together, so you came to the castello, and we met. Perhaps destiny wanted me to buy the castello to meet you, to return your mother's home to you." The way he said it made it seem huge, and a little overwhelming. She hadn't said anything about Saverio to Phillip. After her two weeks in Florence, Phillip had asked her if she'd visited him at his gallery yet. She didn't know what to say, and she didn't want to lie to him.

"Yes, actually, I did. We had dinner together, and I met his daughter and son-in-law. They're terrific, you'd love them. And I met his son in Rome."

"You did? How did you do that?" Phillip sounded a little surprised.

"I'm back in Rome for two days."

"Saverio seems like a terrific guy," he said innocently. He didn't have the remotest idea that his mother was falling in love with him and hadn't left his side for three weeks. It was the farthest thing from Phillip's mind, and not the way he envisioned his mother. She wasn't a romantic figure to him, just his mother.

"He's a lovely man," Valerie said, wondering if she should tell Phillip what was going on. But she didn't want to yet. She wanted to protect what they had. And things were heating up between them, ever since he had kissed her for the first time in Rome.

It was different when they went back to Florence. And after they'd been together for a month, he invited her away for the weekend. She kept thinking about what his daughter had said, that he was more serious than he looked. And not in a million years had Valerie expected something like this to happen to her. But she felt as though she could no longer turn back the tide. And maybe he was right, and it was meant to be. She was no longer sure what she believed.

He took her to Portofino for the weekend, and they stayed at the Hotel Splendido. It was a charming port town, and they felt like honeymooners as they spent long mornings in bed and made love, walked around the little town, had late dinners and came back to their room and made love again. It felt crazy and wonderful and she'd never been so happy in her life.

They were lying in bed late one night and she looked at him in the moonlight.

"Saverio, what are we going to do? I have to go back. I can't just run away forever. I have to say something to my son."

"He's not your father. He's your son. You can do as you wish with your life."

"You wouldn't abandon your children. I can't do that to mine."

"I understand. You came here for the summer. Give us that. Then we'll decide." She nodded, and he made love to her again, and when he did, she almost forgot that she had a life in New York, and a world other than his.

They went to Sardinia the following weekend, and stayed with friends of his in Porto Cervo, whom she enjoyed a lot. They had a beautiful boat, and they spent their days on it, and came back to the hotel at night.

And Saverio took her to Venice on business with him. They flew to London for a day to see a painting he wanted to buy. They were slowly blending their lives and becoming a couple, and she felt totally at ease with him. Valerie enjoyed everything they did together. She wondered if her mother had felt that way with Umberto, when she shared his life.

And in August, they went to the house in Naples and spent a week there, and she could easily understand why her mother had loved it.

And when they got back to Florence, Phillip called and asked her when she was coming home.

"I don't know," she said honestly, not wanting to upset him. "I love it here."

"I can understand why. I love Italy too. You don't need to rush back. Jane and I are going sailing in Maine for two weeks. I just wanted to check in." When he said it, she felt like she'd gotten a reprieve and told Saverio about it that night.

"Would you come to New York with me, and

stay for a while?" she asked him. He thought about it and nodded. He had been rethinking his life too, and trying to figure out how to make it work for both of them. And she had a good point—he didn't want to abandon his children either. And he had galleries to run. Graziella and Francesco did a good job, but he was always close at hand, although he didn't work every day anymore. He did what he wanted, but he was still very much involved. Valerie was freer than he was, except for Phillip. And she was concerned about Winnie too. She had told Saverio about her. "We need to find her a man," Saverio had said, and Valerie had laughed out loud. In that respect at least, Winnie was beyond hope. She didn't want a man. She just wanted to play bridge.

"I could spend time with you in New York," Saverio said thoughtfully. "Not all the time. I don't want to live there. But we could go back and forth. We are very fortunate. We can do whatever we want." It was going to take some managing, but she realized he was right. She could paint anywhere, and he didn't have to be at his galleries all the time. Their children were grown. And he wasn't suggesting they become Siamese twins. They each had a life. And together they had even more. They talked about it a lot now, and by the end of August, they thought it could work. Even Valerie was convinced. Saverio had persuaded her that they could do whatever they wanted. And she found the idea immensely appealing.

In the last week of August, she gave up her room at the hotel, and moved in with him. It seemed foolish to keep the room, she hadn't slept there all month, and preferred staying with him at his sunny little house. And she was going back to New York the following week when Phillip returned from Maine after the Labor Day weekend. She was planning to stay in New York for the month, and Saverio was going to join her in two weeks, and spend the last two weeks there with her. She was nervous about telling Phillip about her romance with Saverio. She had left New York a single woman, and was returning with a man, as part of a couple. It was a totally unexpected change. And all she could hope was that Phillip wouldn't be too shocked.

# Chapter 25

When Phillip and Jane left for Maine in mid-August, Valerie had been in Italy for almost two months. He missed seeing her, but he was happy she was having a good time. And he and Jane had been busy. She had taken the bar exam in July, and she wouldn't have the results until November, but she was hoping she had done well. And she was starting her new job in September. She had had two great offers from well-known law firms, Penny's and another even more prestigious one, which had offered her more money and better terms, so she had accepted, and she could hardly wait to start. They had promised her a junior partnership in two years, if she worked hard, brought in clients, and did well. And Phillip was sure that she would do all three. He had never been as taken with a woman in his life. And he had never gotten along as well with anyone as he did with Jane. They had been dating for five months, and were talking about moving in together in the fall. Everything was falling into place.

And the day before they left for Maine, Christie's put the icing on the cake. They offered Phillip a job in the art department, with a promotion and a raise, effective October first. He would have to travel to Europe more, and there would be more perks. It was everything he had wanted, and waited for, for nearly three years. He had accepted the job immediately.

He and Jane were talking about it one afternoon, after they threw anchor for the night in a small cove. They'd had great sailing that day.

"It's so weird how things work out, isn't it?" Jane said, looking pensive. "I was so upset when I couldn't get the clerkship I wanted, and got stuck at the surrogate's court. But if I hadn't been there, I would never have been assigned to handle your grandmother's safe deposit box, and met you." She smiled at him, as they lay in the sun on the deck, relaxing after their sail.

"And if I hadn't gotten sidetracked into the jewelry department, someone else would have gotten that assignment, to do the appraisal, and my mother would have never found out about her mother, and I wouldn't have met you." He leaned down and kissed her.

"It kind of makes you believe in fate, doesn't it?" she said thoughtfully.

"Or blind luck. But there was a little too much luck here, for it to just be pure happenstance. It all fits together perfectly, and came out right in the end. And fortunately, you got rid of the boyfriend." She had heard from one of her law school friends, who knew John, that he had gone back to L.A. with Cara, and they were starting the business he'd mentioned, with her father's help. Jane was very glad she'd had the guts to leave him when she did, or she might never have gotten to know Phillip, and fallen in love with him.

"How's your mother doing, by the way?" she asked casually. "It feels like she's been gone forever." It had given them more time together. Valerie didn't interfere, but she was a big presence in his life. Luckily, Jane liked her a lot, and Valerie led her own life.

"She's been away a long time," he agreed. "I think it's some kind of rite of passage for her, after finding out about her mother." And after the auction, she would never have to worry about money again, not that she had. But she was secure now, and had a solid fortune behind her that would allow her to do whatever she wanted for the rest of her life. He was happy for her, particularly about the discoveries about her mother, and even finding her father's relatives, which had been a stroke of sheer luck. Yet another. "I think she's coming back right after Labor Day. But she says she wants to travel more now. She might as well while she can," he said, and Jane agreed. "After the auction, she can do whatever she wants. It'll be great for her." And for him one day too. He was cognizant of that. "I think she's gotten acquainted with the man who owns her mother's house now, the place in Naples. I met him in March, when I was doing research on her. My mother said something about meeting his kids and seeing his gallery in Florence. I liked him a lot. I gave her his number. I'm glad she looked him up."

They cooked dinner in the galley that night, and their two weeks in Maine were even better than they'd hoped. The weather was perfect. They ate lobster almost every night. They saw old friends of Phillip's, and Jane liked them. Their two lives were blending smoothly, and they felt even closer to each other by the time they got back to New York at the end of the Labor Day weekend. And they both had new jobs to look forward to in the coming weeks. Phillip was excited to see his mother when she got home, and hear about her trip. She had been all over Italy for the past two months. And he knew from Penny that Winnie was desperate to see her too, and missed her. Valerie had called her regularly, to check on her, and Winnie complained about how long she'd been gone.

*   *   *

It was an odd feeling for Valerie when the plane touched down at JFK. She felt as though she had been away for years, and had come back a different person. Her heart was with Saverio in Florence and Naples and Rome, but this was her home. And it felt incomplete now without him. She was glad he was coming in two weeks. There was a lot she wanted to share with him here. And she was ready to join him in his life in Italy, at least part of the time, and he was right—why let their age limit them from what they wanted to do and could still enjoy? They could do anything they wanted. They had the money and the time, and they had been lucky enough to find each other, or had been destined to find each other, as Saverio said. Whether destiny or blind luck, it was a precious gift, and Valerie was ready to embrace it, and Saverio was too. He had finally told her about the woman who died ten years before. And he wasn't going to wait to lose the woman he loved for a third time. He wanted to enjoy every moment they could share, for as long as they could, and hopefully for a very long time.

Valerie called Phillip when she got home that night—he and Jane had just gotten back too. She was happy to know he was so close. They immediately agreed to have dinner together the next day, with Jane of course. And he told her about their new jobs.

"Fantastic!" She almost said **"Bravi!"** and stopped

herself. Her Italian had improved a lot over the summer. "How was Maine?" She loved hearing the happiness in his voice. Jane was good for him, and Valerie was pleased that he was going back to the art department at Christie's. It was what he had wanted for more than two years.

"Maine was perfect," Phillip answered. "We had a ball. I don't think I've ever eaten that much lobster in my life. And I can't wait to hear all about your trip, Mom. You were all over the map. Sardinia, Portofino, Naples, Rome, Florence, Venice, Siena." She had sent Fiona and Winnie postcards from each place, and emailed him a lot. The only thing she hadn't told him was who she was with on her travels. And she wanted to tell him right away. Now that they knew their plans, Phillip deserved to know.

They agreed to meet at "21" the following night for a homecoming celebration, and she was going to visit Winnie in the morning. She had wanted to call her when she got home, but knew she'd be asleep. She led an entirely different life from Valerie's late nights with Saverio now. Valerie's whole life had changed over the summer. She knew that Winnie would be unhappy about the traveling Valerie would do, but she'd just have to adjust. Valerie was not going to stay in New York full time, and give up Italy, to take care of Winnie. And she was worried about Phillip's reaction too. There was no telling how he'd respond to her having a man in her life.

Valerie unpacked what she'd brought home that night, and walked around her apartment. The painting she'd started of Marguerite was still sitting on the easel in her studio, unfinished, and she wanted to finish it now. And her apartment looked cozy, but different. There was something missing now. It was a relic of her past life, with no evidence of her new one. She set a photograph of Saverio down next to her bed, and felt better, as though to prove he really existed. He called her at two in the morning, when he woke up at eight in Rome, and it was a relief to hear his voice.

"I miss you!" was the first thing she said to him.

**"Anch'io."** So do I. "How was the flight?" he asked her, happy to hear her.

"Long. But I slept most of the way." They had stayed up late talking the night before. There was so much to plan now, and discuss.

"Have you seen Phillip?" He sounded as concerned as she was. There was no predicting how her son would react to him, although she said he had an important woman in his life now. But men were strange about their mothers, and possessive of them. He might take the news of their love affair very badly, although they both hoped that wouldn't be the case. Saverio's children were very pleased, and liked her.

"I'm seeing him for dinner tomorrow night. I'll see Winnie in the morning." Neither of them was worried about her, and Winnie's suspicion and disapproval were almost a given, and to be expected. He was amused by Valerie's descriptions of her. She sounded like a cranky old lady, but he could tell that Valerie loved her and accepted her as she was.

"Call me after your dinner with Phillip tomorrow night. I don't care what time," Saverio instructed her.

"It'll be too late for you. It'll be four or five in the morning. I'll call you when you get up."

"Go to sleep now," he said gently. "It's late for you. Call me when you wake." It would be late afternoon for him. They were going to have to get used to the two time zones now. She loved their little inane conversations, and just having him be part of her life, having him to share things with, and do things with. She could hardly wait till he arrived in two weeks. It seemed like an eternity to both of them, and she had some hurdles to cross first. A big one. Her son.

Saverio kissed her goodnight over the phone, and she lay in bed, thinking about him, before she fell asleep. It was hard to believe, but it was real. They had found love at their age.

The next morning Valerie called Winnie when she got up.

"So you're finally back," Winnie said in a querulous tone. "I was beginning to think you'd decided to stay there."

"I'm here," Valerie said simply. "Can I come by for a cup of tea?"

"I'm playing bridge at noon," she said, annoyed. She needed to punish Valerie now for being away for so long. Valerie had expected it and wasn't surprised.

"I'll come now. I've been up for hours." She had woken up on European time, and called Saverio. He'd been on his way back to Florence from Rome, and he talked to her from the car. She had promised again to call him after dinner, and he wished her luck. It was the operative word now.

Winnie looked well when she opened the door, a little thinner but otherwise fine. And she grudgingly hugged Valerie and was visibly pleased to see her.

"You shouldn't have stayed away so long," she complained. In the end, she had gone to Martha's Vineyard, and stayed with Penny and driven them all nuts. Penny had sent Valerie several emails about it that made her laugh. And Winnie had told her the children were badly behaved when Valerie called her there.

"I was having a good time," Valerie said honestly, and she'd been in no rush to come back. It was the blessing of having grown children. She didn't **have** to come home.

*She followed Winnie out to the kitchen, and they made tea. The housekeeper was vacuuming Winnie's bedroom, so they were alone. "I met a man," Valerie said as Winnie sipped her tea, and nearly choked.

"You what?" Winnie stared at her.

"I met someone." She felt sheepish and a little embarrassed. Winnie was silly, but daunting at times.

"Does he know how old you are?" she said with a look of stern disapproval.

"Yes, he does. He's four years younger. We're both grown-ups."

"You're geriatric, for heaven's sake, acting like adolescents." She had a way with words. "Is he American?" Valerie shook her head.

"Italian."

"Of course." Winnie's lips were a thin line, even thinner than usual. "He's after your money."

"Actually, he's not." She wanted to say "he's after my body," but didn't think Winnie could withstand the shock or the information. "He's a very successful art dealer. He's coming here in two weeks. Would you like to meet him?"

"No, I would not!" She was outraged, but at least Valerie had offered. "I'm not meeting some Italian gigolo." She had completely ignored what Valerie had said about what he did for a living. "So that's what you've been up to all this time! How pathetic! You're lucky he didn't kill you in your sleep." It

was an awful image but was how she thought, and
it was almost laughable that she'd suggest it about
one of the most important art dealers in Florence
and Rome. They sat in silence in her kitchen for a
while, as she digested what Valerie had said.

"Couldn't you be happy for me, Win? It's nice
to have someone to share my life with. He's a
nice man. He owns the château where my mother
lived. That's how Phillip met him. And I looked
him up."

"You could have met someone here, if you were
so desperate."

"I wasn't. It came as a total surprise. Blind luck.
Or destiny, as he says."

"I still think he's after your money. He probably
read about the auction, and was lying in wait."

"I wish you didn't think that way." But she always had. Her parents had been that way too. Shut
down about everything, and angry at the world.
Valerie knew Winnie would come around eventually. She always did, grudgingly. She'd adjust. It just
wasn't pleasant while she worked her way through
it. Valerie left a little while later and told Winnie
she'd call her in a few days. Winnie didn't answer,
as Valerie closed the door and left.

Valerie got to "21" that night before Phillip and
Jane. She was nervous, waiting for them, and tried
to appear calm when they arrived. But Phillip

knew her better and saw instantly that something was happening. She looked great, happy and re-laxed, her eyes were bright, her hair was beautiful, and she had a deep tan. And she was wearing a new dress she'd bought in Rome. Actually, Saverio had bought it for her, and it was shorter than she usually wore, but it was great on her. She looked stylish and full of life, as she chatted about her trip, and Phillip waited for the other shoe to drop all through dinner. He knew her too well, and her surprises weren't always good news. He hoped this wasn't a bad one.

"Okay, Mom, what's up?" He finally broke the ice. He couldn't stand it anymore, as they ate des-sert. The dinner had been delicious, but she had only picked at hers, another telltale sign. She wasn't a big eater, but she ate nothing at all when she was nervous.

She thought about Winnie as she gazed at Phil-lip, and hoped he'd take the news better than she had. But fortunately, Phillip was more like her, open-minded and positive, most of the time at least. But she still couldn't guess how he'd feel about his mother having a romance, since it had never happened before.

"I met someone in Italy," she said cautiously. There was no other way to say it, and he stared into her eyes, not sure he had heard her right.

"A man?" He looked blank, as though he didn't understand, and Jane held her breath. She had got-

ten it on the first try, and didn't know how he'd
react either. Sometimes even adults had crazy ideas
about their parents, particularly men about their
mothers.

"Obviously. Not a woman, for heaven's sake."
Valerie smiled nervously and decided to dive in
fast. "A very nice man. We've been together all
summer, and we like each other a lot. To be honest, I love him." Full disclosure. Phillip looked as if
he'd been shot, as Jane winced. This was a biggie.
She wondered if Phillip was going to feel she was
being disloyal to his father.

"You do? Who is he? What is he? How did you
meet him?" The questions flooded his mind all at
once.

"It's Saverio Salvatore. I met him at the castello when I went to see it. And then I saw him in
Florence. And it kind of took off after that. Very
unexpectedly, I might add. And I know we seem
ancient to you, but it just kind of happened. We're
going to enjoy it for now and figure out a way for
it to work between Italy and here. He'll come to
New York, I'll go there. We both have children and
work and lives of our own, but we want to spend
time together too." Phillip didn't look angry, just
surprised.

"I never thought of that as a possibility. I don't
know why. You're certainly young enough to have
a man in your life." She hadn't expected him to say
that, and tears filled her eyes. "Do you think you'd

move to Italy full time?" He looked worried about it. Even if they were both busy, he liked knowing she was nearby and seeing her when he could.

"I don't think so," she answered him thoughtfully. "I have a life here. And you. But it will be fun spending time in Italy too. We're planning to go back and forth a lot. It'll keep things interesting. So what do you think?"

"I think I'm a little stunned," he said honestly, with a cautious smile. She had always said that his father was the only man she'd ever love, and he was sure she'd believed it when she said it. She had never expected to love someone else. So it was a whole new concept for all of them. But he liked what he saw in her eyes. He saw happiness and peace. "I'm happy for you, Mom," Phillip said generously. "He seems like a good guy, and if you two have the energy to run back and forth between Italy and the States, what the hell, why not? Why would you sit around like Winnie, bitching and playing bridge?" That had never been his mother's style, and never would be, he knew. He smiled broadly at her then. "You look great. He must make you happy. You deserve it."

"He does," she confirmed, "and so do you." It was a coming of age for both of them. She and Phillip were both adults. Being able to accept a new man in her life could have been hard for him, and he was choosing not to let it, and to be gracious about it. He was a man, not a boy. Valerie was proud of him, and happy about how he had taken the news, and so was Jane. She was smiling at Valerie too, pleased for her, and relieved that Phillip hadn't made an issue of it, and respected his mother's right to do as she wished. And she thought it courageous of Valerie to embark on a new life and relationship at her age. It would be challenging going back and forth to Italy, or maybe just plain exciting. Jane loved that Valerie was willing to try something new. She modeled openness and courage and love of life to her son, which was a great gift to him.

And then Phillip grinned mischievously. "Did you tell Winnie yet?"

"I did." Valerie smiled, thinking of their exchange that morning.

"What did she say? I bet she had a fit." Phillip chuckled.

"She did. She told me I was geriatric." Phillip burst out laughing at that.

"You can count on her every time. She'll get over it." Valerie didn't look worried.

"I know she will. She just doesn't know it yet." They laughed about it, and he gave his mother a big hug when they got up.

"You should have told me at the beginning of dinner, then you could have eaten your steak."

"It's okay." She laughed. "I'll eat a sandwich

when I go home." She wasn't hungry, just relieved. He had taken the news like a loving son. They hugged again before they parted outside the restaurant, and left in two separate cabs. He and Jane were going to his apartment that night, not Jane's, so they didn't drop Valerie off downtown.

And Jane told him in the cab how impressed she was by his reaction to his mother's romance. "I've had friends go nuts when their widowed or divorced parents fall in love with someone else. I think most people don't really expect their parents to have lives and relationships of their own, and some people can be real jerks about it." It was testimony to Phillip and Valerie's relationship that her announcement to him had gone over well.

"It surprised the hell out of me at first," he admitted sheepishly. "I just never expected her to fall for someone else after my dad. But why not? She does deserve it. We have each other." He looked lovingly at Jane. "Why should she be alone for the rest of her life? Why shouldn't she have someone too? And if it works, it'll be great. I guess we'll be going to Italy in the future," he said as he kissed her, and he liked the idea. Particularly Florence, which was one of his favorite cities.

"I don't care where we are, just so I'm with you," Jane said, and kissed him. It was almost verbatim what Valerie had said to Saverio before she left.

* * *

Valerie waited patiently until two in the morning to call Saverio again. She got him just as he woke up at eight A.M. in Florence. And he was wide awake the minute he heard her voice.

"How was it? What did he say?" he asked immediately, concerned. He knew that if Phillip objected vehemently, it would dampen Valerie's enthusiasm for their plans. She didn't want to upset or hurt her son.

"He was terrific," she said happily. "He looked shocked for about four seconds, and then he said he was happy for us and I deserve it, and I can tell he means it." She sounded elated and relieved, and Saverio lay in bed and smiled. It was the only thing he had been truly worried about. The rest they could figure out with a little jet lag and a lot of air tickets. He'd been thinking of buying a plane, for business, and that would make things easier too. But even without one, he was certain the relationship would work. They were both old enough to realize how lucky they were to have found each other, to treat each other well, and to know what they wanted and needed and were able to give each other.

"I'm so happy," he said, beaming at his end. Phillip was the only obstacle he had feared, and could have made life miserable for his mother if he wanted to, and been nasty about it, possibly in defense of his father's memory. Instead they had the approval of all their children, which meant a lot to both of them, and made everything easier.

"Now hurry up and come over," she said, and sounded like a woman in love.

"I will be there in two weeks," he reminded her, and they chatted for an hour after that, both of them forgetting how late it was for her. It just felt good to be alive and in love.

# Chapter 26

W hen Saverio's flight arrived from Rome two weeks later, Valerie was waiting for him at the airport, and he took her in his arms as soon as he emerged from customs. He kissed her, and they smiled at each other. It made others smile as they saw them and walked by. They were so obviously in love, and happy to see each other.

Saverio was wearing a well-cut dark blue suit and looked very distinguished, and she was wearing a chic black cotton dress in the heat of the New York Indian summer.

They walked out of the airport, with their arms around each other's waists. They were in no hurry, just happy to be together. The two weeks apart had felt like months to them.

"I bought a plane yesterday," he told her, and she laughed, and told him he was crazy. But she knew that he had bought it for business, for him and his children to use on their trips for the gallery, to see important clients and buy new paintings all over Europe.

They were having dinner with Phillip and Jane that night, at La Grenouille, to welcome Saverio to New York. They were going to have drinks at her apartment first, and then go uptown for dinner. They had a lot to celebrate—Phillip and Jane's new jobs, her relationship with Saverio, and whatever else they could think of.

And when he saw it, Saverio loved her apartment and the atmosphere she had created. It was small, but like a warm embrace. It was a piece of her history, and she didn't want to give it up. And he was interested in all of it and admired her art and her eclectic collection of objects. He had two houses and an apartment in Italy. They would have her place in New York, and best of all, they had each other. They had all they needed. Their life together was a gift. Their meeting each other at all had been a blessing. They had come together through a series of what seemed like miracles now, which included not only them but everyone on their path, each in some special way that met their needs.

The miracles could be explained as destiny, blind luck, or coincidence. But magic had occurred. A woman who had vanished from their lives and virtually disappeared had touched them all in miraculous ways and brought them together. Marguerite had worked magic in their lives in the end, and blessed each of them with immeasurable gifts.

# About the Author

DANIELLE STEEL has been hailed as one of the world's most popular authors, with over 650 million copies of her novels sold. Her many international best sellers include **Blue, Precious Gifts, Undercover, Country, Prodigal Son, Pegasus, A Perfect Life, Power Play, Winners,** and other highly acclaimed novels. She is also the author of **His Bright Light,** the story of her son Nick Traina's life and death; **A Gift of Hope,** a memoir of her work with the homeless; **Pure Joy,** a memoir about the dogs she and her family have loved; and the children's book **Pretty Minnie in Paris.**

daniellesteel.com
Facebook.com/DanielleSteelOfficial
@daniellesteel

# LIKE WHAT YOU'VE READ?

If you enjoyed this large print edition of
**PROPERTY OF A NOBLE WOMAN**,
here are a few of Danielle Steel's latest
bestsellers also available in large print.

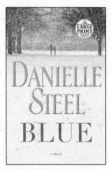

**Blue**
(paperback)
978-0-3995-6680-6
($29.00/$38.00C)

**Precious Gifts**
(paperback)
978-0-8041-9497-6
($28.00/$35.00C)

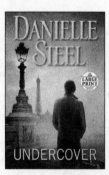

**Undercover**
(paperback)
978-0-8041-9498-3
($28.00/$35.00C)

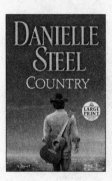

**Country**
(paperback)
978-0-8041-9463-1
($28.00/$34.00C)

Large print books are available wherever books
are sold and at many local libraries.

All prices are subject to change. Check with your
local retailer for current pricing and availability.
For more information on these and other large print titles,
visit www.randomhouse.com/largeprint.